THE
CANNIBAL
PEAKS

U. S. A.
UNHOLY   SLAYING   AGENCY
BOOK TWO

GUY QUINTERO

Sinister Raven Publishing LLC

THE CANNIBAL PEAKS

Book Two of Unholy Slaying Agency Series

Copyright © 2023 by Guy Quintero

First edition: January 2023

ISBN: 978-1-958828-03-8 (Ebook edition)

ISBN: 978-1-958828-04-5 (Paperback edition)

ISBN: 978-1-958828-05-2 (Hardback edition)

This novel is dedicated to the amazing people that I met during my military career. There are too many to name, but all of you have touched my life and helped me grow as a person. Especially to my recon brothers who gave their lives battling terrorism. You will never be forgotten. May your warrior spirits live on in my work.

Special thanks to my beta readers and editors: Carl, Silvestre, Brian, Danica, and Sally.

And a very special thanks to my daughter Nina for always being by my side.

CHAPTER 1
THE HUNTING GROUNDS

Agents waded through swathes of knee-high brush, pushing beyond the sting of freezing wind against exposed cheeks, their lungs pumping hard to absorb the thin mountain air. In a lined formation they weaved between tall bristling pines, and the occasional fluffy Carolina hemlock draping over them with bobbing limbs of flourishing olive and brown leaves.

Weapon barrels remained low at the ready, fingers poised with discipline straight and off the trigger. Their uniforms and tactical armor were a collage of faded browns and greens, blending them with the foliage of the sprawling mountain range. Six pairs of piercing eyes scrutinized every detail before Raptor Team's pace.

I remember this. The Devil's Walk and its beguiling peace before the marauding darkness, Artemis thought. Her gaze scanned over the team. *Everyone appears locked on and good to go. This could be it...*

Birds ceased chirping, leaving only the crunch of foliage underfoot. The chilling caress of the forest swelled in their ears, causing trembles to course down their backs. Gone was the usual symphony of crickets and cicadas ringing in the landscape, replaced with the dullness of white noise emanating from nothing. The afternoon radiance of the sun blurred over the region, unable to penetrate the dreary mists that lingered with the cold of a departed morning.

Too quiet. I didn't notice it the first time. I was so naïve to the signs. Aris would claim I'm being too hard on myself, that I was just a girl. But I should've noticed it.

The quick advance continued, their conditioned lungs matching the rapid pace. The agents' hard glares searched onward, their singular determination acknowledged through glances and exchanged nods.

Agent Rivers held point, carrying the pace for the team. Behind him was their heavy weapons specialist, Milton, carrying a short barreled M240L machine gun.

"Actual, what makes you so sure this isn't just a wild goose chase?" Milton turned to his team leader Artemis Coleman. "I mean how do we know that anonymous tip isn't just trying to string us away from a real issue?"

"Yeah, Actual," Agent Corwin, her second, agreed. "I'm not one to question orders but we haven't seen anything out here, not even so much as a deer."

"Mira, don't you think that's reason enough to be suspicious?" Agent Rodriguez countered as she wiped sweat from her brow. "Besides, the scryers were sensing something big going on here. Are we just going to ignore that fact?"

"Have I ever given you reason to doubt me?" Agent Coleman responded.

"No, Actual, you haven't," Milton answered. "I apologize. I'm not trying to be insubordinate, but this mountain range is huge, and a hunt could take weeks. Searching this tiny portion with just our team and no definite coordinates seems like looking for a needle in a haystack. Pardon my cliché."

"It's fine, I know you're trying to think outside the box, as I taught you." *He wanted us to see the first snap tonight. I know the tickets weren't cheap. I hate canceling on him after he makes these wonderful plans. But I know the scryers' tip isn't a ruse. I could never forget this place. I could never erase that night from my mind.*

Artemis smirked as she caught the man winking back. Firmness returned to her face once a rank odor of rotting flesh mixed with tartness of expired body fluids invaded her nose.

Agent Rivers halted, raising his balled fist to alert the others. He lowered the muzzle of his weapon, reaching into a pouch on his combat vest for his cellphone. Dried blood remained caked into the crumpled foliage below the girth of a towering hemlock. Stains of rust brown and red surrounded them, splashed about in a haphazard tapestry of scratches, raking the bark in desperation. Sour reek from fetid puddles invaded the agents' nostrils as their boots squished into it. Life fluids reached the upper portions of their view, dripping from leaves and branches. Sections of dirt were rived away, with deep and wide streaks torn into the earth, exposing moist soil. Among the stains were tufts of cloth, stuck between the foliage and wading in the forest breeze.

"Someone was trying desperately to pull away," Agent Rodriguez noted.

"Actual, there's dried blood everywhere. I think we found the hiking party," Agent Rivers said. "You need to see this. It's exactly what you anticipated."

As Agent Artemis Coleman hurried past the rest of her team, the barrels of their readied weapons lowered with discipline teeming through muzzle of awareness. She shouldered her M14 with its camouflaged synthetic stock, advancing to a position next to Rivers. Agents Pippen and Corwin took a knee behind a tree, watching the rear and flank with rifles snug in their grip, pressed into their bodies, scanning the environment.

"Damn, that looks messy!" Milton exclaimed.

Artemis' face remained as chiseled stone, her fierce stare gathering the details. No bones or morsels of flesh remained among the greasy scraps of clothing. Ripped laces and crumpled steel guided their scrutiny to a pair of boots, wrenched apart and strewn about the kill zone. Shining metal appeared among the foliage. Agent Rivers reached for it, withdrawing a gold watch that continued its dutiful ticking.

"An Arthur Poirier watch, popular with the Wall Street types and celebs. It must be worth at least ten grand and whoever did this just left it," Rivers mentioned to Artemis, handing it over. "Another possible confirmation. We know they're not after wealth."

"Rich pendejos." Rodriguez shook her head. "Probably had no idea they were being hunted until it was too late."

"The kill sack is too tight, despite the mess. It was an ambush, timed too perfectly for my comfort." Artemis noted as she tapped her communication earbud. "Carver, are you getting the images from my body cam?"

"Affirmative, Actual." Carver responded over comms. "I see it on my monitor. Does it smell as bad as I imagine?"

"And then some," Rodriguez replied.

"Lovely. It's times like this I'm glad you all leave me behind with the vehicles. Hey, Rod, let's hope this didn't make you lose your appetite."

"Why?"

"Ugh, no reason. I'm going to transfer these images to headquarters for further analysis."

"Actual, is this it?" Corwin wondered. "Is this what you expected?"

"Yes. Did all of you bring incendiary rounds?" Artemis' grim gaze searched the distance, resting a straight finger over her weapon's trigger.

"Roger, Actual," Corwin acknowledged. "Just as you advised."

"That means we're hunting—" Pippen started.

"A ravenous vector," Corwin interjected. "Stay sharp people, we know how fast they move, and how clever they can be when stalking."

"Before we Charlie Mike, we're falling back to the nearest town," Artemis ordered. "I have to make a phone call."

"Cryptic as always, Actual. But we trust and acknowledge," Rivers replied.

Artemis patted the agent on the back, before turning to the horizon rising beyond the tree line. An involuntary torrent of memories flooded inside. She was a little girl again, watching quick flashes of images plaguing her mind's eye. Desperate and shrill screams rang into her psyche, rushing through her with a quivering torrent. Flood gates opened with images of blood spewing from flesh cleaved to the bone. That day ruined her family and shattered the masquerade of youthful ignorance.

The radio's crackling noise vanished, along with the faces of her teammates. She was no longer with them, but a child again, a little girl with her twin brother, rattling in the cabin of their family's SUV, cruising through a dilapidated and narrow road.

A cool chill from an autumn breeze flowed through sparse buildings in a small mountain village. Rear lights from an SUV flared to life, as the rolling vehicle stopped before one of two rusted pumps outside a gas station. 'Jasper's Pitstop' was written along the graying white walls, in a red blocked print, that had long faded into pink. Vehicle doors unlocked and opened in quick eagerness, the family's exit announced with yawns and stretches to the orange sky.

Mario looked to Adonis. The eighteen-year-old nodded, entering the store with cash in hand as his father inserted the pump's nozzle into their thirsty vehicle. The twins Artemis and Aristotle stepped out. Cornrows lined their scalps in tight and neat fashion, pushing underneath their winter caps. Sandwiched between was their younger sister, walking with them hand in hand. Her feet dragging, the little girl's curious eyes peered in wonderment at the frosted tips of mountains stretching around the landscape, rivaling the clouds with their towering height.

This was the beginning. Where it all changed. My thoughts used to shout whenever I saw it, playing back in my head during the few moments I manage to get sleep at night. 'Artemis, plead with him, tell him to turn around.' He wouldn't have listened. Dr. Mario Coleman always knew better. Probably where I got my tenacity from. His career as an anthropology professor commanded an aura of respect he carried beyond his professional life. The black Indiana Jones. Were it so elegant! My father's greatest strength was his pride, but it was also his Achilles' heel.

"Arty, Aris, you better keep an eye on Persephone," Mario ordered. "If anything happens to her, that's your hides."

"Okay Dad, we got her," Artemis yawned as her brother Aristotle stretched his arms to the clouds.

"I mean it, she's your responsibility!"

"Howdy," a voice greeted them from the porch of the station.

A worn face draped with thick and heavy wrinkles scrunched together with a jovial smile. The man's ears flanked wide on his head, looking akin to small radar dishes, reddened from the mountain chill. Saliva stretched where the majority of his teeth should have been. Calloused and wart-covered fingers came together in a wave.

"Well, howdy back to you too, good sir. I'm Dr. Mario Coleman. How's the evening treating you?"

"Mario, you say? I'm Jasper. It's settin' for a big chill. I can feel it in these ole bones of mine. I'd reckon we got about three hours o' sunlight left. Where you headin'?"

"Good to know. I guess we're going to have to push it if we're going to settle in before dark. Taking the family camping deep into the Jefferson by the Devil's Walk. Hoping to give them some time on a hunt and hiking. Passing on my knowledge, making sure the young ones have time to practice. It's a big part of our family."

"Pardon me, but if I were you, I wouldn't be headin' up to the Devil's Walk. Folks like you should avoid those parts, wouldn't be doing my Christian duty if I didn't tell ya to steer clear of it."

"Those types, huh?"

"Yea, partner—"

"I don't let backward thinking fools impede my life."

"No. You don't seem to unders—"

"No. I don't think you understand. You won't be scaring us away just because you don't like seeing black faces around here. This is our country, too."

The station door closed behind Adonis as he walked back to the car, smiling with a bag of beef jerky. Mario's face remained stone etched, his lip curling with disgust as he turned away from the old man and completed fueling. Stern grumbles ushered his children to hurry. Mario peeled out from the station, leaving the town in their rearview mirror and trees whipping past their peripheral. He shook his head, muttering with fists wrapped tight around the steering wheel.

There are those moments in a person's life when they have to deal with that which they wish they did not. Racism came fleeting, drifting away but always rearing its ugly head back. My father had grown up seeing it more. Although, he liked to pretend that it was gone at times, it always made an unwelcome appearance in his life. At least that's what he anticipated at the time. Hindsight has that strange way of clearing the muck of chaos and emotion, organizing the objective, until only the truth rises to the top.

"Dad, you were kinda hard on that old gentleman back there." Artemis broke the silence.

"Arty, don't say 'kinda', like some hood rat. We've been over this."

"Sorry, Dad." *I miss that curly salt and pepper beard of his...*

"You don't understand. I've dealt with this longer than you. There are people like that who are going to try using fear to manipulate you. He just doesn't want us around."

"Dad, I don't think—"

"Arty, stop. His kind are dying relics from a bygone era. I'm just upset that you all had to see it. Even if he tried masking his condescension."

"What's that word, Daddy?" Persephone asked.

"It means to say something from an ideology where you feel superior to others."

"That's not good."

Mario chuckled. "No, it's not, sweetie."

"GPS isn't helping much," Adonis stated. "But the map says we're almost there."

"Good work, Son."

Dad found a camping site for us before the end of the evening. Nothing staged like the glampers. We did everything from scratch, from setting up our tents, digging latrines, and starting a campfire. I remember the smell of baked beans hovering in the air, just as Aris and I were overwhelmed with wanderlust. The beauty of the forest draped in the dwindling gleam of the day had mesmerized us. We enjoyed our adventures back then, although nothing ever came of them except for tired feet and voracious appetites. That was until...

Thick fog blanketed the mountains with a gentle and cool whiteness trailing into the surrounding forest. It rolled into the campsite, weaving between the tents and around the shallow pit dug for a fire. Mario popped in and out of the three tents, searching with Adonis in tow.

"Artemis! Aristotle!" Mario called out and shook his head. "I bet they wandered off. I told them to stay put until we could reconnoiter the area at dawn."

"You know how they are," Adonis said, taking Persephone's hand. "Although, I managed to keep this one in my sight. You're not going anywhere."

Persephone giggled as her older brother's fingers tickled into her arm pits.

"So be it," Mario continued. "Adonis, you and Perse gather more firewood for the night while I get dinner started."

Adonis saluted, taking his sister by the hand as they meandered to the perimeter.

Shrubbery crumpled under the quick steps of Aristotle and Artemis. They peered overhead to purple hues claiming the sky along with twinkles of distant stars that ushered in the evening. Aristotle continued their rapid pace through the wilderness.

"Why have you been so quiet lately?" Artemis asked.

Aristotle shrugged. "No reason."

"Oh, don't give me that. I know something's wrong. Like you can use that bull-donkey on me, right? Out with it!"

"I just keep having dreams lately about Mom. They feel so real. I had another when I was napping on the ride up here."

"What are they about?"

"She was warning us. I dreamt she was on the side of the road. Pleading with us for something. Waving away at the vehicle."

"Creepy. Are you becoming a ghost whisperer? Like on that show where that chick can see dead people?"

"Don't be so callous!"

"Sorry—"

A visage of gleaming eyes halted their steps. From behind the cover of shadow and foliage, a young feminine face peered. Sharp and tiny protrusions rose from her thick matted curly auburn hair. The girl's thin serpentine pupils met theirs.

"Papa..." the quivering girl murmured, shaking with apprehension.

"Hi—"

Branches and leaves rustled as she receded into the wilderness.

"Wait!" Artemis said. "Come back. Are you lost? Do you need help?"

"Way to go," Aristotle murmured.

"I didn't see you doing anything but freezing, dork!"

"Let's go see if we can catch up and help her. She looks a mess. Were those rocks in her hair?"

They rushed through the thickening wilderness,

following the shadow that darted away from them. Around the trees the girl went, between bushes, and through swathes of grass, until they arrived at an opening in the earth. Shadows covered the expanding vastness before them, descending into a cave's mouth. Riddled along the ground were strips of metal immersed in thick brown corrosion, surrounded by tall weeds rising in sections amid the worn path. Broken flakes peeled away from heavy rust that surrounded a cart, the wheels long gone from its snapped axles.

"I swear this looks like a mineshaft," Aristotle mentioned. "Like the type Dad lectured about on the drive up."

"Yeah," Artemis agreed. "Crazy. Looks as if we finally found something. So, when we get back, we'll have a reason to curtail the pending reprimand!"

Aristotle nodded. "My sentiments exactly."

"We lost that girl. Here I thought I was fast. She could really move."

"Should we go in the cave and check it out, Arty?"

There's always a lingering sense of urgency that comes when I think of this moment. Part of me wishes we had gone back. It's irrational of course. We would've ended up like them.

Adonis and Persephone sat in their nylon fold out chairs, smiling as the warm aroma of baked beans and salty bacon flowed into their nostrils. Mario stirred the large boiling pot and tossed another branch on the crackling fire below.

"Some bacon, some chives, some Himalayan salt, some

peppercorn," Mario rattled off with a grin as his youngest daughter clapped with excitement.

"Yes, sir!" Adonis matched his father's expression, until a rapid movement caught his attention in peripheral sight.

Adonis gazed past Mario, staring into the surrounding darkness of the evening. Shadows rifted among the backdrop, straining the young man's eyes.

"The night playing tricks on you?" Mario followed his son's gaze. "You see something?"

"I thought I did."

"Our minds tend to graft together the shapes and images we see in the dark. Same thing happens when we're gazing up at the clouds. There's an innate eagerness to make sense of it. It's called pareidolia. Fascinating concept. It's also how we're able to recognize art."

A silhouette formed in the darkness. With smooth and noiseless steps, it circled the camp, disappearing behind one of the tents. Adonis stood up, his eyes straining to scrutinize what he followed. Mario ceased stirring, turning around to see the figure as well. From the darkness Artemis stepped out, her cheeks perking with a toothy giggle.

"Girl, quit playing games with your brother!" Mario snapped. "You know he's jumpy."

Adonis remained silent. The recesses of shadow refused to leave his sister. Artemis' smile continued, expanding with her exuberant eyes. Persephone shuffled behind Adonis as Mario turned back adding another pinch of salt.

"Arty, where's Aristotle? Are you hungry? I'll have dinner ready in a few minutes."

The gleam of nocturnal predatory eyes appeared from the depths of shadows, hovering several feet behind Artemis. Persephone dropped her plate, the metal of its structure clanging with rocks amidst the grass. In slow steps the little girl tucked herself behind Adonis.

"Perse..." Mario raised a brow to his little one. "What's wrong with you?"

The quaking of their bodies sent a shiver through Mario, hair rising on the back of his neck. The freezing grip of apprehension seized his limbs, washing away warmth from the camp's hearth. Breathing grew in pace with their escalating heart rates. Mario followed their stares, seeing the inhuman gaze of ravenous intent looming over them. Others appeared, encircling their position.

Tall weeds shuddered under the approach of the twins as they continued into the mineshaft, with beams from their flashlights guiding their path. A cloud expelled from the depths. Thick warmth laced with sulfur invaded their nostrils, forcing an involuntary gag. Aristotle coughed, the stream from his flashlight twirling on the surrounding walls, escaping his hands.

"You, okay?" Artemis patted her brother's back.

The boy continued to convulse, though his coughing subsided. He screamed. Artemis grabbed him, patting his back to no avail as he fell over.

"Hey!"

Aristotle continued his cries, mouth agape, his face distorted with horror, clinging to his sister with a trembling grasp. She took him in her arms, cradling her brother, helpless to watch tears streaming down his face.

"Please, tell me what's wrong!"

It was his psychic awakening. Of course, I didn't know the signs at the time. Probably still wouldn't be able to recognize it, seeing how they differ from case to case. My brother didn't regain his ability to speak until a time after that, making only silent appearances with his long face and dreary eyes, until I was older. When he finally talked, I wished he hadn't informed me of what he saw... what he knew.

Mario kept his sight on the first pair of eyes, waving for his daughter to come. The ladle escaped his grasp, stepping back to his other children. He looked over to the tent, yearning for his hunting rifle.

"That won't do you any good," Artemis declared.

The parody of her voice was deep like a man's, carrying a tone of sinister purpose. The girl's crazed smile never left her unblinking gaze.

"Artemis Coleman, stop this!"

"Daddy, come get me," Artemis mocked until all attempt to feign softness in her voice was gone. "Daddy, please save me."

Artemis twitched, stomping forward, plowing through the boiling pot and roaring fire. Her feet trudged with the shadows still over her lower body, pulling the unseen with her approach, save for the girl's torso, reaching with ravenous delight.

Fingers extended with the darkness, curved and sharp in their final design. Like knives they punctured Mario's stomach. Bellowing laughter filled the campsite. Howls from the surrounding presences echoed deep into the night air. The frenzied cries passed through the mountains with an unceasing fervor and ringing pitch.

Artemis' head lurched back, bearing a grin widening with cracks in perceived reality. Her skull stretched, dropping back, opening a visage of endless barbed teeth and strings of saliva reverberating from deep cackles. When she snapped her head forward, Mario's torso crunched under the impossible force of her slamming maw. Convulsions were all the man could muster, as hundreds of thin fangs punctured his body. Ribs snapped away, shattering under the pressure, his chest cavity collapsing.

Persephone screamed. Adonis sobbed. Resistance withered from Mario's kicking legs, until they dangled before his children. The being looked into their eyes, slurping the remains of their father down its gullet.

With staggered steps it approached, the shape of its head remaining wide with the horizon of a warp in reality. Fangs punctured its own lips, sending an ooze of saliva and blood careening from the wounds. Adonis screamed, running into the night. Howls in the darkness followed. Noiseless steps carried tall beings in rapid pursuit of the teenager. Between heavy breaths he looked back, seeing the eyes in the distance, closing in seconds.

Cries grew louder, their whining pitch screeching into Adonis's ringing ears. His legs pumped with everything he could muster, but they never lost pace. Their near gazes remained upon his back, with intention burning a hole in Adonis despite adrenaline numbing his senses. From the shadows and foliage, a claw reached, grabbing the boy's arm. His shoulder popped, disjointing out of socket, under the immense strength that refused to unhand him. The pain of dislocation didn't register over the insurmountable fear as the boy thrashed for dear life through haggard screams of desperation.

Predatory screams closed on Adonis, until becoming one. His pursuer released him. The boy fell over, sobbing and crawling with his working arm. A thin frame seethed with fury and sinew, pouncing from the darkness. Eagerness flexed through its fingers, ripping through Adonis' back. Others joined the frenzy, shredding away and devouring the stolen morsels of his body, until all that remained were stains of gore riddled with tufts of material.

Artemis looked to Persephone with whom she now held hands. "Dinner is served."

Rasping inhuman cries carried through the night, mixing with the howling winds of the late evening. Hulking silhouettes appeared in the distance, clawing at a mess below them.

Artemis helped Aristotle over her shoulder, catching glimpses of the beings. She saw an image of herself standing adjacent to the frenzy; the twisted parody of a grin over her face sent the shiver of fear rumbling down her back, paralyzing all senses with its unwelcomed pulse. Persephone's eyes shot over to her sibling. The light of her soul extinguished, replaced with an unblinking addled lack of self-awareness.

"It seems we have more dinner guests," the other Artemis stated.

The head of a lithe being rose, its gore-stained maw

chomping at the flesh squeezing between its flat teeth. A howl followed. Its pitch directed at the twins. In hushed steps they bounded, save for the heavy breath of anticipation that escaped their mouths with the fervor of unceasing hunger. Aristotle pushed his sister away.

"Run, Arty!" he said, picking up a large branch to clutch in his arms while shaking away the daze. "I'm your big brother. I have to protect you."

"I can't. What about you—"

"I'll catch up, I promise! Just go!"

Artemis ran, her legs pushing with all the zeal that her lungs could summon. She continued to run. Despite leaving the howls in the distance, their echoes continued to ring in her ears.

The residue of fear lingered within Artemis, despite her mind drifting back to the present. She continued with Raptor Team until they arrived at a break in the trees, leading to a small roadside town. Amid the outskirts she spotted the glare from their black trucks parked in a nearby field, facing outboard in a squared formation. The vehicles each possessed large antenna, the light of active radio equipment inside blared from transmissions passing over their receivers.

Artemis approached a vehicle, spotting their intelligence agent, Carver, leaning back in a seat, with his hands folded behind his head of blond hair. He jolted when a shadow crept up, finding Artemis glaring at him through the tinted window.

"Hey, Actual…" the intelligence agent greeted her after opening the door.

"Get off your ass and get me an AD on the horn," Artemis ordered. "Another thing, get your head out of your backside. This isn't going to be a standard hop. Do you get me?"

"Yes, ma'am." The agent brought his posture upright, his face firming with discipline and focus.

"I mean it, Carver!" The team commander pointed her finger with grim resolve. "You're the weak link on the team. No showing your ass on this mission. I don't care how bored you get back here. I need everyone with their head in the game. I want you to be the agent I know you can be. I've had my thoughts to dismiss you from the Raptor Extreme Climate Warfare Team because I felt you didn't have the mettle of the others. Prove me wrong, Agent, or go home."

The others stood behind their leader, staring down Carver. Rodriguez drove her finger across her neck, gagging in silence, before scowling. Corwin nodded in agreement with Artemis' sentiment.

Carver's glance shot over to Milton who mouthed the words 'ouch' before seeing Pippen statuesque and stone-faced as usual.

"Yes, ma'am!"

"We have something alarming here that needs reporting."

"There's smoke?"

"No. Fire."

"Acknowledged." Carver grabbed the radio mic. "Tac-com this is Raptor6India, we're in need of further guidance from a top. Over."

"We copy, your last, Raptor Team," Tac-com transmitted. "All tops are pressed in operations. What's your status?"

"Roger. There's fire we need extinguished."

"Acknowledged, we're alerting the head-shed now. Stand by for response."

"What do you have for me, Raptor Actual?" a deep voice asked over the radio's speakers.

"It's AD Hughes," Carver whispered with apprehension. "The Curmudgeon!"

"Give me that!" Artemis snatched the mic. "Curmudgeon, this is Raptor6Actual reporting from the Jefferson AO. My team found dismembered campers. It's a mess, sir. Hard to tell how many are deceased, but I'm going to assume there were no survivors. Very similar to..." she released the transmission.

"I know, Raptor Actual." Hughes' voice softened. "I cannot provide any backup; all teams are tasked with major operations at present. The Agency is stretched thin. Monarch is still being utilized by QueenBee for her clean-up operation in the Los Angeles aftermath. You're riding solo until further notice. I'll send HoneyBadger to reinforce when they become available."

"I see."

"Hector hasn't seen you in a while. I'm sure he'll be happy—"

"I'd rather not. I hate having him watching over me. Makes me feel like a little girl again."

"You're going to get whatever is available, Raptor Actual. Now, it's your call whether you want to proceed or hold."

Artemis looked to the rest of Raptor, listening outside of the door. Solemn faces of resolve and nods were given.

"We're Charlie Mike."

"Continuing mission, okay. I know you don't fuck around, Arty. Run it heavy, if you must. I'll keep checking in on Raptor and so will Sanchez, whenever she's available. If this becomes more than a simple hunt for uglies, then you hold until relief is in place."

"Acknowledged, Curmudgeon."

"Be safe out there, Raptor. Curmudgeon, out."

"What now, Actual?" Corwin asked with the other Raptors surrounding their team leader.

"I'm going to call for another backup. You all grab some chow and rest your feet. We're not going to challenge these vectors until sunrise."

Raptor Team dispersed among their vehicles, fetching convenient Meals-Ready-to-Eat in plastic containers for their dinner. As the evening sky ushered away the last of the sunlight, twinkling stars greeted them, along with the bite of an unrelenting chill.

Artemis grabbed her cellphone, its monitor blaring with light in contrast to the darkness. She punched in the emergency contact, seeing the name appear on the device, 'Aristotle.'

"Hey sis, I thought you were on a mission," he said with the slowness of residual sleep.

"I'm in Jefferson, Aris. They're back."

Artemis waited a minute with no reply.

"Aris, did you hear me? It's happening again. We found—"

"I don't want any part of it. Besides, every time you're in the mountains, you think we've found it and then it turns out we're just hunting a sasquatch or dogman. I know I promised to always be here if you needed a scryer augment, but... I can't this time. I haven't got the motivation in me to keep going like this. I know what you're feeling. Let it go."

"Don't give me that crap! You can't do this now! I need you! My team, they're damn good agents, but they don't understand everything we went through—"

"Arty—"

"Aris, please. I'm alone. The flashbacks... they're overwhelming. I can't get my mind off it because there's no one to talk with. But this is it. Remember how we found Adonis? The victims today, they were brutalized in the exact manner. The species in this area leave a particular calling card."

"I can't believe I'm letting you talk me into this again. Damn it... damn you, Arty. I'm on my way. But only because you're the last member of our family. I couldn't handle it if something were to happen to you. I'll be there in the morning."

"Thanks, big bro."

"Don't thank me yet. If you're right and we find these entities, let's survive this war you plan on starting with them, first."

CHAPTER 2
FRAGMENTARY ORDER: INNOCENCE STOLEN

Sunlight began its slow approach among the lazy clouds of the morning sky. Prickling cold faded from the exposed portions of skin within their uniform. Artemis and Corwin approached the town on foot. Corwin grinned, rubbing his hands together in anticipation.

"Beef jerky!" Corwin proclaimed. "We need some jerky before starting this hop. Small towns like this usually carry the best."

"Roger that, they do, and with luck we'll run into someone I once knew," Artemis agreed. "As much as I love MREs, nothing beats a good bite of jerky."

"You love MREs, Actual? The hard to swallow, make your stool into jagged rocks, tasting all vaguely the same, MREs?"

"Yes."

"You're insane!"

"Yes, but you already knew that about me."

Chuckles evaporated upon approaching the small gas station. A middle-aged couple stood before them. Graying strands of brown hair stuck to the woman's damp face from the tears streaming through red-rimmed eyes. The man comforted her with gentle pats, a morose expression of longing defeat covering his face. His head lowered in sympathy with his wife's cries that escalated into deep and gasping sobs.

"We was just heading out to speak with ya," the husband addressed the agents. "We supposed that by them fancy vehicles and uniforms, that you're some kind of feds? Can you help?"

"Yes, sir," Artemis replied. "You are correct. I am Agent Artemis Coleman, and this is Agent Adam Corwin. What seems to be the problem?"

"Our daughter Julie..." The woman's harsh sobs mixed with her words. "She's been gone since yesterday when she went out looking for herbs."

"She likes to collect them plants, making remedies to sell folks on the internet," her husband added. "One certain plant grows near Devil's Walk. She knows better than to go around that area this time of year when its colder... but... she wanted to earn enough for a new car."

The Devil's Walk. This is it... everything is becoming clear again... The weight of doubt faded from Artemis, her composure straightening, her face hardening. In her mind's eye a fish was grasped in a hand of gleaming light. *That image is back, the fish and the hand, always when... No. Coincidence. But this. I've always known it was here... the familiarity of the buildings, the twang in their voices. All doubt is gone. I'm back where it all started. I've searched for so long. Why did I have such trouble finding this place again?*

"I see," Artemis replied.

"I'd get my shotgun and hound, and go out there myself, but I'm in no condition to deal with those lunatics in Cray."

"We'll search for her," a familiar voice announced from behind.

You came after all. It's great to have you at my side, Aris.

Artemis glanced over to see her brother approaching. Despite wanting to smile, her face remained stony and grim as her brother reached her side.

"I'm feeling this all ties in together, Arty," he said.

"What do you think, Actual?" Corwin asked.

"We're going to search for her. We're heading that way for our investigation, so we should help these good folks. Tell me more about the inhabitants of Cray, please."

"They're not right," the wife sobbed.

"I went out there one time as a boy," her husband said. "You may think our town is small and backward. You ain't see nuttin yet. Cray Village doesn't even have running water. They provide for themselves, shunning the outside world a long time ago. They just refused to join us. I've seen one of the villagers a long time ago. I hate judging like this, but he didn't look... like us."

"What do you mean?" Corwin asked. "Please, spare no details, sir."

"Never mind the fact that his lumpy back wasn't straight, but his lips, they weren't all there. I don't know the medical terminology for it, but you know. They're all like that out there. Something's off with how they look."

A hand flipped the 'closed' sign in the dusty gas station window to open. The owner peered at them before stepping out on the porch. Strands of wiry hair escaped underneath his faded baseball cap. His wrinkled and withered face hadn't changed since the first time the twins had seen him all those years ago.

"I remember you," the old man said. "I could never forget

those haunting brown eyes of yours, the evening you pounded my door begging for help. And now you're back, geared to the teeth. Lookin' for some vengeance, Artemis?"

"Your memory is sharp."

"Plenty o' bacon grease to keep the old brain lubed." The man snickered.

"What does he mean, Actual?" Corwin asked.

"Just givin' me too much credit." He continued, "Not much else happens around these parts. So, judging by the Johnsons lookin' like they're pleadin' with you, and Julie not being here, she was taken. Crays needing to keep up their stock?"

"Don't talk like that, Jasper!" Julie's father snapped. "Damn it, you can be so inhumanly callous at times!"

"Earl, Sara, stop sugar coatin' the bits. Our grandies and elder folk told us all they do out in those parts. We both know what happens to folk that wander near Cray. I do my good Christian duty to warn people, mostly to no avail."

"Jasper," Artemis interrupted. "What do you know?"

"They ain't bible thumpin'. They believe something different. Something unwholesome to decent folk. If you're darin' 'nough to go, you'll see their idols. I know some history of this place. They sparked off from our town a long while ago. Started their own settlement back in the 1800s. Wanted to believe what they wanted to believe."

"Cultists?"

"Not my place to say with freedom of religion and all that. But Artemis, if you get captured like Julie, save a bullet in that fancy rifle for yourself. You be sure to pass that on to the other women folk with you."

"The layers are speaking to me, their words flowing with the energies around us," Aristotle said. "I don't know exactly how it all correlates, but the ether is telling me this is the path,

Arty. We have to help them, in order to accomplish our mission."

"We're going to get your daughter back," Artemis announced to Earl and Sara. "Tell everyone in your town not to venture off. I'm not sure how the inhabitants of Cray will respond, and I don't want civilians getting caught in a crossfire."

"Thank you!" Earl shook Artemis' hand.

Sara gave both the agents a big hug.

"These parts been troubled for a while," Jasper said. "What made you government types decide to come out now after all these years gone by, Artemis?"

I wish I knew the answer to that myself...

"Our specific agency specializes in handling issues of the paranormal variety. While we have access to resources, our numbers aren't enough to contain every issue. There's also the matter of internecine trouble within the nation. We attend the dire situations as they arrive, the best we can."

"You don't sound too confident in that regard."

"We'll bag your cray-crays," Corwin interrupted. "Don't you worry about that. Actual discovered this hot sector. She decided to investigate after a plethora of campers went missing in this area over the last hundred years. You should be thanking her, buddy."

"There's something else." Jasper continued. "A group of young fellas went up them mountains about twenty days ago. Their vehicles are still parked here. It's not like folks to stay that long in the mountains."

"Acknowledged." Artemis replied. "We'll keep an eye out for them."

Jasper nodded.

"I never had the chance to apologize for my father's

behavior toward you, Jasper," Artemis announced as Corwin raised a brow. "The circumstances never afforded me the opportunity. Had we listened to you then, my family would still be alive. Well, I'm listening now."

Jasper met the gaze of the Raptor Team leader and nodded with respect. "God bless ya, Agents."

"Can I please buy some of that jerky, now?" Corwin smirked.

Artemis and Corwin approached their camp, the latter with a large grin and arms filled with bags of jerky. Raptor Team poured from their vehicles, stretching and yawning. Rodriguez ran her fingers through her pixie cut, before strapping her combat helmet back on. Milton stood behind his truck, stuffing his backpack with MREs and extra drums of ammunition for his machine gun. His eyes connected with Artemis, her solemn gaze raising his heart rate.

Milton reached out to caress her hand, but she pulled away.

"Not on mission," Artemis murmured, before reaffirming her command presence. "I know you're carrying a lot of firepower already, big guy. Do you think you can ruck the SMAW, too?"

"We're breaking out the Serpent? Heck yeah, I can, Actual!" Milton grinned. "I'd hump it coast to coast if I knew I had a chance to blast something with it."

"Good. And thank you."

The heavy weapons specialist unclipped a large black case,

opening it with a smirk and a nod. Within its foam confines was the SMAW Serpent, an electronic 83 millimeter warhead delivery system. The menacing weapon looked akin to a large tube with a pistol grip and advanced scoped targeting system along its flank for the wielder. Milton strapped the Serpent to his pack using thick green nylon cords, held together by quick release clips.

"Hmm... I'll have an HE loaded in her, and I'll take two HEDP high explosive dual purpose, and just in case we run into something particularly tough and unfriendly, HEAA high explosive anti-armor."

Milton secured the rocket cannisters to his pack.

"Excellent." Artemis concurred.

"I scored heaps of jerky," a grinning Corwin chirped.

"If you are what you eat, then you're going to have a shriveled, limp little piece of meat!" Rodriguez snickered.

Corwin frowned at Rodriguez, stuffing jerky in his pack. "You know that's not true, Pattie! I caught you looking during my leaks on the march!"

"Will you two knock it off?" Artemis snapped. "I swear after this hop, you both need to get a room and have it out already."

Pattie scoffed, holstering her pump action Mossberg Maverick shotgun on the side of her pack, where a catching mechanism locked it into place, before slinging her UMP45 over her shoulder. "Starting to think I'm not his type. He loves putting meat in his mouth a little too much."

The two women exchanged smirks.

Corwin shook his head.

"Gather around everyone," Artemis called out.

Raptor hurried toward their team leader, with Agent Pippen being the final member, shuffling up in his shaggy ghillie suit of green and brown hues, imitating moss and leaves. Slung over his shoulder was a nylon case, carrying his bolt action Barret MRAD sniper rifle. After he gave a thumbs up to Artemis, she began the briefing.

"Listen up. We've grown accustomed to our missions, hunting down lone or small packs of rogue tangoes. That won't be the case this time. From the sound of things, we're definitely outnumbered. So, staying together, utilizing combined and coordinated sectors of fire will be key to suppressing their numerical superiority should it come to that. We are going to infil via vehicle and take it by foot once the terrain becomes too inhospitable for the trucks to move safely at combat speed."

"Roger, Actual." Head nods followed.

"Understand this isn't going to be one of our usual hunts. This isn't some territorial sasquatch, or hungry dogman. There's rumored enemy coordination happening within a village, dozens of klicks into the AO."

"Let's talk about the FRAGO, Arty," Aristotle reminded.

"There's a fragmentary order I'm issuing this hop, for a rescue mission."

"Oh jeez, someone's been captured by these backwater loonies?" Milton asked.

"Unfortunately." Corwin shook his head. "Actual and I promised her family that we would search for her during our mission."

Glances wandered during a momentary silence for the unfortunate soul.

"The hostage we're searching for is a young adult Caucasian female," Artemis said. "So, maintain awareness of where you're placing any lethal intent. Put the finishing touches on your combat loads before we infil sector. Once we stop at the recognized perimeter, we'll dismount and proceed. Anticipate for prolonged field deployment. You have your orders, Raptor. Be ready to move after the hour."

"Acknowledged, Actual." Unanimous replies came from the agents.

"Without fear," Artemis said.

"Without limits!" Raptor Team roared.

Hang in there, Julie. We're coming.

Julie's consciousness returned, her swollen eyes struggling to open from the mixture of apprehension and sticky tears. Agonizing pain pulsed around her body, curled on the filth encrusted surface in the fetal position. Blood had stopped flowing from her crushed nose, long dried and caked within her nostrils amid swollen warmth. Exhaustion possessed her body in a haze of stillness, clouding her perception. Bruises spotted along her tender skin, reminders of the futile struggle. The ache between her thighs registered again with memories of stolen purity. Sticky wetness oozed from the torn remanent, bearing the stinging heat of repeated violation.

Her gasping chokes pulled in thick stagnant air. The recollections of a deep musty stench returned in waves upon her taste buds. Quaking channeled through her shattered nose, from a fierce blow that silenced her defiance. Julie's eyes followed one of the many flies buzzing around her, as it landed on the dusty floor. Its back legs kicked up several times before retaking flight.

"You were good," she recalled a voice announcing through

cleft lips, from a salivating mouth of teeth more akin to dispersed and jagged rocks. *"Shame we have to give ya to the master."*

The hulking man had stood over her, his silhouette haloed with bristling salt and pepper hair. Despite his distance the buttery reek of his pungent body odor still clung to her. He rocked on his heels, tugging up his pants, before putting on a large straw hat.

"After ya boys have your turn, set up a watch to make sure she don't escape before we can trade for her. Break her legs."

That's when the other ones joined... what's to become of me? My life is over. All over. The pain hasn't stopped since... I wish daddy were here... I'm so scared...

CHAPTER 3
A TRAIL TO THE LOST

Raptor Team's convoy halted in a lined formation, with their noses facing outboard, next to a creek of quick flowing shallow water. Mists of the early dawn continued to blanket the wilderness, having grown thicker the further they traveled into the range. Between the numerous trees the white coldness roamed, surrounding their vehicles, whose headlights beamed into the mass.

"Visibility is going to be low," Artemis announced over comms. "Maintain noise discipline after we dismount, only whispers and hand signals."

"Acknowledged, Actual," Corwin replied.

"Actual," Carver said. "I'm having difficulty reaching Taccom on communications via retransmission. Your orders?"

"Stay with the vehicles and keep troubleshooting."

"Understood, Actual."

"Ready for a synchronized dismount, Raptor. Five... Four... Three... Two... One..."

The engines switched off in unison, followed by doors thudding closed as the team exited their vehicles. Into the white mists the team disappeared, pushing deeper into the mountain forests.

Rivers spearheaded Raptor, guiding the team with a wave of his hand, signaling a forward movement, and closing his fist for momentary halts. With an M4 carbine and attached M203 grenade launcher at the ready, Raptor Team's point man proceeded, each step planted in a controlled fashion, mindful of whatever came underfoot.

Their eyes scanned the silhouettes of graying detail coming into view upon approach. Grass rustled with the scamper of squirrels, their chirps accompanying desperate scrambles into the cover of trees and bushes.

"Something is living around here after all," Aristotle whispered into his sister's ear.

She nodded.

Aristotle added, "The mineshaft has something to do with all of this. Remember? How close were you to it when you first started the sweep?"

"No idea," Artemis replied. "It's not on any of the maps and I'm no psychic. I'm good. I'm not omnipotent."

"Fair enough, Arty." Her brother bumped shoulders with her before giving a playful chuckle. "Jeez, I still can't budge you."

"You never will." She grinned. "Pussy."

Rivers halted, bringing a fist high into the air. Raptor Team ceased their advance with Milton and Corwin taking knees, raising their weapons outboard of the formation, and scanning around. With quiet steps Pippen moved back into the shrubbery and mists, his ghillie suit blending him away from sight. Rodriguez approached with caution, her UMP45 submachine clenched tight in both hands, shadowing Rivers who scrutinized the ground with hawkish countenance.

"Contact, gordo?" Rodriguez wondered.

"I know that means 'fat boy' in Spanish!" Rivers snapped. "I should've never told you about my childhood!"

"Easy! Sensitive much? I'm just playing. You know you're my bro. Chill."

"What do you have for me, Rivers?" Artemis asked.

"The ground in this area has been disturbed." Rivers pointed. "I can see the faint trace of a line surrounding certain patches."

"How you're able to move that quick and take in all those details is beyond me, George," Rodriguez murmured.

"Not bad for the guy who grew up being the fat kid, eh?" Rivers smirked.

"I would've never guessed."

Artemis followed his finger, guiding her vision between breaks where the grass parted with slight space between the sections. A thin coat of brown dirt remained adjacent on other patches, fading, and blending save for the thicker spots.

"Damn good eyes." She patted her teammate before taking up a large stick from the ground.

After stepping close, Artemis poked the soft ground. The middle of the patch began to push downward. With more effort she continued until the masquerade of the top layer gave way, crumbling as it plummeted into a deep pit. Wooden sticks sharpened to angular perfection appeared below, puncturing with ease through the collapsing layer. Brown mud covered the makeshift spikes. A pungent warm odor spread through the air, forcing Artemis and Rivers to step away with a gagging cough.

"What the fuck?" Rodriguez raised a brow.

"Punji sticks," Rivers informed. "At least that's what they were called during the Vietnam War. The trap is common around the world to slow the advance of intruders. Cheap, easy, and efficient."

"And what the hell is that smell?"

"Dung," Artemis said. "That's not mud covering them. It serves as a poison to cause infection and septic shock."

"That's it," Rodriguez scoffed. "I can't wait to fill these assholes with buckshot."

"Nasty way to go," Corwin murmured.

"They've been busy." Rivers pointed to the other patches weaving between the trees and bushes. "This place is riddled with them."

"Everyone save Pippen will be in line astern formation on patrol," Artemis announced. "Keep it tight and single file behind Rivers until he announces we're clear."

"Roger that, Actual," Rodriguez acknowledged with a twisted expression of disgust.

"Pip," Artemis called over comms. "You got our far-side overwatch?"

"Roger, Actual. I'm in position and shadowing."

"Raptor, let's keep moving. Watch your step and prepare for contact. We're drawing near."

Rivers pressed onward, the team following his slow steps in single file formation. The others remained with eyes searching outboard to their flanks, double checking the ground before each step. Sweat raced over their bodies, despite the morning coolness still clinging to their uniforms. After moments passed, Rivers raised his fist again, turning back with his palm to the team.

He's got eyes on something! Artemis pushed forward to join him. Peering out into branches, she spotted cabins sprinkled amongst the forest. Moss covered the craggy logs forming the dirt encrusted walls, topped with a thatched roof of dust-covered hay faded from its original tawny hue. Yellow and brown grass remained matted and withered around the township, with a trail of dirt weaving through the middle. A stone well flanked one of the larger buildings, with a wooden bucket resting on the ledge, tethered by a rope attached to its handle.

Trees stood among the village, with their branches removed. The tall trunks had been stripped of bark, the remainder of their pale surfaces smoothed over and etched deep with lined sigils formed by overlapping slashes. A further scan spotted the parody of a serpent carved into another. Six wings extended from its body, with the tail curling around a circle.

"They weren't kidding," Aristotle whispered. "This place has definitely been forgotten by time. How many chickens and cows you think they would trade me for a young healthy lass of breeding age like yourself, Arty? Just curious, that's all."

Artemis rolled her eyes and turned to her team. "Give me a near-side overwatch from here."

"Roger, Actual." Milton pressed a button on his front grip. Thick plastic legs extruded from it, stretching outboard, forming a bipod. He took to a prone position between bushes, lining the machine gun's buttstock snug into his shoulder, while scanning the village with the red sight dot of his scope. "Set."

"Corwin, you accompany Milton. Keep fire off the housing units until we can get eyes on their hostage."

"Acknowledged, Actual," Corwin responded taking to the prone with Milton.

"Rodriguez, Rivers, with me."

"Roger, Actual."

Artemis sensed a looming presence, stealing attention in

her periphery. She turned, finding only the endless swathe of trees amidst the surrounding wilderness. Pulling away, her attention shifted as they stepped into the village.

Milton's gaze applied an unseen pressure, the long face of his trepidation usurping her thoughts, ushering forth images of the tall blond man's disposition.

He's worried. He always gets like this. I'll be fine, big lug.

"Without fear," Artemis turned and mouthed to Milton.

"Without limits." He sent a nod that restored his determination.

In slow and silent steps, the three walked into the outskirts of the town. Artemis led the way with Rodriguez and Rivers in tow. Reek from salty urine swelled into the air, mixing into a tartness with the pine scent around them. It grew stronger as they approached the buildings, searing in their nostrils with each breath. Artemis' eyes followed her nose, guiding to the yellow-tinted stains along the foundations. She stepped past, teammates following in tight formation, keeping close to the walls without brushing them.

Artemis peeked inside, catching the glimmer of a smoldering fireplace, with a black kettle suspended over it, via a three-legged steel fire crane. A few stools were spread throughout, along with sleeping bags strewn across the floor and blackened from thorough use. Glimpses of rapid movement appeared on the floor, tiny dots scurrying through shadow. Flies buzzed past Artemis' head, escaping into the light of the morning.

"Nothing," Artemis mouthed.

As they moved to another cabin, the double doors leading across the way to the entrance of a wide domicile swung open. Out strolled two hulking men, struggling to button their black wool pants, and slipping on matching shirts. The team hurried, slipping just past their view to the other side of a cabin. Artemis peered low around the corner, with Rivers leaning over her, sharing the view.

"It doesn't seem like they saw us," Rivers whispered. "What the hell is wrong with them... look, Actual... their faces..."

Cleft lips rolled back with glee revealing near toothless smiles, arrayed with something more akin to jagged brown rocks than teeth. Twisted were their chins, pulling away from their faces to eliminate any modicum of symmetry in their countenance. Drooping soulless eyes peered from them, more like beasts than men, hanging far lower than their wide rolling foreheads.

"Fun, fun, fun!" one chanted with a deep voice elementary in its tone.

"Ya, had fun, too. I wanna marry her." The two shuffled away, heading deep amongst the village until out of sight.

"She's in there," Artemis whispered. "Those bastards..."

Raptor Team maneuvered from their cover, along the cabin's flank until dashing to the entrance. Rodriguez raised her UMP45 tight in her arms, leading through the double doors. A stale odor hit them first, with the contrast of shadows opaquing their vision. The familiar hint of copper and salt grew stronger. Shadows surrounded them, their steps creaking with the uneven floorboards as they walked farther inward.

Hay was strewn about the floor, crunching underfoot. The buzzing of large flies grew evident, humming into ears with their ceaseless drum. Artemis scanned hard, seeing a table, and chairs, then following the trail of hay that grew thicker. Their steps drowned out a faint noise.

"Stop," Artemis whispered. "I hear something."

A whimper followed struggling breaths coming from the

far corner. The team continued down the trail of hay, until arriving to a large pile. Within the shadows, writhing on a sleeping bag, was the bare body of a young woman.

"Give me a controlled beam," Artemis ordered.

Rivers removed a small flashlight from his vest, clicking once with his hand over the brightness, then twice to lower its red intensity. When illumination was brought over the young lady, her twitching swollen eyes rolled upward into her skull. Fresh blood streamed from her smashed nose, contorted from blunt force trauma. It trickled down her neck, over her bare chest into streams of red cascading in various directions. Breaths heaved from her petite frame, escaping through her gaped mouth of shattered teeth. Artemis knelt beside her, nodding back to Rivers as she checked the girl's limbs, helping her upright with a gentle embrace.

"This has to be her," Rodriguez exclaimed. "Dios mío, what have they done to you?!"

"Shh... Rod," Rivers warned, pulling his medical kit from its pouch. "Hey there Julie, my name is George Rivers, and that woman holding you is my commander Artemis Coleman. This is our team member Agent Patricia Rodriguez. We're with the US government, sent here to rescue you. I'm going to need you to remain perfectly still while I stabilize your wounds so we can get you out of here safely, okay?"

Artemis braced her as Rivers went to work. He drew the contents from a small bottle of Lidocaine into a syringe. The sharp plunger of the needle was guided with slow grace, piercing near the ridge of Julie's nose, next to her swollen eyes. Numbness came, ushering away the myriad of pain. The last of its contents were dispelled into her cheeks, still dark bluish with traces of red veins blaring through her agony.

"You're checking her tongue?" Rodriguez asked when Rivers drew a thin wooden depressor.

"No, I need to straighten the broken parts before I apply the gauze. I don't have the right tools, Pattie. I'm doing my best here."

"It's a good idea." Artemis nodded, holding tight to Julie. "Do it."

The wooden device went into Julie's nostrils, guiding with a gentle but assertive force. Rivers looked at her with his big eyes of reluctance. A loud crunch followed quick grinding as he aligned the remnants of her nose. Artemis' hand went over Julie's mouth with a tight seal, muffling the girl's cry, when she floundered in the commander's arms.

"It's straight again," Rivers announced. "Thanks, Actual."

Blood greased his fingers, packing her nostrils with gauze. The gushing flow of red ceased. Rivers finished with copious amounts of medical tape forming a splint over the ridge of her nose.

"Julie, stay with us." Patty helped her fellow agent repack his medkit.

"That's the best I can do until we get back to civilization," Rivers said.

"You did well, George." Artemis said.

They heaved the girl's limp body on to Rivers' shoulder. "I got her."

"Good, let's rendezvous with the rest of the team."

"I say we get on the horn with Curmudgeon, call in HoneyBadger Team to wipe this town off the map."

Artemis nodded.

Light flooded into the room from both doors opening. Illumination flashed inside, over the cracking wood and dust particles floating through the air. Yellow whiteness washed away their vision with the heat of sunlight, rendering a large silhouette void of detail.

"More! I want more!" The deep voice reeked of desperation laced with carnal desire. "Gimmie 'nother turn!"

Raptor Team's view adjusted, matching stares with the confused villager. His malformed lip curled upward along with a twitching brow, examining them with beady misaligned eyes. Rounds spurted through Patty's submachine gun, peppering the man's chest with bullet holes ripping through his overalls. Squeals filled the air from the floundering villager with lead boring in his wide frame. He took steps back, before looking up at Rodriguez and growling through his jagged teeth.

"What the fuck?!" Patty exclaimed.

A bellowing roar came from the villager, plodding forward, the floorboards creaking with his heavy steps.

Rodriguez released her grip on the UMP45, its sling keeping the weapon draped to her person. In one quick motion she drew her twelve-gauge, spewing buckshot. Hard force collapsed the man's chest, sending him careening into a pile of furniture.

"And the whole of Cray just heard that!" Artemis said. "Raptor Overwatch, we've been spotted. Ready the defense cordon, we're coming in hot."

"Roger that Actual," Milton replied over comms. "We're in position and ready."

"Let's move!" Artemis ordered the others. "Double time!"

Patty led through the double doors, with Rivers following and Artemis bringing up the rear. Rodriguez halted on the patio, seeing another villager with an ax in hand. Shoelaces of saliva dangled from the roof of his mouth, shuddering with an unintelligible roar clamoring through the area. Doors swung open from adjacent buildings, their thin frames slamming, as denizens of the village stormed forth.

A blast of buckshot smashed into the combatant before them. Rodriguez cocked her shotgun, sneering at the malformed man reeling in pain. His wailing continued, until another burst ripped into his throat and lower jaw, tearing the later until it hung from a tuft of flesh. The team proceeded, maneuvering around their foe's corpse plopping to the ground.

Numerous footsteps beat and trampled through grass, bearing heavy breaths eager with anticipation. Roars of anger laced with animalistic tone erupted through the town, mixing with anguish when the pursuit carried them in view of their downed brethren. Metal and wood clanged as they beat their weapons together. The shot of a rifle echoed through the village, sending the reverberating twang of ricochet through the buildings.

Artemis spun around, raising her M14 and aligning its sight to the villager carrying a lever action rifle. A smooth pull sent a 7.62 round bursting through his forehead, spraying brain matter and skull fragments over his comrades who didn't miss a stride. Among their numbers, one towered in a wide straw hat with his minions zipping around him.

There's… nothing. Artemis locked with his blank eyes, unsure if they were cognizant of her or something in the distance. An unwholesome grin pushed through his coarse beard that extended well to his chest. Sharp rusted sickles gouged the ground, dragged by his elongated arms.

"Interlopers, kill the lap dogs of El!" their leader bellowed. "Bring the flesh of their men so we may feast and capture their women."

"Arty," Aristotle cried out. "We're here! Keep moving!"

Artemis fired two more controlled shots, dropping the first

pair of the crowd. *Too many!* She rejoined her teammates, sprinting past another building, before spotting the heavy woodline of the surrounding forest. Muzzle flashes and carbon spewed with rapid bursts tearing through the shrubbery, cleaving down a few of their approaching enemies. Milton continued firing, putting room between his comrades and foes.

Corwin rose from cover, taking Julie from Rivers. "I got her, bud. Catch your breath after that crazy sprint."

Raptor Team turned to their foes, many pushing out to the flanks, their gunfire nullified by the buildings they wove behind. Shots chimed from a few doorways with lever action rifles pointed outboard, returning fire to the team's position.

"They're maneuvering around the kill sack," Artemis warned. "We need to fall back before their numbers split our sectors of fire and collapse on us. Bounding withdrawal."

Continuing with a salvo of fire into the charging remnant, Milton rose from the prone. "Ready, Actual."

"On me," Rivers called out taking point, heading deeper into the forest.

Through bushes and ferns they pushed, stepping through tall weeds and over rocks in hurried fashion. Artemis and Rodriguez turned back, firing shots as Milton pressed forward to rejoin the team.

"Set!" He took position behind a tree ahead, continuing the hail of bullets into the swarm of enemies letting the other two catch up.

Raptor Team watched hooting and howling rise from their far flanks. Grass rustled, shredded from the hapless kicks of fast paced feet. Bushes exploded with clouds of leaves and debris, the residents of Cray bursting through them, eager to pounce on their former position. Instead, the pincer failed, with all enemies flowing into the same position short of the agents.

"Great call, Actual," Corwin said.

"We're not out of it yet. Careful with that girl, Cor. We don't know how much she endured."

"Roger." Corwin patted Julie. "How you doing, Jules?"

Faint and unintelligible murmurs left her blood encrusted lips.

"Hang in there, sweetie. We'll get you back home. Just stay relaxed for the carry."

"Fuck this!" Milton grumbled looking over to Artemis.

Yeah, he's right. We need to end this. These tangoes are resilient. How are they taking so many shots to bring down? Do it, John. Give them the business!

"Steer clear of my backside!" Milton continued.

A rapid exchange of nods signaled an agreement. Milton took off his pack, unstrapping the SMAW II Serpent. The rocket launcher payload tube extended behind him while he rested into the shoulder pad to stabilize his aim. Through its scope he gazed, seeing the white thermal signatures of targets congregating amidst the gray foliage. His body shifted, breaths growing deep with anticipation. A flick of the thumb removed the safety. Then he fired.

Exhaust spewed from behind, the rocket soared forward, leaving a graying white trail in its screaming wake. Cray villagers watched the warhead colliding with one of their own. The thunderous impact that followed shuddered the forest, blinding those near it. Screams joined the ruckus as the explosion ripped through a large portion of the foes, tearing asunder their gathering. Gore pelted those behind the impact, chunks of flesh and blood splattered the landscape. Dust and leaf fragments billowed through the air, giving arise to choking coughing from those outside the kill zone.

Survivors screamed. Many flopped about, their bodies reeling with the pain of shrapnel. Ear drums gave, collapsing under the immense pressure of sound expelled from the calamity. Cray warriors staggered, their expressions glazed with wide-eyed, surreal disbelief, and the dilated pupils of concussion.

Raptor Team continued unleashing fire, with Milton dropping to his machine gun letting rounds fly. Cray denizens dropped. Their numbers thinned, with survivors withering away, fleeing back in the direction of their village.

"Top off, and maneuver," Artemis ordered. "We're getting Julie home before we Charlie Mike."

"Roger, Actual."

Patty removed the payload feed tube from the SMAW, loading in another rocket, as Milton switched the ammo drum of his M240.

"Status check," Artemis called. "How's everyone?"

"All in one piece from the look of things, Actual," Corwin announced after inspecting the others. "Except this poor thing." He added, gesturing to Julie.

"Right, let's move!"

Stragglers walked into Cray, shoulders slumped, their heads hanging low like their dragging weapons. Others limped behind, some falling just short of the village, being raised, and carried by their kin. Mathias Cray watched his children wander inward, surrounding him with long looks, some not able to hold eye contact from shame, bringing their faces low.

Mathias placed both sickles into one of his gorilla paw-like hands before removing his wide straw hat. Sweat caused his balding head to shine where his matted jet-black hair grew around. He nodded to himself, his vision wandering to the depths of the mountain forests as a smirk overcame him. Those gathered began to scratch their heads and follow his sight, shrugging and turning back with eagerness.

"The master warned us they'd be comin' one day," Mathias said. "He done warned us and we knew this would happen. And we failed because we lost focus. Carin' too much about desire led us to bein' blinded. Never mind 'bout all that now. We know them agents ain't stoppin' with just a rescue. Send warnin' to the kingdom. Tell the High Priestess there's trouble. She'll know what to do."

Quick nods came from a pair, turning to scamper off into the wilderness.

"I know who put them agents up to it. We'll handle that later. Ya'll stay indoors for now no matter what. Don't come out until I say so. The master gunna release the hungry ones…"

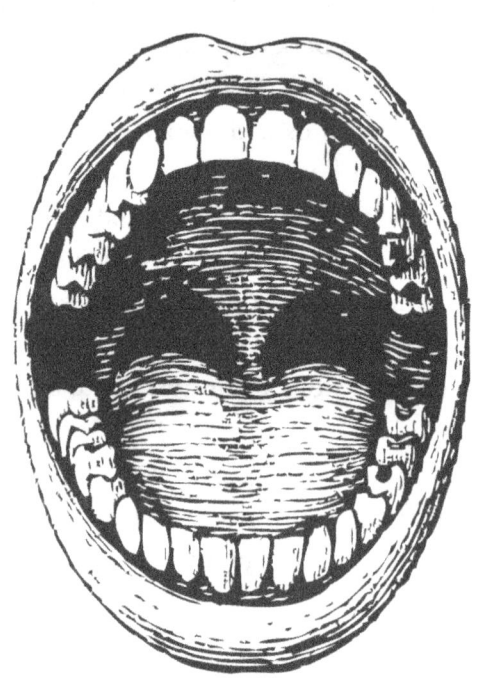

CHAPTER 4
EAT

Are they still behind me? I think I lost them...

Rapid breaths pumped through his lungs, becoming clouds of white contrasting with the freezing air around him. Sweat on his body crystalized into ice. Chilled tingles passed through the clothes sticking along his back. Bright snow remained as far as the eye could see, blinding with whiteness save for the gray rocks that jutted from the mountainside. Howling wind brushed against the hood of his thermal winter coat. His heart pounded, as if trying to leap from his chest.

Clenching tight to a hatchet, he spun around with it raised and ready. Teeth bared, his trembling face grimaced, heavy with the wrinkles of apprehension. There was only the descent of snow, leading beyond the clouds that now drifted below his position.

Just the wind... just the wind... again. How many days now? This coat... it's not doing anything anymore... I've no idea where I am. Get hold of yourself, Robbie. I can't! Frankie, he was the navigator... I don't know what the hell I'm doing!

Pain erupted in his rumbling stomach, squeezing his body with a torment that shot through his weakening core. *My wife's warm apple pie... the delicious... sweet chunks of fresh fruit that went between your teeth with each bite. I wish... it should've been you, baby. I chose them instead to prove my manhood on this godforsaken trip... how many days again? What did I do to get here?*

Weakness took Robbie's steps, his shuddering body falling over. The whimpering man's vision plummeted into a face full of snow. He pushed up, brushing away the clinging flakes of cold. As the gloved hands cleared from his eyes, blowing strands of long raven hair came into view. She turned, her luscious pink lips pressing together in a smile. Robbie's blue frostbitten nose managed to inhale her lavender scent. She sashayed closer, her wide hips shifting in a pinstripe pant suit.

"Robbie Mills," his wife called out with her sultry southern rhythm. "Hurry up, you're going to be missing out. I made an extra pie just for the two of us. The kids are asleep, they won't be a bother."

"Maggie, I should've never gone on the trip. I should've stayed home with you!"

"It's fine, I'm here now, that's all that matters, right? You sound delirious, hun."

"Maggie... aren't you allergic to lavender?"

"That's vanilla, silly. As I said, delirious. You're not all there in your head right now, mister. Now are you going to keep me waiting? I know you're hungry. It's been what, twenty-three days now? Three weeks or so with just roots, berries, and your fingernails to munch on."

"I don't know anymore..."

"Well, if you keep dragging your feet, there's just going to be more pie for me!" Maggie giggled, sauntering through the snow.

The woman walked up the path, moving through the thick layers with ease. Robbie trudged on, head lowered, shoulders drooped, breathing heavy to summon the last of his strength and make it up the steepening climb. Each step forced a whimper from Robbie as the shock from his blaring blisters grew from rubbing on his crusted socks.

I'm remembering now...

Screaming rang in his psyche, with the familiar voice of his brother and friends. Goosebumps rose on his chapped skin, prickling at his body the louder the memories grew. Tearing nylon resonated in his thoughts, their tents peeled away with ease to razor-like claws during their camp's invasion. Hungry bites, hoarse with desperation devoured those he knew with greedy abandon.

Couldn't see them... they were so fast. The rifles did nothing... they were so fast. The bullets did nothing... even when we did hit them... nothing!

"Maggie..." he sobbed. "Wait... you don't understand... there's things... they killed Petey... and Frankie... they... killed... everyone! And ate them... I've been stuck. Every time I try to leave, they... I can't explain it... they're corralling me..."

"Shh... it'll be okay. It's all over now. I promise. Save your strength. Don't go getting yourself all worked up."

"No! They're still here, I can feel it! Evil... the presence of real evil! Okay, not that stuff we imagined as kids playing video games... Maggie..."

"Easy, Robbie. You're still delirious. Just hungry and tired, my love. It'll be okay. You're home now. We're almost there. I rescued you, remember?"

"The things—"

"The doctor said you'd be suffering from a little mania

until you've completely recovered. I didn't realize to what extent—"

"Maggie! You're doing it again... stop lawyering! Be my wife... just be that and listen!"

"Okay, we did speak with the counselor about my over-assertiveness in communicating, as he put it. But try calming yourself first, you're scaring me. I think the pie is almost done cooking. We'll get you a few slices ASAP! Doc said it would be good for you to do familiar stuff and get some food in your tummy."

"The things, Maggie... they're still out there. I thought they were bears... but they're too smart. In the glimpses... they looked like men, skinny men... we have to tell someone, Maggie! Are you listening to me? Stop laughing!"

"Oh my. Just calm yourself, hun. We're almost there."

"Maggie... please! The things!"

"I told you already, hun. The kids won't be a bother."

They arrived at an area leveling off from the rest of the climb, surrounded by an array of graying boulders. Soft stones underfoot made their steps uneven. Underneath the soles of his boots, Robbie felt them being driven into the snow. Maggie spun around with a tender smile, hoping to connect with her husband's maniacal gaze. But Robbie had stopped, picking a stone from his footprint. What he held possessed a long shape, although natural, had been created with purpose long expired. He turned it, examining its faint yellowish shade with stains of pink and red embedded down its center and corners.

This... is not a rock... what is this?

Shadows moved within his peripheral vision. The stone fell from Robbie's hand as he raised his hatchet, staring over to the boulders. Snowflakes entered a gentle cascade in his view.

Maggie raised her hands and backed away.

"They're here!"

"Easy, Robbie. You're really still back there, aren't you? I'm never going to get my husband back..."

The hatchet lowered. His shoulders deflated with jerking sobs. Aching continued, from his frostbitten toenails, into his swollen feet, up his throbbing knees, and convulsing stomach that churned with ever growing torment. Hunger climbed throughout his body, gripping his mind with the fog of desperation.

A beer, a steak, chicken fingers, tacos, French fries, a burger... my Maggie's warm apple pie.

"Maggie... Maggie," he sobbed, shaking his head. A cold wind shut his eyes. The hatchet fell from his grip, during an attempt to rub the freezing tears away. "I'm sorry... I don't know what's happening. So tired... so hungry..."

"I know, that's why I brought you some pie, silly." Maggie smiled. "Your favorite. Doctor said you needed to eat more. I don't approve of all this deliciousness in one sittin'. Better not brag to the kids later when you come to. I already told them they couldn't have it."

What... why does she keep saying that?

"Maggie... what are you talking about? We don't have any children..."

Burning from the wind's embrace clamped his eyelids together. A chilling bite forced groans from Robbie. Darkness and blurred images took their turn in his view. When vision returned, his beloved wife stood holding a bundle of cloth blankets, swaying with gentle care for its contents. Her full cherry lips and thin alabaster face went into a loving smile. She waved Robbie closer with excitement. He staggered over, dizziness beginning to usurp all clarity, rendering the surroundings of his immediate focus into mottled images.

Can't keep going any longer... I don't know how... I've managed this far...

They stood rubbing shoulders, holding the bundle together. Maggie leaned in, removing layers of the blanket until a small, soft, round infantile face appeared. Robbie stared, unable to see beyond its withered newborn eyes, scrunched together, refusing to open. Its fatty little arm slipped out, pawing with open palms at their hands.

"I don't understand..."

"You're just confused. You haven't eaten anything, hun. You gotta eat."

"What? What are you trying to say? I can't... I can't—"

"Can't eat an apple pie?"

Warmth radiated from the blanket and the dish sitting in his palms. Maggie slipped away, returning from behind, patting her husband's shoulders. In his hands was the apple pie, heat channeling into his palms from the center of its body. Sweetness carried into his nostrils, driving his stomach into an excruciating shudder, coursing through every inch of him. A milky odor battled for his senses, driving away the smell of apples and cinnamon. Fingers dug into the fattiness of the plate's underside. The pie shook in his grasp as it moved, its little hand touching his index finger.

So hungry...

"I know, hun. It's been a long time. The pain isn't going away until you get something in your system. You have to eat."

I can't...

"I saw this on the Life Channel. This girl had anorexia. She just couldn't get over her mental blocks. Poor thing. Robbie, look at me."

He met her loving smile and big eyes. Maggie's gentle hands slipped into his hoodie, caressing the back of his neck, until her touch disappeared when she traced over the deadened skin of his frostbitten ear.

"Maggie—"

"Eat for me. No, eat for us."

Blurs moved in his peripheral, but he saw only the boulders again. Trembles continued, into his shaking hands. Cinnamon and apples flooded his senses, carried by the fog of desperation, bringing thoughts into chains of incoherent words.

"Eat for us..." Whispers slipped into his thoughts, neither Maggie's voice nor his own.

"So... hungry..."

Sharp pain jutted through Robbie's face when his frozen lips peeled back. Teeth sank into the pie, its soft flesh rolling over his tongue with the hot taste of salt and iron. Meat filled his mouth. Shrill screams rang into his ears with a harsh and unceasing plea for mercy. Robbie bit down harder, soaking his mouth and chin in the sticky juices of the pie. Another bite and his tongue brought small bones to crunch underneath his molars. Down his arms flowed trails of red. The screams stopped.

Strings of blood and saliva dangled from the roof of his mouth with each desperate bite growing more powerful and aggressive in succession. Gnawed tufts of flesh slipped between his fingers as they bored into the pie. A growl rose from the depths of his stomach. He hunched over his meal, coiling with predatory vigor.

Robbie howled into the wind, biting down again. The fog grew heavier in his mind, possessing his vision. He wandered, staring away into the grayness that surrounded him, wading with his arms only finding vast emptiness. His body was still animated, but without his consent. Strength returned, flooding through his thinning frame with an aura of writhing shadow. The remains of the mangled pie fell, staining the snow with a gushing slap of blood.

Fingers grew long, his blackened nails pushing outward, curving, withering away any softness of humanity. The daylights of his eyes faded, replaced with desolation signaling a lack of cognition. He ripped at his clothes, claws streaking away until baring his emaciated body, leaving gashes of dripping crimson across his thin frame.

Robbie fell to his knees, devouring the morsels of the pie that remained until only the small bones escaped into the snow. His eyes became as amber, shimmering like a nocturnal predator, looking for Maggie. She remained at his side, smiling with approval.

"Still... hungry," Robbie's voice resonated with eldritch fury. "Must... eat..."

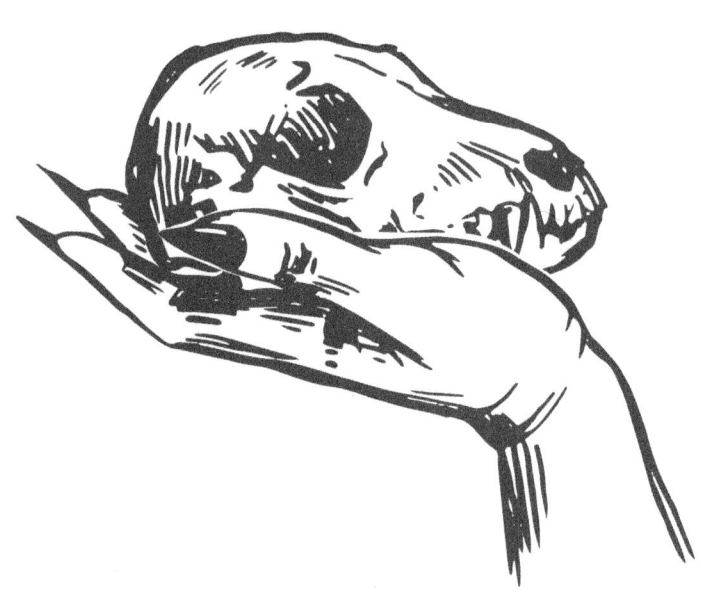

CHAPTER 5
A TIMELY ARRIVAL

R aptor Team continued through the wilderness. Rivers led with a brisk pace, his eyes searching every blade of grass before they passed over it. Trees appeared thicker and lush around them, some hugging close to each other, their massive branches mixing the emerald barrier of leaves into a canopy. A long caress from a chilling breeze swept down into the forest, sending shivers through them. Aristotle tailed his sister, trying to tap her shoulder, before she sped away with her rapid movement. Rivers raised a fist, halting the team. Artemis pushed to join him.

"Something isn't right, Actual," the point man whispered, his face narrowing with fierce scrutiny. "We should've been back by now. It was practically a straight shot from the vehicles. One of the easiest trails we've ever cut. My compass has been going haywire, too."

Rivers showed his team leader the device, its needle spinning counterclockwise in fast motion.

"It's as if we're heading deeper into the forest— look how

heavy the vegetation has become, Actual. I didn't make any wrong turns, but I'm lost—"

"I know, mine is doing the same." Artemis' hard stare shifted around the area. "This all seems surreal, as though there's a fog of confusion over my mind."

"I felt it, too." Rodriguez interrupted. "I just chalked it up to shitty sleep. Anyone else getting a headache, though?"

"Arty," Aristotle called out. "I've been trying to tell you. The energy in this area isn't just negative. It's like nothing I've ever felt before. This is beyond demonic resonance or dark sorcery. What are you seeing in our surroundings?"

"Trees, fat ones, tall grass wading down our steps, thick weed bushes—"

"No!" Aristotle shook his head. "Everything around us is dead, Arty. Everything. There's just mountain snow, large-jagged stones, and husks of wood that were once trees."

"We could start marking some of those trees you mentioned, Actual," Milton suggested.

"While you're all deciding, I'm going to check on our precious cargo." Corwin placed Julie upon the ground with slow care, brushing away a few wild strands of hair sticking to the dried blood on her cheek. "Try not to move; save your strength."

"You can use my med kit if she needs clean bandages," Rodriguez volunteered.

"Thanks, Pattie. Why can't you always be sweet like this?"

"Hmph!"

Pippen remained poised while shadowing Raptor Team. He moved with a calm control, each step slow, but direct, to provide the best field of fire to overwatch. The stock of his MRAD remained locked into his shoulder. He gazed through the scope that oversaw Artemis' movement to a tree. She drew a knife, slicing a large cross into the trunk. The vision of his team leader faded as a dull throbbing developed in his skull. Pippen shook it off, bringing his view to Corwin and Patty applying fresh bandages to the battered girl.

"What do you see?" a deep whisper asked from his righthand side.

Pulling away from the scope, the sniper hopped from his kneeling position, turning to draw his pistol with one smooth motion, leaving his rifle dangling from his vest with an attachment cord. The alignment of his weapon found nothing but the forest.

"Well now, you're a little jumpy today," Milton said from behind.

"Quit playing stupid games!" Pippen grumbled. "It's not like you to act so immature during an op, Milty. I could've blown your head off. You know better than to joke around with me during a mission."

"Sorry, Pippen. I couldn't resist. How you holding up?"

"Not well, I'm getting a headache from hell. It wasn't much earlier, but now it's growing worse. Fine time to get one. Got any ranger candy?"

"Ranger candy?"

Pippen brought his focus through the scope again, watching Artemis and Rivers continue their markings.

"With how long you were in the service and agency, you can't be serious right now? Quit fucking around. You know what ranger candy is. It's Motrin, you know, the good stuff."

"Didn't bring any this time, bud. Sorry."

"It's my fault, for not packing it. The damn bottle I brought was empty save for the freshness tab I mistook for pills. I'll live, I guess."

After shaking his head for a second, the sniper brought his view over Raptor Team in the distance. Artemis and Rivers nodded, exchanging words. Rodriguez had finished placing Julie back on Corwin's shoulder with Milton helping.

"Don't be so sure about that, Pippen."

The agent turned. His teammate was gone.

A delicate hand of russet complexion reached with slender fingers to one of the few small caskets upon an altar. High Priestess Sarai lowered her head away from the candlelight, a sigh escaping from her.

Memories flooded into her psyche when she held the cooing life in both her arms; its body already nearing the size of a toddler despite being only minutes old. Agony surged across her body, with stitches holding together the long incision lining underneath her stomach.

The second I saw them, I wanted to squeeze them, holding close to never let them out of my arms...

She looked into her child's eyes, glowing like headlights from its cone shaped head. Tingles of belonging attached her to the little being, making the pain of her shattered body fade away.

How long has it been since your faces have withered? The priestess wondered, shaking away the urge to open the boxes.

No longer can I look upon your glory, that once emanated the light of my beloved.

A tether came from her mind, latching on to the baby, energizing her arms with the limitless endurance to hold. Yearning rose in her spirit, wanting to protect and gaze with endless wonderment into the little being's shriveled face. Then his small breaths had ceased. The little body in her arms went limp. A shuddering sigh brought her back to the candlelight, and the aroma of buttery wax that dripped from the high shelf above her altar. She followed the floating wisps of smoke from burning sandalwood incense until it brushed with her face.

One more attempt, and I could fulfill my duties to my lord. I will risk it all with gestation until the final—

"*You cannot withstand it,*" a reprimand came whispering into her mind. "*No mortal woman can. Their size would tear you asunder. This is why I forbade it. While the others remain imprisoned, we must act with haste and precision. Then, through the might of our children, I will be able to rule the surface once more. Neither El nor his minions will be able to interfere.*"

Yes, my love...

Tears swelled into Sarai's vision, dripping when she blinked. Her fingers caressed the box, giving a reluctant nod.

You won't recede. I promise, my little ones. We seek the answer to your salvation. Please be patient. I know it has been long since we guided your spirits to the Glowing. That place your father fears to tread, but the energies of the earth pour through. It will sustain you, until we succeed, so you do not share the maddening fate of the others. Fortune has smiled upon us. A solution arrives soon. I can feel it...

From the negative etheric reaches, two energies stumbled into range of her senses. The souls read like speckles of dirt within the ocean of darkness that immersed Sarai. From the corner of her eye, she glowered at the door, rolling her fingers into tight fists with nails driving into her palms, until scratching out droplets of blood.

No! How dare they interrupt my lamentations. They will suffer!

Mathias gave me a death sentence. Either I disobey him or prolly get eaten by them. At least they won't do the funny business with my corpse down here.

Leather shoes scuffed in the hurried shuffle of a desperate rush, echoing through the halls. They remained in the light of the few torches holding back the creeping shadows. The pair slowed; whistling breaths grew deeper through their malformed lips, exhaustion weighing their legs to a walk.

"We almost there, Fudd," one of the Cray runners said. "This be your first time in the kingdom. You don't know how they can get. Just lemme do the talkin' and follow my lead."

"Yup. There any water down here, Garr?"

"Keep quiet!"

I pray to the serpent mother that this idiot don't get us killed...

The underground passage continued, leading them deeper into the subterranean recesses of the mountain. Sandalwood smoke drifted in the air, erasing the musty earthen reek. They arrived at a door. Garr's eyes widened, sticking out an arm to stop Fudd.

How long has it been watchin' us? Was it following?

"What now?"

"You don't listen to anything anyone tells ya! Shut up!"

Garr reprimanded between clamped teeth. He punched the younger runner, sending him to the dust of the ground.

Oh God, I almost done it! Remember what Mathias said, the loud noises rile'em up.

The older Cray villager's head lowered like a submissive dog, his hands following, dropping to the side like limp noodles. Garr's eyes made momentary contact with the shadows surrounding the door, shifting away with a tremble beginning to climb through his body.

What he say about them last time we was here? Don't stare. No sudden movements in their direction. No frowning. Don't stand straight up and tall. No showing teeth, not even to smile...

"We umm... we beg for your forgiveness for coming unannounced... to the High Priestess' chambers like this..." Garr's voice quivered.

Fudd watched Garr's vision rise high into the darkness, where the rifting waves of torchlight dared not touch. A faint outline of something loomed over them, the shadows folding around its movements of perfect silence.

"Stop!" Garr slapped Fudd with a ferocious backhand, before leaning to whisper. "Don't be eyein' them. They will take it as a challenge. Especially their Alpha."

The older Cray runner turned back to the being in the shadow, his shoulders aimed at the door while his head lowered once more.

"I apologize a thousand times for my buddy's behavior... he don't know any better. But Mathias sent us... there's urgent news from Cray... the master will want to know."

From the shadows, a long hand reached outward. Its blackened digits, more akin to talons, folded together leaving only its foot long index finger pointing at the doorway.

Garr bowed his head, helping Fudd to his feet.

"Thank you, thank you," he murmured, rushing through the door.

Eureka! I might make it out of this.

Garr sighed when they closed the entrance behind them. The scent of burning sandalwood grew stronger, mixing with that of myrrh as ashes of incense passed by their faces. Tables lined the walls of the room, covered in an array of bones. Wax pooled, dripping off the table from large candles holding aloft dancing flames. Creaking brought their attention back to the door drifting open. They saw nothing but the shadows behind them before their attentions turned onward.

I thought I closed that damn thing... I need to be more careful. I'm cutting it too close with these casual mistakes...

Across the way was a large pile of soft animal hides. A woman with skin of pale cinnamon glared at them, rising from her rest. Rattling came from a necklace of ribs draped over her delicate shoulders as her thin frame stretched with a long yawn. Drool escaped from Fudd's gaped mouth, admiring her petite and chiseled frame, following her ample hips clad in a deer skin skirt up to the thin top hugging her pert bosom. She watched his eyes trace the thick cesarean scar extending over the bottom of her abdomen.

That idiot better not try eye-fucking her. That ain't gunna go over well.

"Two servants from Cray, I see," the woman announced with a smoky voice of authority, her eyes narrowing over a growing frown. "I can smell you from here. To what do I owe this displeasure?"

Garr dropped to his knees, bowing his head to the ground. He peeked up to see Fudd still admiring the woman. A hard slap to the back of his leg sent the younger Cray runner following Garr's example.

"Great goddess of the kingdom! Guiding light of all that we behold! High Priestess Sarai!" Garr announced. "Mathias sent us to warn you that they here!"

"You are referring to the U.S.A. Agents?" Sarai asked. "We are aware of their presence. My beloved is attending them as we speak."

"The master?"

"You two are expecting some kind of reward for your initiative, correct?"

"No, my goddess. Serving you is enough—"

"Yes!" Fudd interrupted and grinned. "I want reward!"

Fudd rose from his bow.

Garr looked to him, mouth dropping in horror.

"Very well, give them what they deserve." Her sight rose to something in the darkness behind them. She turned away, her thick brown locks of tangled curls swaying when she left their sight.

Long claws reached from the darkness, snatching Fudd from the ground. Screams echoed into the chamber, growing harsher in pitch. Rapid munching brought forth the wet sound of fresh meat being devoured. Garr pressed his face into the hard floor. His body convulsed with sobs pushing from his trembling lips.

Teeth slammed together, and lips smacked, every audible bite into his partner sending a jolt through the Cray villager. The warmth of Fudd's life fluids sprayed across Garr's back. Red stains seeped into the cloth, sticking to his quaking frame. Tears left Garr's eyes, pooling into a small circle of mud. The door closed as Sarai returned.

"Oh, you're still here, Garr?"

How does she know my name?

"My mind is beyond what you could imagine, simple little

Cray vermin. The powers of the universe flow strong within my bloodline. Does that answer your question?"

"Yes, my goddess."

"Send word back to Mathias. The master wants you to attack the town. It's time to consolidate our power. Do what you Crays do best, fetch us sacrifices and offerings. Tell Mathias not to partake in any of the stock that you wish to offer the master. A god will not be content feasting on your leavings. Away with you."

Garr rose from the ground, slow and rigid in his attempts to battle through the fresh memories gripping into his thoughts with echoes of lament. It resonated through his being, well into his shaking hands and feet. A long yellow stain of wetness traveled down his pants, but shame was the last thing that registered through his desperate rush out of the kingdom.

Raptor Team gathered around Artemis. She held the button on her communications earbud to reset its resonance.

Pattie looked to Corwin, nudging him with her elbow, and winking when he rolled his eyes.

"You owe me a drink when we get back to the rear," Pattie declared.

"Yeah, yeah, Rod."

"Not the whole team, just us. Understand?"

Milton chuckled at the two. "I don't think he understands, Pattie. He's a little slow."

"Okay, just us. I promise, Pattie."

"Raptor6India, this is Raptor6Actual, radio check, how copy?" Artemis asked over comms. "I haven't heard anything for a while from Carver. He's probably wondering where the hell we are. Carver, you better not be napping at the radio!"

"I hear you, Arty. Sorry about that. Just grabbing a bite to eat."

"What the fuck?" Milton mouthed to the others, raising a brow.

"Did he just refer to Actual by her first name?" Corwin recoiled. "He shows his ass once in a while, but this is a whole new level. During an operation, too."

"That ate-up motherfucker loses his mind sometimes. We all know this. I'll slap him upside the dome when we get back," Rodriguez threatened. "That should reset him back to factory settings."

"Calm down, Pattie," Artemis replied before turning back to comms. "Raptor6India, we're getting strange interference. It's imperative that you remain utilizing proper radio linguistics. We don't know who could be listening. We're going to talk about that when I get back. But for now, I need you to get on the Force Tracker's monitor in the vehicle and give us an exfil route."

"Why?"

Artemis' eyes narrowed. She shook her head and balled her fists. Raptor Teams' eyes widened with revulsion, Milton backing away from his beloved when Artemis' face hardened to a death stare.

"Showing his ass today is an understatement," Rodriguez chuckled. "Boy, is he going to get it!"

"Raptor6India, you are testing my last nerve. We have a wounded civilian, dark magick is afoot, and we are deep into enemy territory without backup or orientation. I'm not explaining any further, save to work out the details of your Non-Judicial Punishment for conduct unbecoming an agent during an operation. Do you get me?"

"I think I understand," Carver replied. "Yep, I see you on this tracking device. You aren't far from me."

"Good, give us direction and distance."

"Just continue north, you'll find it."

"That doesn't make any sense." Milton raised a brow. "If we continue that way, it'll have us going deeper into the mountain range."

"Hurry, Arty. It'll be good to see you again."

"Whiskey Tango Foxtrot!" Rodriguez lifted a brow. "That boy is asking for it!"

"I concur," Artemis answered. Her eyes connected with Aristotle who was shaking his head in doubt.

"Actually, there's been a change of plans. I have reinforcements closing on your position. Just sit tight, Arty. They're coming."

"Carver, what are you going on about—"

Blurred movement registered in their outlying vision. Amongst the trees they ran, whisking like the wind in their rapid and noiseless strides. Artemis tried to recognize one, struggling to gain a semblance of detail on their unfocused form.

"We're surrounded!" Artemis announced.

The team closed together, their backs to each other, weapons outboard with fingers ready on triggers.

From behind a tree one of the creatures stepped out, revealing half its tall and gaunt frame. Long blackened claws scratched at the trunk. Bark flaked away with ease, leaving huge gashes across the base. A glossy black eye peered from around its cover. The dull listless stare was a window to the emptiness within its vessel, despite a subtle aura of shadow rising from its stained pale figure.

Artemis locked eyes with it, gazing into the dark globes that read with nefarious intent. The jaw of the creature dropped to impossible length. It leaned forward howling with the pitch of a hundred echoing screams.

"Raptor Team, ready your incendiary rounds!" Milton ordered.

"Indeed," Aristotle agreed. "The wendigo are upon us."

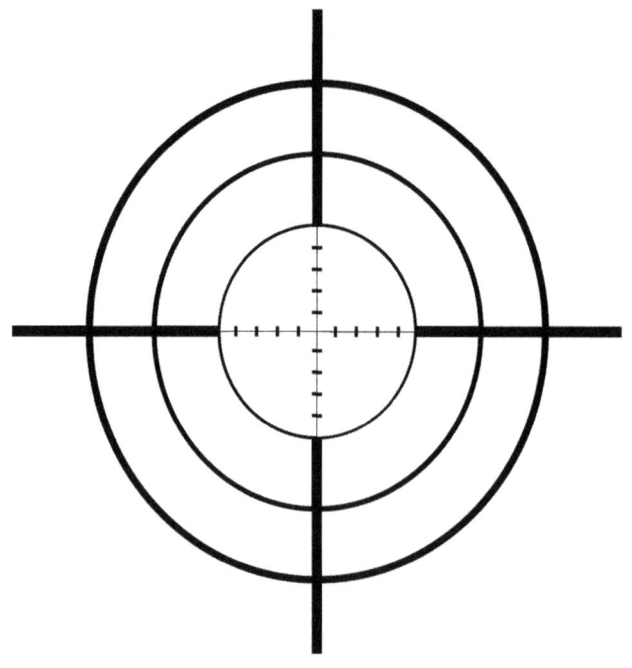

CHAPTER 6
HUNTER'S GAMBIT

"Pattie, I'm a man, and you're a woman..." Carver slapped his forehead. *Yeah, real smooth. She'll sock me for talking like that. What am I thinking? She's not even here and I'm nervous. Okay. Stop, Ned. Focus.*

The intelligence agent sighed as he looked into the rearview mirror, clearing his throat, and straightening his posture before continuing.

"Pattie, I find your smell intoxicating." *Meh, probably not the best thing to say after a field op. It'll make me look creepy. Damn it, man. Get it together.* "Pattie, I'm crazy about—"

"Raptor6India, this is Raptor6Actual, radio check, over."

That's a relief to hear them. I was wondering if my radio was still working. Carver shook himself from the amorous stupor, jabbing the steering wheel before grabbing the radio mic. Fluster withered away with discipline, his stern face returning.

"Roger, Actual, this is India. I read you, Lima Charlie."

"I beg your pardon."

Is she being serious right now? I can never tell with Actual. She's strange at times. Meh, I should just trust her by now and stop being an asshole. After all, she's saved my skin a few times. "Loud and clear, Actual."

"Understood. Listen up, India. We need you to bring up a vehicle for one of the wounded hostages; it's going to be impossible to get her out of here by foot. She's in a bad way and I don't want to risk further injury by moving her. How copy?"

"That's a solid copy," Carver responded, peering over to the Force Tracker's monitor. "I'm en route to your position marked by Corwin. Give me a little time to maneuver safely through this terrain. It's the village, right?"

"Yes."

"Is it still hot?"

"Negative. All enemies have been slain. There weren't many threats. You'd think they would send more than just this knuckle dragging gaggle of apes to challenge us."

Slain? Not neutralized? Odd verbiage today. She must be too exhausted for customs and courtesies. Must be one hell of a story. "That's motivating to hear, Actual! I'll be in your position in twenty mikes. Moving one of the vehicles now. Without fear!"

"Excellent. See you when you get here."

"Without fear—"

"Yes. I heard you the first time, India. Is that supposed to mean something?"

"No..." Carver's face scrunched together with scrutiny. "Nothing at all, Actual. I'm just being a goof again. Raptor6India, out."

"Load incendiary rounds!" Artemis ordered. "Weapons free!"

"Let them have it!" Milton added.

Muzzle flashes filled the landscape. Rounds spewed from rifle barrels. Clouds of carbon erased the scent of the pine and grass, surrounding them with the warm aroma of expended gunpowder. Shots punctured tree trunks, blazing dots across the forest that trailed behind the rapid abominations.

A creature halted, its glossy dark eyes reaching out to Corwin, then shifting to Julie. Saliva glistened along its lips, gathering in greater amounts that trickled out the sides of its hissing maw. The agent aimed on the monstrosity, his fire hitting it in the shoulder. Howls of fury released in defiance, the wind-like pulse of the calamity reverberating into their ears. Flames emerged from the creature's bullet wound, sputtering as it reeled back into the snow.

"Tango down!" Corwin announced.

Wendigo hounded them, darting among the trees, through the bushes. Their strides closed the distance. Pattie aimed with her UMP45, but lost sight as one spirited out of view. Her peripheral vision beamed in alarm to a darting shadow. She whipped to the left flank, missing with shots pouring into a tree it dipped behind.

Milton's machine gun blared, its ammunition belt zipped from the drum, spewing copious amounts of lead aggression at targets pacing in and out of his sector.

"How are there so many?" Milton yelled. "I thought these things were solitary creatures!"

"This is weird!" Aristotle announced, ducking behind the heavy weapons agent. "Don't stop firing! It'll keep them off! They're like felines, waiting for an opening, a moment of weakness from a lack of focus so they can slip into our defenses!"

"Keep firing!" Artemis ordered. "Control your shots! Maintain your sectors! They're trying to mix our fields of fire to confuse us!"

"How the fuck did wendigos learn about battle tactics?" Pattie barked. "This is bullshit!"

Dark blood sprayed across the snow with an adjacent shot ripping through a wendigo's skull. The creature buckled, falling into a limp heap over a barren frost-covered bush. A gout of flame fizzled and hissed from the gaping hole left by the large caliber round.

The ground is covered in snow, now? Just changed like that? The trees no longer have leaves. The bushes are long dead, nothing more than a cluster of bristling branches. What am I seeing? Think, girl. The team is counting on you. The landscape just shifted before my eyes, morphing into something radically different. Sorcery? Artemis looked over to the crouching Aristotle.

Her brother mouthed the words, 'I told you.'

"Great work, Pippen," Artemis stated over comms. "What's the view for overwatch?"

"I see them closing on your position, Actual. You have to move! At a minimum there's a dozen! They're too damn fast! I'm barely getting a sight picture. I can't keep them off you!"

A chevron reticle directed the magnified aim of Pippen's scope. Raptor's marksman remained poised behind bushes in a kneeling position, the barrel of his weapon hidden within the multitude of branches and the dead shriveled leaves still clinging to them. Shots from his teammates zipped through the landscape, around a wendigo taking cover behind a tree. The creature hunched over, poised to leap out like a coiled spring.

Engagement sequence; field of view minimal due to natural obstructions. Approximate range from tango; 700 meters. Calculating the curvature of the earth, combined with the fleeting target's movement and direction versus my muzzle velocity. High windage, making rounds careen left. No time to dial. Need to make a holdover shot.

Swift computations played through Pippen's mind, bringing his aim over to a wendigo's right flank. The reticle sat just outside the creature's profile, following its quick sprint to another tree, drawing near Corwin.

The loud roar of a single shot clapped into the mountainside from a large 7.62x51 millimeter bullet racing forward, smacking the creature. Its chest caved, the round burrowing deep. The wendigo clutched tight to the fizzling wound. The abomination's snarling demeanor never gave during its racking death throes, reaching out with a claw for Corwin. The agent unloaded more shots into the downed wendigo, turning to acknowledge Pippen in the distance with a nod, finding only the wilderness cover of the elusive sniper.

Another wendigo dashed through Pippen's sight. He followed the creature sprinting with a wide arc around the team's position. Dead foliage came into view, impeding the path of a shot. Pippen rose from his knee, locking his arms tight, trailing the monster.

Damn it, the angle is awkward... have to gooseneck this one.

Pippen's cheek left the comfortable warmth of the stockweld he was accustomed to resting on with each shot. His shoulders rotated, sweeping with the tango's path. A smooth pull of the trigger and the next shot found its mark. The wendigo's jugular exploded with blackened blood spraying over its shoulder. The creature spun from the momentum, collapsing into a writhing pile. Its claws reached up, scratching in vain at its throat set ablaze.

Black eyes searched the distance for the sniper, the wendigo crouching low and hissing in the direction of the accurate fire. Two of the fiends raced toward Pippen's location. The sniper kept low, moving behind a wall of bushes with quick and controlled steps, shifting along the flank of their trajectory.

Damn, they move fast. There's not much time. "Actual, this is Raptor6Sierra." Pippen said. "My hide is compromised. Overwatch will be down until I can relocate. Moving to supplementary position bravo now to reestablish hide. Over."

"Roger, Sierra. I see them. I'll try to divide their attention." Artemis fired at the creatures, her shots whisking into the bushes and trees.

The marksman continued until repositioning. Overwatching his old hide from the new. Quick moving gaunt figures swarmed the area, halting, raising their listless grimaces into the air. Claws flexed, curling with readiness to lash out. Hissing broke the delicate silence, passing like a threatening breeze from their lips trembling with rage. Pippen brought his scope's reticle into view, centering over the rib cage protruding through its pale skin. Heaving breaths of growing animalistic fury expanded from its chest. Howls of blood roiling anger followed claws raking through the bushes, sending splinters of debris into cascading clouds surrounding them. Their ravenous cries grew louder, resounding with insurmountable rage.

A smooth trigger pull sent a roaring shot slamming into the heart of the creature. The wendigo buckled as if trying to hug itself, falling back into a nearby shrub. Flames rose within its open wound, scorching its innards. The second screamed in Pippen's direction, resonating on the sniper's skin with the throbbing of a hundred anguished cries. Its voice carried from a depth beyond the physical realm, entering Pippen's psyche with an eldritch evocation seething in hatred. The creature's black eyes searched, devouring every detail, until their pupils engaged. In the moment they locked, it sped toward the marksman.

Judging by its speed, I've only one shot at this...

Pippen brought the quick moving profile into view, his arms and breath relaxing. Into the stock his cheek dropped, holding the weapon snug to his shoulder. The length of his finger wrapped around the trigger. The reticle of his sight centered on the sneering target. Ringing grew louder in Pippen's ears from its furious cries, competing with the escalation of his throbbing heart. Its echoes swelled in his mind, resonating deep in his soul with a coldness that hollowed resolve to the rising surrender of impending violence.

Another smooth trigger pull brought the rifle's roar against the monster's scream. Its face caved around the large bullet hole puncturing clean through its skull. Blackened chunks of brain matter sprayed out the exit wound, raining across its backside. The screams stopped, along with the ring of its chilling gasp.

"I've cleared my hides." Pippen sighed with relief. "Overwatch will be back up once I can get set, Actual. Hang tight."

"Acknowledged. That's some good news. We're about to perform a withdrawal. Our ammunition won't last if this continues."

✡ ✡ ✡

"Weapon down!" Milton yelled over the last cases and links spitting from the weapon. He dropped to a knee, opening the feed tray cover with a sweeping motion clearing it of debris, before snapping on another two hundred round container. Metal from the ammunition belt raked over the plastic drum's mouth as it was drawn into the machine gun's smoke-laced confines.

"I got you covered, big guy!" Rivers announced, taking his sector of fire.

Weapons continued ripping off shots at the elusive beings, weaving in and out of cover, continuing their encirclement of Raptor. Black eyes seething from snarling countenances stared down the agents, careening to cover when barrels and sights aligned with them. Shots peppered into the trunks of rattling trees, setting some ablaze. Bushes swayed with bullets passing through, the hot payloads of their incendiary rounds languishing in the snow. Flames grew in slow climbs up the tall remnants of hemlocks, creating a hot bastion between the hunters and prey.

How can this be? It looks as though there're more. We've never encountered this many wendigo before. A mated pair at the most, but never in such numbers. This is our chance. The fire, their greatest weakness. It'll keep them away. "Get ready, we're moving!" Artemis announced. "Wedge formation. I want Milton at point with the suppression weapon. Everyone line up adjacent to him, Corwin keep center with our rescued hostage."

"Roger, Actual." Agreement came from Raptor Team in cohesion.

"Raptor6Sierra, scratch the hide, regroup with us at your discretion."

"That sounds swell, Arty."

"Okay, we're moving, Raptor!"

Black eyes swelled with hatred across growling visages of the bestial creatures, rearing away from flames consuming the landscape. Those that circled around were suppressed into cover by the hail of fire Milton released, sending shards of wood flying and fizzling holes into the snow. The bulk of the salivating creatures remained pinned behind the fire, receding into the cold depths of the forest.

"It's working, Arty." Aristotle cried out. "That huge fire is repelling them!"

"We're not out of it yet. Raptor6Mike, we've lost eyes on your hide. Give me your status. Pippen?" Artemis asked after a heavy pause.

A tug of dread usurped Artemis, calling her view over to the wall of fire. The others stopped, their quizzical gazes falling on their team leader then following her line of sight. Rifting movements appeared in hazy and swift steps through the brightness of the conflagration. Light blended as something passed through, coming beyond the flames, between the mayhem and the team.

The blending light appeared in a humanoid outline stepping before them, towering to the center line of the tree. Smoldering foliage crumbled as it dragged something large and heavy, darkened with burns and bruises. Then it raised the corpse for all to behold. In its clutches was Pippen. The sniper's body was stripped of its clothes, covered in deep gaping gashes, overflowing with streams of blood and smears derived from the callous hauling of his corpse.

"The fuck is that?" Rodriguez exclaimed.

"What is that thing?" Artemis asked.

"I... I don't know," Aristotle replied, scrunching his brow.

"We've an unknown vector!"

"It has him!" Rodriguez cried out. "Pippen..."

"Hold! Follow protocol. Do not engage. Keep distance and maintain eyes on. Pippen is already gone. I don't want to lose anyone else."

Tension rose as goosebumps on the back of Raptors' necks, climbing down their backs with limb rattling shivers. The being stared back at them from where its eyes should've been, its translucent light form becoming apparent when it stepped closer. With a quick jerk it hurled Pippen's corpse into the depths of the forest. Piercing shrieks from wendigos rose into the sky, with dozens of quick movements darting through their peripheral vision, chasing the blood scent, hounding after the snack.

They pounced, their flat incisors biting. Muscles in their faces strained with each desperate chomp down into the warm flesh. Blood flowed with every bite tearing away meat from the corpse, convulsing through the ravenous act. Desperate scratches followed, laying claim to a leg, a hand, an arm. Flesh tore as the creatures pulled away their bounties, scampering to hunched over cover and cramming their mouths with the salty remnants. Their feet shuffled away from the deep red stains in the snow.

When Artemis returned her gaze to the being, she froze. Through her, the surreal energies of wanting and desire surged. Artemis gazed at the visage of familiarity that stirred a love stemming from longing and regret. Mario stared at her with a warm smile, his arms widening with the open invitation of a father's embrace.

Memories flowed, and Artemis became that little girl again, with stains of pasta sauce spotted on her yellow flowered dress as she sat at the family's long oak dining table, adjacent from the unlit kitchen. Her pencil marked across the science worksheet. Mario's large hand wrapped around her own, guiding her to the correct answer before she could circle the wrong one. She felt a kiss on the top of her head when he got up, leaving her to finish.

"You've come back to me, my Artemis," Mario announced with a deep, heaving voice, soulful but laced with an eldritch presence.

"Actual, your orders?" Milton asked. "I want to blast this thing already!"

"Actual?" Rodriguez waved a hand in front of Artemis' glazed eyes.

Barrels raised as the light being was brought into weapon sights. Aristotle shut his eyes, the scryer forcing his mind's focus to flow with the surrounding energies. The tumult rose around his senses like a boiling cauldron. Strain gripped within his head, rising like an inward convulsion. Focus shuddered with each step, the tenuous grasp on his projection slowing his spirit approaching beyond the material veil. A growing euphoria of dizziness fogged over Aristotle's view, reaching for a connection with the familiar vibrations of his sister.

What is this? The scryer wondered. *It's willpower from something, beyond... Artemis? There she is. She's been enraptured into the mind's eye, but how? A sorcerer?*

The vision of his sister as a little girl sat at the table, circling answers on her homework. She turned her head and smiled. Aristotle rubbed her shoulder, but heavy steps pulled away his attention, emerging from the darkness of the kitchen archway. Mario stood before them, grinning with a rising unwholesome chuckle with his presence resounding into Aristotle's senses.

You're not part of the dream. You're sentient. You're not supposed to be here!

"*Neither are you!*"

Screams erupted from Mario, sending the scryer on his back. Pressure grew, sliding Aristotle across the cold floor. Snow surrounded him, and the roars continued, pounding through the scryer's mind, and washing away his thoughts. Torrential force pressed his body, sending him rolling. Aristotle gripped at the table's leg, floundering in his struggles to remain.

"*No, Daddy don't!*" Artemis cried out. "*Don't!*"

"*Arty, listen. It's Aris. Please, he's not our father! Wake up!*"

"*Daddy, don't hurt him!*"

"*Arty, I can't... hold on... much... longer... fight it!*"

Artemis sprang from her seat, gear rattling, having replaced the dress, her full height now apparent with her actual age. She grabbed Aris, helping him to his feet. Her grim gaze fell back on the being across the way in the snow, shaking off the stupor with arched brows of contempt.

"Yes!" Artemis ordered Milton. "Neutralize that bastard!"

The machine gunner released constant bursts from his M240. The large caliber 7.62 rounds passed through the being of light, disrupting its shape, blurring the presence of its outline. It reached out, before evaporating into nothing. Deep booming cackles resounded around them, carrying through the forest with ever growing echoes compounding into wince-inducing fervor.

It was just a thought projection? Aristotle wondered. *The presence. I can still feel him, all around us. His willpower and command of the etheric layers are immense.*

Milton turned the fury of his weapon upon the encroaching wendigo. Voracious eyes glared back, while they sped away to cover. In the distance was the red stain that stretched across the snow; the remains of their comrade. A growing headache thumped in their skulls with the laughter. Artemis looked over to the depths of the forest. Approaching wendigo doubled back, swinging around their position.

Cat and mousing us. We're not going to last out here much longer. Not like this. We're being toyed with. This was an ambush. Every detail of it planned! "Retreat!" Artemis declared. "Rivers, cut us a path out of here. I don't care if it's not to the vehicles, just get us away from this kill zone!"

Raptor moved, their wedge continuing a hail of fire keeping those that hounded them at bay. They pressed on, jogging at quick pace, their gear bouncing as they hurried through the forest.

Mario reappeared, the wendigo gathering around with unblinking gazes fixed on their master. He grinned, watching the agents leave his view, reaching over to pet the wrinkled bald scalp of a minion.

"That was entertaining, my children. Indeed, she is worthy. Let the morsels go, there is no need to pursue. Make them feel safe, as if they have control, and they will drop their guard. El's warriors are heading right where I want them."

Assistant Director Troy Hughes' sat at the war table with his shining bald head leaning over, resting in his palms. Deep controlled breaths left his flaring nostrils, and his shoulders rose in the jacket of a sharp pressed black suit, over a crisp white collared shirt brought together by a tie in the perfect Windsor knot. Tapping from keyboards of surrounding secretaries faded from the background, disappearing along with the bright lights and cooling breeze from the vents overhead. The churning waters of the AD's mind calmed, the waves of thought slowing until becoming a lake of stillness.

Breathe in, and out. Achieve oneness through mindfulness and focus.

Creaking door hinges announced an arrival as Hughes left his meditation. A narrow pale face riddled with heavy stubble peered at him from behind bushy dark eyebrows that mimicked the unkempt blades of hair on his head. The drooping bags below their eyes matched in dark complexion, along with a slouched demeanor hidden amongst sharp movements.

"AD Grimes," Hughes greeted his colleague. "Fix your tie, damn thing is hanging lower than my blood sugar levels."

"Then take a second to grab a bite, big guy?" Grimes shrugged and smirked, slapping his tie with apathy.

"Can't, waiting for reports from a few of my tasked teams."

"Oh, that's why I'm here." Grimes placed an envelope down. "Comm room bubbas mentioned they got word from Raptor over text via their Force Tracker Network. I took the liberty of printing it up and running it here. No need to thank me or anything, Troy. You know I have your back—"

"Why wasn't I notified earlier?" Hughes snatched the paperwork.

"Probably because they saw you meditating and figured it

could wait? Besides, from what I read seems your protégé, Coleman, has it well under control."

Hughes' eyes scanned the print, before narrowing. "We are winning?" The AD shook his head. "No fucking way."

"What do you mean?" Grimes asked. The towering AD rushed past him. "Troy! Wait up! I have to talk with you about —" The door slammed in his face. "Damn it! You're not getting away that easy."

Brightness from the overhead lights of the main hall brought a wide gleam to the polish of their Oxford shoes. Steps clapped in rapid pace with one another. Hughes and Grimes rushed across the shining floors of the immaculate hall. The larger Assistant Director banked into a room, exploding through the door. Static filled their ears from the stations where agents were situated, monitoring radio devices that hummed and chirped with each transmission.

"What time was this sent?" Hughes asked, raising the paperwork.

"Oh, hey Assistant Director," A radio operator swung around in his chair. His face scrunched, while he scratched his chin. "Hmm... those particular ones came in late this afternoon."

Tapping on Hughes' shoulder took his attention as exasperated breaths caressed his flank. "You move fast for a big guy. I can't believe you're still in combat shape—"

Hughes glared at the radio, his lips curling back like a dog ready to bite. The paper crumpled into the tight grasp of his mighty fists that shuddered with growing rage.

"—I'd be able to keep up with you better had I not drank a whole pot of coffee. Wait... Troy, what's the deal? You're about to blow a gasket."

"Mr. McDowell," Hughes called out.

"At your service, sir," the radio operator responded.

"Send word to Team HoneyBadger, that I need them to augment Raptor in the Jefferson Mountain range AO once they're done sweeping. It's an emergency. I know they're finishing up a major operation. Tell Badger Actual his favorite is in trouble."

"I'm confused."

"He'll understand. Trust me."

"Acknowledged, sir! Sending it now."

"Troy, you going to tell me what all this is about?" Grimes demanded.

"The message was a lie. I don't know how, but that wasn't Artemis. I know my agents."

"What do you mean?"

"Artemis and I had a talk long ago when Badger Actual and I began her recruitment. She told me that there can never be a victory for her. That the best she could hope for was to prevent the nightmare from spreading to another family."

"Oh." Grimes' eyes widened.

"So many questions remain. Who the hell was comms texting with on the encrypted Force Tracker Network? How did they crack it and how long has our equipment been compromised?"

CHAPTER 7
WHISPERING MEMORIES

Carver's black SUV left the cover of wilderness, entering the open area upon the outskirts of Cray Village. The agent stepped out, greeted by the lingering scent of gun smoke. He peered toward the buildings, his eyes skimming past moss rising along the wooden walls, beneath thatched roofs splintering into a frayed parody of their original design.

This place is even more of a dump than that mountain town. Why can't we ever get missions in places like Aspen? Good to stretch the legs though.

Carver reached back into the vehicle for the radio mic. "Raptor6Actual this is Raptor6India. I am at the designated sector. I've no visual with you or tangos."

He paused, looking to the radio with a scrunching brow line. *That's not like her. Usually, she's a hawk on comms.*

"Raptor6Actual, this is Raptor6India. I've reached the grid coordinates, but I have no visual on the team, over."

Static returned over the radio. Carver grabbed his M4 from the front seat.

A fine time to be having comm issues when we're about to wrap this up. The agent sighed, strolling forth. "Hey, Raptor! I'm here! Let's evac the—"

A thin wooden door opened wide with a slam, snatching away Carver's attention. Villagers poured from their hovels, swarming the area with an array of jagged knives and rusted pitchforks waving overhead. Lever action rifles shook in their meaty grips with eager trigger fingers popping off shots to the gray clouds above.

A villager's hard stare met the agent, inflating with deep breaths of insurmountable rage. His blinking left eye protruded higher than his right, leaving the agent unable match the glare. Through lips more akin to shriveled bacon the villager loosed a shuddering growl.

What the fuck...

Rounds flew from Carver's M4, peppering the malformed man and sending him squealing in agony down the steps of his front porch. Primal howls of anger rose throughout the village signaling the mad dash of tangoes closing on the agent's position. He shifted his sight picture, bringing another into view of his alignment. Two successive rounds hit the next target, the recoiling weapon shaking in his controlled grasp after each smooth trigger pull. The first struck into the target's chest cavity, puncturing his heart. The next entered his forehead, snapping his skull back.

The tango collapsed as more sprinted past his position, weapons held high, gripped in paw-like hands with fingernails outlined in dirt. Their plodding movements, hindered in the chopping discoordination of eagerness, melded with bestial rage. Carver lowered his rifle, opening his field of view. Dozens of them were emptying from the village, surrounding his position.

"This is some bullshit!"

Carver ran back to the truck, slamming and locking the doors. The villagers swarmed around the vehicle, their weapons beating against the thick ballistic-resistant windows. Small dents began spotting Carver's view of the outside as impacts pelted around him. The truck rattled and swayed like a tremor unfolding. One of the villagers climbed on to the hood, sledgehammer in his grasp. After standing upright he took the weapon to the windshield, roaring and pounding hard. A massive spiderweb indention spread from his repeated onslaught, cracking along Carver's entire front view.

"Holy crap!" Carver yelped, finding the ignition, bringing the truck's engine to life. "Come on, girl! Get us out of here!"

The vehicle roared to life with the four-wheel horsepower of its reverberating engine. Carver's foot dropped on the gas, bringing the truck's heavy grill crashing into a few inhabitants. Underneath the thick tires they went, their bodies sucked beneath rubber and heavy steel. Bones crunched in the agent's passing, leaving moaning and writhing victims in its wake, their skin indented with the pattern of tread. Carver slammed the brakes, sending the villager upon the hood flying into the air. To the ground he soared, arms slapping the earth from momentum launching him into a tumble.

Carver punched into reverse, bringing the tail crashing into those massed behind him. He jostled in his seat as the truck's tires ground over villagers, their muffled screams carrying through the cabin, drowning away the engine's purr. A hatchet slammed on the driver's side window. Rifle shots popped off around him, sinking into the hood and frame, with clouds of gray and white carbon growing amidst the chaos.

The truck circled, heading into the wilderness. Figures in

the rearview mirror gave chase in sprints that died once Carver rode beyond their reach.

What the fuck was that? Where was Raptor? Damn, I hope they didn't get overwhelmed. But that's not what Actual said over comms. What the hell is going on? Carver wondered, gripping the mic. "Raptor Team this is Raptor6India, does anyone read me? Anyone?"

Boots ceased their rapid crunching of snow as Artemis rose her fist, bringing Raptor Team's retreat to a halt. Warm clouds expelled from gaping mouths, gasping for oxygen. Sweat rolled down their bodies, soaking into their fatigues, staining undergarments with clamminess that clutched to their skin. Artemis gazed around at Raptor, turning to Aristotle, who put an arm around her and squeezed. She looked to her twin, his long brow and frown melting from her smile when she mouthed the words 'thank you'.

"I have to check on Julie," Corwin announced, placing the girl by a tree, and kneeling to tend her. "We have to keep these bandages fresh to prevent infection."

"Good call," Artemis acknowledged. "I think we're in the clear, but you're covered for all the time you need. Take care of her, Corwin."

"I'll help," Rodriguez volunteered.

"Any idea what that new vector was, Actual?" Rivers asked.

"None. At first, I believed it to be a sorcerer. But whatever we encountered is too strong for that. Far too strong."

Artemis looked to Milton, standing by himself, staring off

into the white wilderness. His fierce glare remained unflinching despite cold flakes of snow sprinkling his chiseled face. A sigh escaped the heavy weapons specialist when he turned to acknowledge Artemis.

"Whatever it was, Actual, it needs to pay for what it did to Pippen." Milton announced. "He was a good agent. He didn't deserve to die like that."

"We'll get it and bring it to justice. That's what we do."

Rivers had taken a knee and was digging through his pack. The agent unfurled a map, while withdrawing a compass from a side pocket. He peeked at their surroundings between studying the topography, aligning the device to get a sense of direction.

"Actual, I have no idea where we are," Rivers announced. "And I can't orient our location until we find a significant landmass. After what's been going on with the electronics, I'm not using the grid finder. We have to go old-fashioned with land navigation."

"That's fine, Rivers. It's obvious the Force Tracking Network is compromised. Just get me an idea. We'll work from there."

"Roger, Actual. I'll get us something."

"Everyone, conserve your energy. Now is the time to hydrate and eat. Check ammo and gear. You know what to do, Raptor. Just give me any status reports from the ordinary." Artemis took a few steps away from the rest of the team, watching the perimeter.

"Arty," Aristotle called as he caught up. "That thing—"

"Thank you. It had me back there. I was in its grasp, and I had no idea what was happening. I thought it was twenty years ago, back in our old home... before... it felt so real. The cold was gone, the weariness of the mission. I was there again, with Dad. Some of my happiest times were learning from him. He was such a good teacher. I could remember the confidence I felt whenever I learned something new, but more so the pride that he radiated. When I was a little girl, I lived for that, Aris. He was always so proud of me. Of us. And I needed that feeling again. Whatever we encountered knew I needed it..."

"It's not human; you're right about that much. The grasp it had on your psyche. I could sense that he was able to read everything about us at once. I'm calling it a 'he', but what is it really? I've never encountered such a being even in all my studies as a scryer. At first, I thought it was a rakshasa, or maybe a djinn, but those wouldn't have the power to make the environment change on a whim or read our thoroughly trained minds with such ease. That thing was peering into our souls! I could feel it, reading us like novellas... with the same quick pleasure."

"Aris, it's that thing we saw, that night. The wendigo answer to it. Those cursed things are able to turn off their ravenous hunger to actually obey something. I didn't think that was possible. This is what we've been looking for our entire lives."

A slow and doubtful shake came from Aristotle's head. His eyes lowered away from his sister.

"You're still not sure? What else could it have been that night? What else did we just now see attacking the team?"

"No, Arty. It's not that. I'm in agreement. I just think we're in over our heads here. We need to find a way out of this mess and get back to the Agency and the order."

"Whatever it's doing, we are its prisoners. There's only one way out of this. That's by fighting. At this rate, I'm worried none of us are going to make it back."

Nodding came from Rivers while he studied the contour lines along the map shaping the framework of the landscape. His vision continued darting between their perimeter and the topography. *Jeez, it's difficult to make out anything from the ordinary. I'm going to be hard pressed shooting an azimuth to find our position. This is trying. Can't fail the team though. The mountain slope seems to follow along... well this doesn't make sense. The map is saying to the east, but the compass is saying otherwise. The slope rises to the north.*

The agent sighed, taking a large gulp from his canteen. The cool refreshing water flowed down into his body, revitalizing him despite the warmth still radiating from exertion. Memories came, changing the bland water to the sweetness of fruit punch. From the mind's eye appeared his father's stern gaze of hateful brown eyes. Along his scowling face was a five o'clock shadow topped with a ponytail of slicked black hair. The man stumbled through the doorway in wobbling steps. The caress of his mother came next, delicate hands smooth from lotion subdued the fears threatening to grow.

"Drinking like a—a fucking piggie again," his father scoffed through a drunken slur. "Boy, about the only thing you're good at is stuffing your face. If only you applied the same effort to your shitty grades. Maybe you wouldn't be reading like a goddamned retard!"

"Henry, stop!" his mother pleaded. "You had the same problem at his age!"

"Shut up, Miranda! Now I've told you that porky here, is eatin' too damn much. Look at him. Looking like a stuffed pig!"

"Henry, enough!"

"We got money to feed this fat son of a bitch, but not money for me to leave long enough to stop looking at him?"

Mom don't go!

Miranda rose from the table, storming out of the kitchen. Henry's eyes never left Rivers. The boy sat, trembling as his father staggered toward him. Heavy breathing overcame Rivers, his short and rotund frame heaving through a tight shirt with a faded cartoon bear displayed. His thick arms shook. Urging for release, his bladder pulsated between his legs, rising into his stomach with the alarming resonance of impending failure.

No, I peed the last time, when he busted my eye, leaving it swollen shut for two weeks. He knocked out my baby teeth, too. I can still remember the laughter. No, I won't give him the satisfaction.

We can't. He'll only enjoy tormenting us, knowing that's the kind of fear he provokes. Remember his cackling when you lay upon the floor barely conscious? The stain in your shorts. Lying in a puddle of our own mess. That's what they do. They feed off fear. You have to be fearless. Anger is the quickest remedy for that. The old cliché has rung true since the dawn of time; don't get mad, Rivers. Get even.

"You, fat fuck!" Henry continued. "Sip, goddamn it! You— you don't have to guzzle everything down!"

Fat fuck. He always called us that, remember?

"Look at you, boy. You ain't shit. You're never gonna be shit, either." Sharp words left spit on George's face.

"Durr... I wanna be a marine!" Henry continued, mocking his son's aspirations with a deep and slow tone. "You keep saying that but how, piggly? Marines aren't fat and stupid! Like I said, you're never gunna be shit. Never!"

"Here, take it!" Miranda demanded. She stormed back with a roll of dollars. "Take it and just leave us be, damn you!"

Mom, she did her best to protect us, taking the brunt of the beatings… you wanted to endure them for her. But you didn't have the courage. He broke you down and not just physically. The others don't understand and how could they? They never saw it. Artemis, keeping the team so professional, do you all truly know each other? Does anyone know the truth about George Rivers? How that bastard father of yours left you an empty shell, going through life waiting to be filled…

"I should slap the shit out of you, bitch!" Henry snatched the money. "Talkin' to me like that! Where'd you get this money? From your boyfriend, or selling your cunt around the park? Eh, I don't give a fuck."

That bastard never had anything positive for you. Always jeering, always full of hate. His life was miserable from his own poor decisions. That's why he took it out on you. He was a coward, unable to face the truth, my precious boy.

Henry began a slow stagger out, neglecting the door on his departure, leaving the neighbor's trailer visible. Miranda's delicate palm rubbed her son's cheek, raising his dejected head.

"You don't ever pay mind to the negative. You're better than that, George."

Rivers nodded to the love of his mother shining through her warm smile. Energy blanketed the boy, who welcomed it with an open heart. George smiled back as Miranda placed a kiss on his forehead. The fear withered, replaced with a longing for that moment, the confidence and pride she instilled to take on anything. That's what got him through basic, through the toughest of training and most arduous of times. It spread through his soul like wildfire, consuming his mind.

"Remember, Mom is always here for you, George Rivers. If you ever need me, I'm only a whisper away."

Just a whisper away, waiting for you in the darkness that looms.

"I need you right now, Mom." George's voice cracked with tears pouring over his cheeks. "I always need you."

"Just let me in, my son. You never have to doubt. I'm here with you already."

CHAPTER 8
FOLLOWING THE NIGHTMARE

lakes of cold ice cascaded down to the highest peaks of the mountain range. Gusts of heavy wind wailed, sending ice flakes adrift upon spiraling currents, where they landed at the apex of the tallest mass. The etheric layers remained placid, like an undisturbed ocean, its waves carrying with the rhythm of the universe and the energies of old.

It's similar to the aura of the great trees that my sons removed so long ago. Until... his birth replaced the darkness we brought to the material plane. Washing away a millennium of effort with one miserable mortal existence.

Amongst the nothingness he sat upon the summit, gazing down at the vastness of mottled paleness that stretched across his kingdom. Chiseled muscle moved with ease in its flexion, as he shifted to rest his chin upon a fist. Perfect was his form, save for the quartet of massive scars stretching across his upper back.

These creatures are even more pathetic than their predecessors, allowing themselves to be led by subhuman creations, serving purpose only as pleasurable breeding tools. Their loathsome figures are a parody of their inane sire. I can still hear his declarations echoing into my thoughts, the day the war started. A reminder of his harsh words brought upon us for their own disobedience, despite our warnings.

Cursed be her daughters, in their generations. Before the wrath of flames and chains, I took them, by the dozens, invading their wombs despite their pleas for mercy. I relished in watching them being ripped apart by my emerging seed. In their screams they served as my bloated symphony of pain. Their flesh; the bread of my ravenous spawn.

Strong their will may have been, these challengers will surrender their reality or succumb to the madness I bring in my wake. They think themselves warriors. Humanity is nothing more than a resource. Their prideful leader, how foolish of her, willfully returning to my grasp. She will feel agony from the vice of psychosis, closing upon her mind and soul. In her screaming lament of hubris, she will birth my new prince. There is no choice in the matter. I will not risk the well-being of my beloved. But I will gladly forfeit hers. The DNA is close enough. I will take delight in ravaging her, humiliating her, my delicious Artemis. Watching the meaning of her life and hope seep from her existence as I make known the only purpose of her design.

The glaring expression of his sharp eyes resonated with the faint glowing of a light that wanted to rise, but withered, staying only in a glimmer of potential. The aura of golden pupils followed distant specks maneuvering closer. He focused his hearing, closing off their conversations of planning. The sizzle of anger from his annoyance subsided after the disappearance of their heavy pants. Irritation lingered with his narrowing view upon the quarry.

"*You squander yourself with too many games.*" A voice invaded his thoughts with a velvet tone woven in contempt. *"Did you not learn your lesson when my brother imprisoned you here after that humiliating defeat? Speaking of whom, I can sense his wretched grace. He is near."*

My Queen? How long has she been watching? Mind your thoughts...

"You incorrigible thing. How much pain must you endure before awakening to the truth of my strategy?"

"I am honored by your—"

"Save the hollow pleasantries. Your attempts to play coy with me will not be well met. Despite my predilections, I have come to warn you that this dangerous game you are playing, jeopardizes my stratagem. These mortals aren't the same breed as the wandering cattle you've enjoyed feasting upon. You must address their intrusion, the fault of which is your own."

"I have. I've been in control the entire time. Fate is in my favor. They are guided by my whim, ever closer to my kingdom where they will bring her—"

"Your faith has always been misplaced like your motivations. Perhaps it is due to your attachments to the material. You are no better than they are. I have foreseen it, child. You underestimate that which El has made in his image. Especially his daughters, who you seem to have no issues indulging yourself with despite your irrational trepidation."

His head rose from the contemplative pose, turning from that which surrounded him. The aura of her energy rivaled the sun within the etheric layers, bearing upon him impossible light that washed away his vision of the beyond. The strength of his eyes gave with his pride when he tried to pull away. Hot flashes of redness emanated, resisting his ruler as the levees of discipline became subdued by anger.

"You do not take this seriously, my Queen! he rumbled back. *You never did! Ever since the day you jeopardized our great plan—"*

"My great plan."

"I remember the declaration. Do you, my Queen? Crushing our heads as we bruise their heels. I have worked tirelessly before the deluge to hinder his proclamation and now I sentry myself at the gates to continue that purpose, while you seek to appease their consent. I take what I want."

"Bold words, child. Then why not murder them outright?"

He paused, shutting his eyes tight until the lids squeezed together. *"You know the answer."*

"But do you?"

"I will not alter the course I have chosen. This is my domain."

"Mighty Azazel, suffering to contend with mortals. That is where you're wrong. It is your prison. As it has ever been."

Raptor continued their trek, pressing through lush green grass and thick bushes. Rivers continued blazing their path, a renewed vigor coursing through him, leading with assertive steps. Artemis looked to the sun, concluding its course through the sky. Its light entered the dim stages, beginning the day's completion.

Wild green foliage instead of a deadened snow-covered mountainside. Artemis pondered that, following the lush and flowing leaves around them with their wide and jagged patterns. The crunch under boot changed to what had fallen from the branches, crumpling into the debris that decorated the endless swathes of grass.

Nothing in our view shifted. No warnings, no signs of magick, nothing to alert us of these changes. I'm sure the others recognize it, too. But they're keeping calm about this. My Raptors, always with their steely discipline.

Aristotle's nod pulled her away from the ruminations for a quick moment.

He knows what I'm thinking. He always does. It's getting late. If Rivers can't maneuver the team out of here by dusk, we'll be forced to contend with the wendigo in the darkness. Those relentless fiends know well that they rule the night. Even with our optic devices, it will be near impossible to face them in a prolonged engagement. Damn it, this isn't good. Must keep my cool for the team to get us out of this situation. But I can't shake it, that guilt starting to weigh heavy on my shoulders. I pushed this, always keeping an eye on this region; wanting answers to what happened. Now we're in over our heads, facing down something that we've never encountered in the history of the Agency. Its power is immense. I let my personal desires get in the way of my better judgment. Has my wanton hunger for vengeance damned the only family I have left?

Artemis looked back to see Milton bringing up the rear, his fierce gaze watching the surrounding woodline, searching for the quick glimpses that would herald the arrival of their foes. Corwin carried Julie over his shoulder. Rodriguez took his flank with her ever watchful eyes serving as sentry. Artemis turned to her twin beside her, a frown of concern usurping her gaze guiding to Rivers. *Aris is right. He seems more determined than usual.*

"Raptor6Echo," Artemis called out.

Rivers continued, unimpeded.

"Rivers?"

"Hey, pendejo!" Rodriguez scolded. "George! Don't you hear Actual?"

Rivers halted. His back remained toward the others when their patrol stopped. "What?"

"Distance, direction, what's the report?" Artemis asked. "Where are we heading?"

"We're heading out of this place. Going to safety. Can't you tell we're heading downward?"

"George, what's gotten into you? I'm just saying the map doesn't make sense. How did you get our orientation?"

"How do you expect us to trust you, when you can't even trust us, Actual?"

Artemis paused, pressing her lips together before a reluctant nod. "Very well. No argument about that. I'm just trying to understand."

"We must go this way."

"That doesn't answer my question, Agent."

"George, you all right?" Milton asked.

Rivers continued, leading the formation with a scowling frown.

Milton patted Artemis. "I think he's just hurting about losing Pippen. That's all. We handle these things in different ways."

"Understood. I'm feeling it, too. Save that I don't have the luxury to express it. We'll do something special for Pippen, to honor his memory once we get back to civilization. He won't be forgotten. I promise."

The heavy weapons specialist winked at his team leader, before breaking contact and continuing his search of their surroundings. Cold winds brushed against Artemis' face, making her blink. Within the rapid closing and opening of her eyelids, swift glimpses of shadow caught her attention. Her search found nothing, save for the caress of wind and the towering brown trunks in every direction.

"You see something, Actual?" Rodriguez's weapon barrel raised, her sight shifting around them.

It's called pareidolia. Artemis recalled one of her father's repetitive fact-riddled speeches. "I have no visual."

"We need to keep moving," Rivers announced.

The team paused under the hard stare of their point man, statuesque and unblinking in their direction. His focus falling to none. Milton looked to Artemis, then Corwin and Rodriguez.

"You sure you're okay, Rivers?" Corwin asked.

"You're bugging, man," Rodriguez added.

The twitch of movement in Pattie's peripheral brought her spinning to the ready position with her submachine gun. The glowing reticle of her close combat optic went over a swaying tree branch. Her tense shoulders deflated, lowering her weapon.

"Hijo de puta!" she exclaimed. "The forest is playing tricks on us!"

"Easy there." Corwin patted her. "False alarm. We're all on edge."

"I'll get us to where we need to be!" Rivers snapped, storming ahead. "Enough with the spazzing and questions. It's only delaying us."

"His energy," Aristotle said. "It's not the same. Something is off about him. There's a negative aura surrounding him."

"Could be the lament, like Milton said," Artemis countered. "We all handle grief differently."

"Could be. I haven't worked with Rivers before. They're your team, so you would know them better than I, Arty. But I remember his signature being different in the etheric layers."

"Yeah, that's definitely lament." Corwin nodded. "I feel his pain. Go easy on him, team."

Coldness crept in, flowing through the air with its

inescapable touch nipping at exposed skin. Lips grew chapped. Rosiness protruded from cheeks. Clouds of breath grew thick as streams from nostrils billowed around them.

"Arty, we're not going to make it," Aristotle whispered. "It seems we're nowhere near our destination. You have to order your team to dig in for the night. Fire is our only salvation now."

"Wait!" Artemis ordered. "We're not going to make it at this rate. It's almost dark."

"We keep moving," Rivers said, stepping forward to disregard her. "We're almost there."

"The hell we are!" Rodriguez snapped.

"Rivers, stand down," Artemis reprimanded. "Our only chance to stave off the wendigo is by building fires around our area. Now we have about an hour of sunlight left. That's enough time to set up a fighting position to get us through the night."

"I agree with, Actual." Corwin added. "If we don't make it back before night fall, we're going to be caught with our pants down." Rodriguez bit her lip and winked at him. He rolled his eyes, continuing, "Besides, it's about time that I gave Julie here some rest and changed her bandages."

Rivers glared at his fellow agents, placing their rescued victim against a nearby tree. Milton began digging through his pack, removing an entrenchment shoveling tool, snapping it together so that it locked into place for work.

"I'm taking Rod and we're going to fetch the tinder," Artemis announced. "We need to round up ample amounts."

"So, a fuck ton?"

Artemis nodded and smirked. "For lack of a better term."

Rodriguez put her arm around Artemis. They walked away whispering in their embrace. "Chica, we need another girls-only vacation at the resort after this one! Beach, sun, and giant margaritas! Hey, don't give me that look! You know I'm a tropical creature."

"I'll get to work on the perimeter," Milton announced. "Rivers, watch my six while I'm digging."

With finger resting on the trigger, Rivers shadowed Milton who chopped at the earth with the shovel's edge. His narrowing gaze of disdain fixed on the large agent.

"So be it, Raptor..."

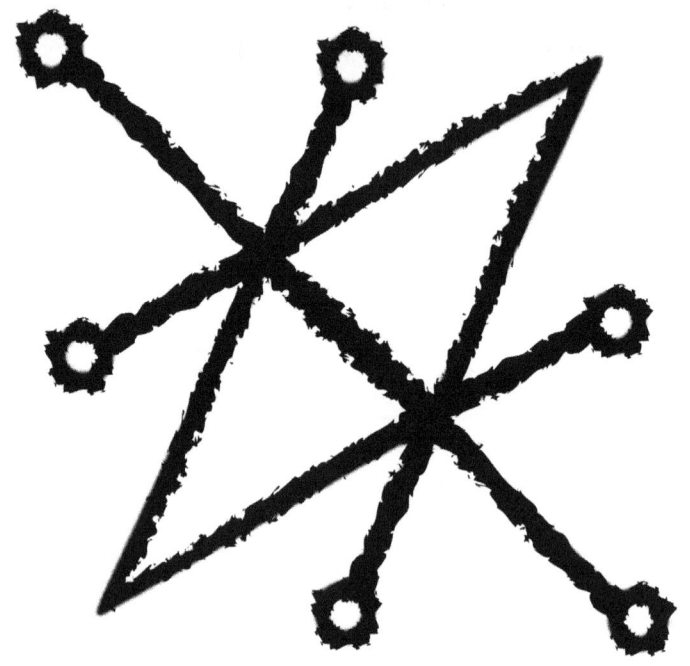

CHAPTER 9
TWO VOICES

The rifting light of tall flames blazed along the trenches surrounding Raptor's encampment. Fluctuating hues of yellow and orange stretched around the agents, pushing waves of heat that ushered away the dry biting cold. Darkness from the night's overcast encroached, its reach halting just beyond the perimeter of their fortifications. Grass and weeds were trampled underneath a pacing Rodriguez, who stopped for a moment to inspect beyond their warm breaths, dissipating into the smoke-laced surroundings.

"We should've kept moving," Rivers murmured.

"Mira! Enough with your bitchin'. You're acting like a real cabrón lately." Rodriguez continued trekking between the gathered pile, tossing new tinder to keep the barrier alive. "Pinche wendigos going to have to earn this meal."

"We're getting you out of this." Corwin kneeled beside Julie, clearing strands of hair from her swollen face. His head lowered with a sigh. "I wish there was more I could do for you.

Just stay strong. You've already proved tougher than most by staying alive through all this injustice."

Milton and Corwin exchanged nods.

"A fuck toy for a bunch of malformed retards; that's what you call tough, Corwin?" Rivers smirked, his voice carrying a biting contempt. "She's dead weight like most bitches."

"Something's gotten into you." Corwin raised a brow and recoiled in disgust.

"What the hell is your problem, George?" Milton snapped. "Spouting that misogynistic crap!"

"I think I know what's wrong," Corwin interrupted. "I'm trying not to think about it myself. Not until we get back to the rear."

"You're all my fucking problem, Milty."

"I know you're upset about losing Pippen. You used to be a hell of a guy. So, drop the bullshit before I drop you!"

"Oooh, so tough, huh? Big guy? What happened to being a devout Christian? Either way, I'd love to see you try."

"Lock it up, everyone!" Artemis ordered. "You're bickering like children! We are federal agents. The enemy is gathering. For the first time we're facing the terrors of the wilderness and they're united. So now more than ever, Raptor needs to be a team. Or we're not making it out of here..."

"She's right," Corwin agreed. "Wendigos are masterful hunters. In this low visibility even with our NODs, we're not going to be able to combat so many. They'll outmaneuver us with ease. We'll never see them coming."

Artemis searched past the inferno, into the endless distance of trees and brush. Snowfall cascaded within her view, her eyes following the drifting cold flakes, touching down to the layer at their feet.

The team leader's brow arched with her rising anger, disgust filling her face. "It's here."

"How do you know, Actual?" Rodriguez paused. Her gaze dropped to the snow, then the trees covered in white. "Wait! The environment! It changed again! Carajo!"

Artemis nodded. "Keep an eye out for the manipulations and anything else that may occur."

Milton pulled back the charging handle of his machine gun, before patting another drum clipped on his hip. "Let the games begin. I'm ready to play."

Glimpses of shadows appeared, within the speckles of moonlight escaping through the tall foliage. The night wrapped around them. Agents watched in all directions, staring outboard with backs and shoulders brushing in their movements. Weapon barrels faced the vast width of their firing sectors, fingers poised along each trigger's length.

The things... they're here... killing without mercy again... it's just a function for them at this point, like a force of nature. Their relentless hounding... I can't escape, no matter how far I run. The hunger... so hungry... always hungry... I remember their black and soulless eyes ushering me onward, their screams carrying through the forest... here I am stuck. I can't... I'm scared...

You know they are relentless in their nefarious pursuit of death.

I know... I saw... they killed them... their loud noises, ringing in my ears as they dispensed death to all of them. But how did they do that—killing with just their gazes?

They're dangerous, beings beyond your comprehension.

So much blood. The others didn't stand a chance. How did we go from a camping trip to this?

There's no time to deliberate the choices that led you to this point. You're here now and all that matters is survival.

So hungry... the pain... always in... pain! I must... eat...

You've no choice in the matter. You have to survive. The monsters are here, ready to kill you like they did other hikers and campers. What you witnessed is just the beginning of their viciousness. The tip of the iceberg that floats into fathomless depths of the icy beyond. Survival is all that matters. Make it home to your family.

Family? I have... family? I see... images of a woman... pretty... long raven hair... my wife? Who is this? Yes, my wife... the little ones... their happy smiles... glistening teeth... thick... meaty... juicy... cheeks... meat...

Face the monsters. Kill all of them save for their leader. Coral her to the Glowing so that I may trap her within it. Now is the time to take a stand or there will be no tomorrow for you. This moment you must find the strength to fight back. To survive at all costs.

Survive... must... eat...

Beyond the flickering hot bastions and the waves of warmth that rose from them, screams carried through the dead of night. Lamentation carried through the ear-ringing noise, a growing rage pulsing through and erasing the initial desperation. The pitch grew higher, blending into the howling winds with an onslaught of voices that called from the hidden beyond.

The agents poised themselves, facing the predatory calls in the distance. Their weapons remained with barrels up and at the ready. Buttstocks pressed into their shoulders, knees bent, breaths staying controlled and shallow through conscious effort against the call of death.

"Damn!" Milton murmured. "They sound more riled up than usual."

"Stay poised and ready, Raptor." Artemis ordered. "Without fear!"

"Without limits!" the team roared back.

Humanoid eyes glimmered in the distance, upon a shadow whisking behind a tree. Beyond the reach of the camp's light it remained, it's ravenous intent blaring through a twitching predatory gaze. Cries of anger and desperation continued to haunt the night. The pitch reverberated on the agents. Fiends darted amongst the foliage in the distance.

The reticle of Corwin's ACOG scope rose into view, lining on the head of a wendigo. The illumination of a tracer round sparked out from his M14, exploding through the creature's dome. Brain matter splashed against the tree's trunk. Its corpse toppled to the ground. The blackened hole in its skull fizzled with its twitching body.

Roars erupted from Milton's machine gun, bullets raced through the receiver, launching bursts of fire. Trees shuddered as rounds hit, following the wendigos' movements closing around the encampment. Fire rose from the impacts, bringing light to the distance with each incendiary round sputtering like celebratory sparklers.

The red glowing reticle of Artemis' sight followed the gaunt frame of a tango. She carried it just beyond the target's path, and with a smooth trigger pull, a round flew. A cry was cut short. The creature shuddered, falling back to the snow. Blazes of orange and yellow erupted from its chest, burrowing into the heart.

Screams continued gathering. Moisture gathered in the air.

"Arty!" Aristotle called out. "I'm sensing a change in the etheric layers!"

A droplet of water fell from above. Artemis peered upward with a gasp, her eyes widened watching the rain fall. Pounding rose in her chest, channeling into her palms. *No! Please, God. No! Not now!*

The drizzle came in sprinkles of wetness clinging to their skin, saturating their uniforms. It grew heavier, soaking into the ground that glistened to Raptor's dismay. The bastion's fire receded in puffs of smoke. Darkness lurched forward with the call of bestial fervor moving closer.

"NODs!" Milton screamed. "Lock 'em in!"

Vision returned with the glowing green tint of their night optic devices. Rodriguez yelled in defiance, her submachine spewing rounds at something in the shuddering bushes. Black eyes appeared, whisking deeper into the foliage, its swift movement carrying like a breeze around them. Rodriguez hounded it with her weapon's barrel, until it disappeared in the barrier of her vision's tapered peripherals through the NODs.

"It's right here," Rodriguez hollered. "They're closing on us!"

Corwin turned, hurrying for Julie. Four streaks of pain raked across the back of his leg, sending the agent stumbling. Deep breaths sucked in the air behind him. Corwin rolled over. Water mired the lens of his NODs, smearing his vision. Muzzle flashes burst into view as he fired into the wilderness.

Wendigos stepped from cover. Corwin felt himself raised from the ground by mighty arms grasping at his armor. Tension poured into his body, flooding through with the intense pumping of his heart.

"Easy, I got you," Milton announced.

Corwin sighed with relief, until Julie's squealing screams rang into his ears. Her cries became distant as she was dragged away. They carried her by their claws punctured deep into her arms. Agony rose through her lungs, her loud sobs floating on the wind. Teeth chomped down, biting away morsels of tender flesh into the ravenous mouths gushing with the blood of their prey. The wendigos' cries rallied in the dark, each of the voracious hunters reaching for a portion of the living spoils. Julie's screams withered, until the only sound carrying in the night was the feeding frenzy of gnashing maws.

"No!" Corwin cried out, stumbling on his wounded leg. "No! Damn it!"

"She's gone!" Rodriguez cried out, grabbing him.

"Activate beacons!" Artemis ordered. "Grab your packs! We're moving!"

A flick of the switch on their helms gave off glowing lights that pulsed into their night-vision goggles. Plodding steps squished through the wet grass and mud from Rivers' sprint. The team remained in tow, struggling to keep pace with the fast-moving point man.

"Rivers, keep us together!" Artemis ordered. "Corwin is wounded!"

They continued moving, whipping past trees and bushes. Howling gales carried around them, the seeping cold bringing their bodies to involuntary quakes. Rodriguez grunted, summoning every ounce of strength, pulling deep from her muscles stinging with fatigue to help Corwin, groaning through his limp.

"Rivers, damn it! Slow it down!"

Milton glanced over his shoulder. In the distance, he saw the lithe figures of their nemeses gaining ground. He paused, dropping to a knee, fingering through his pack.

"Milty, there's no time. We have to move!"

"This will buy us some time, Actual." The large man continued withdrawing a small-curved device, straightening out thin legs along the bottom. Along its face were the instructions 'Front Toward Enemy.'

With the device placed snug into a bush, Milton ran a line of wire to a sapling, before heading back to the device and attaching it to the fuse well along the top.

"A claymore mine." Artemis nodded.

"Complete with snag line."

"Good thinking. Won't kill them, but that'll definitely slow them down."

"Let's just hope it works," Milton murmured, continuing to run.

"Where the fuck did that pendejo go?" Rodriguez snapped.

"Over here!" Rivers called out in the distance.

Raptor sped toward him, but Artemis and Aristotle slowed their pace. Rivers stood at the mouth of a cave. Adjacent to them was an abandoned cart, layered in years of thick rust, most of which had broken off into flakes melding into the wet mud and grass. Tall weeds grew around strips of metal that lined the ground, leading into depths of stagnant darkness.

"Arty, it's the place..." Aristotle came to a halt.

"This means we're back where it all started..."

"We should take cover inside," Rivers called upon entry.

"Come in, take shelter and we'll create a sector for fire on the wendigos. It'll become a fatal funnel."

"That's a damn good idea," Milton agreed, turning to scan the forest as Rodriguez and Corwin hobbled past him. "Actual, are you okay?"

"Yeah, I'm fine."

Artemis' uniform was soaked, weighing around her limbs. Water escaped down her helm and nods. The droplets finding their way into her nose and mouth. The fatigue of her burning lungs faded. There was only the blaring alarm of dread that channeled through rising instinct. Rivers glared at her. The whites of his eyes were visible since his NODs were no longer worn. His vision followed Artemis through the pitch darkness of the cave's center where he remained. She stayed poised, circling, and glowering back.

"What's your problem, Agent?" Artemis demanded.

Rivers smiled at her, reaching out to caress her hair. She went to slap away his touch, her hand passing through nothingness.

"Who were you yelling at, Actual?" Milton asked, walking inside.

"Rivers... he's still being weird."

"Are you sure?"

"Positive, he's starting to work my last nerve."

"Actual... Rivers was just outside with me." Milton pointed at George now entering.

Artemis shook her head. "Why aren't your NODs on?"

"They're dead." Rivers shrugged. His face stretched with a wide grin. His unblinking stare remained on her as water dripped from his helm. "Are you okay, Actual? Seems you're seeing a lot of ghosts lately."

Artemis turned away, kneeling beside Corwin. Rodriguez

rustled through their medical packs. "We used it all on Julie, Damn it!"

"Here!" Artemis handed over some of her own bandages. "Pattie, you get him stabilized and rested at all costs. You hear me?"

"Yes, Actual. I'll take care of him," Rodriguez answered, her face softening into longing worry, stroking Corwin's face.

"Let me know if you need more, Rod," Milton added, watching the entrance with his machine gun poised over a tipped cart. The weapon's bipod scratched through the corroded brown layers as he zeroed his sights and position with the mouth of the cavern.

"I failed her," Corwin murmured through grinding teeth while Rodriguez cleaned his wound. "I promised..."

"Mira, papi! You have to stand still so I can make sure I clean it all. We can't risk it getting infected."

"I promised I would get her out of this... and I failed her..."

Artemis placed a hand on the agent's hip. "You're a good man, Corwin. And the best second a team commander could ask for. I know you genuinely care about the civilians we save. But you can't blame yourself for that one."

"Actual, I—"

"Agent, please save your strength. We're going to need it for escaping this nightmare."

Corwin nodded.

"It's deep, Actual." Rodriguez announced as she prepared a needle and stitching. "I'm going to close it. But his hammy's cut deep."

"Understood. At sunrise we'll find something to splint that leg for the trek out of here."

Loud clamoring swept through the forest and mountains. Raptor exchanged grimaces of confusion at the noise that appeared more akin to the long blaring of a trumpet, and the whining squeal of an elephant's call. The commotion grew heavier and deeper, reverberating through their core until becoming the rumbling growl of a predator. Echoes of its negativity remained etched in their minds, lingering in their souls beyond the quaking of their hearts.

"What the hell was that?" Milton looked to Artemis.

"I have no clue."

Rivers stared out into the wilderness, his squared shoulders rising and falling with the depths of eager breaths. He turned with a wide grin and uncompromising stare, falling on Artemis once more. "War has been declared. He will no longer wait to punish your trespasses. He will no longer wait to claim his prize."

"What prize?"

"You. Artemis."

Milton's gaze rose from the sight of his weapon, glaring at Rivers. "What the fuck are you going on about, George? Start talking."

"Who is he, Rivers?" Artemis asked.

"The master. He taught us the hunt, fashioning weapons, and making war."

"You're still not making any fucking sense!" Milton snapped.

"I am subjugation!" Rivers' voice grew deep, each syllable touching them like the lash of a whip. His countenance grew heavy with an aura of dark majesty as the shadows reached to embrace his form. An unearthly and sinister echo rang through his tone, calling from a world alien to their comprehension.

"I am violation incarnate, the rapist of countless women, the devourer of flesh and soul. I am the corruptor of your form. I am Archon of those that gave their heavenly estate in the years forgotten of the time untold. I am your nightmares made manifest, the caress of fear when your innocence is forced to expire. I am the one that suckles at your misery."

Rivers lowered his glowering face.

"I am Azazel, highest of the B'nai ha Elohim Grigori Anun. Warriors of El, I will break your will, until all you shall know is torment eternal."

CHAPTER 10
MOUTH OF FEAR

Tread marks were left in the wake of the truck's speedy advance, leaving tufts of grass and sprinkles of dirt riddled behind it. Agent Carver's trembling grasp loosened on the steering wheel. Echoes of thudding attacks still rang in his mind, along with the unintelligible cries of violence. A deep exhale and his foot eased from the gas, bringing the vehicle to coast as the blurring streaks of brown and green became trees once more.

An ache climbed through his stomach, rising into his throat, despite attempts to swallow it away. The sweat continued to trickle down his forehead, flowing with heavy breaths that matched the rapid pulse of his heart.

What the fuck? What the fuck? Get ahold of it. Damn, what the fuck! Get ahold... Artemis and the team... shit where could they be? Back there? Dead? Did they get overwhelmed by that wave of insanity that almost claimed me? Check their signals.

The truck came to a stop. Carver leaned to examine the glowing monitor of the force tracker. He reached over to the passenger side, shifting it while scrutinizing the map details. Blue dots moved along the brown contour lines of the terrain.

Okay, so they're in this location roughly—

The dots disappeared.

Strange. Their beacon's turned off.

Raptor's signal reappeared, twenty-five kilometers west of their last position. Carver slapped the tracker. Their beacons blinked before vanishing again.

This fucking thing on a delay?

They reemerged along another side of the monitor. Another set of dots appeared adjacent from them.

Damn, this must be broken. It's reading them all over the place!

More signals appeared, forming a circular image. It tapered with the dots shifting, forming cheek bones, and narrowing into a strong chin. They overlapped each other, melding into a pointed nose with eyes below an arching brow. Carver dropped back in his chair. The face turned to address him. White static grew loud on the radio, rising from the speakers like a hissing serpent.

This isn't happening.

But it is, Ned.

I'm losing it! I must be...

This job is taking its toll on me.

Arty is back there. She has to be. They've spared the women. I didn't see a female amongst them during the attack. The others are dead. And I ran. I left Actual and Pattie to their fates. I have to go back.

But you can't do anything for them. Not to mention the court-marshal that will most likely await you upon return to headquarters, right? How do you expect to live down these failures? One of the Assistant Directors will do an inquiry as to how you're the only one to survive. Then what? They'll dig up something on you; dereliction of duty, cowardice... or perhaps treason.

Material from a crisp and pressed suit brushed with Carver's skin, replacing the sweaty combat uniform. Imagination had carried him to a spotless room before the line-up of Assistant Directors. Irate and grim stares took in every bit of him, dismantling each detail with scrutiny, building animosity and resolve to his fate. A coldness formed in his stomach, developing into shakes, tremoring down his boots.

No. The Agency wouldn't—

Wouldn't find a scapegoat for the catastrophic defeat of an entire combat team? Don't be so naïve. They are a government entity like any other. You return home alone, with this story? You'll be finished not only as an agent, but as a free man.

Moisture swelled into Carver's tear ducts, his head shaking.

I just wanted to serve humanity. Now this? No, I can't. There has to be another way. I can't survive in prison. Especially if they find out I'm a government agent...

The tether of a gentle force guided his view until settling on the M1911.45 ACP pistol resting on his hip. In a smooth motion he pressed the holster's release and withdrew the handgun.

I'll never make it in prison. I—

You'll never make it. This is for the better.

Cold metal radiated into his skin from the weapon's barrel he pressed underneath his chin.

This is the best resort. On your terms, not theirs.

Carver pulled the pistol away, drawing the weapon out. The loud roar of shots echoed through the cabin. Thick rounds punched into the screen of the force tracker. The crumpling device sparked and crackled, the visage it held fading with the drift of smoke.

No! Carver snapped back. *What the fuck was that? A demon? I felt all of that... I need to get back to town. Have to call HQ for back up.*

A twist of the key started the truck's engine.

But how do I get there from here? I got it! Have to go old school.

Carver opened the glove compartment, drawing out a folded paper map.

I'll find my way or make one.

Heavy droplets of rain continued in rapid showers tapping along the mine's roof. Swelling cool mists rose waist high, covering the forest floor in a floating gray haze. Gaunt silhouettes took position behind trees in the distance, their shapes distorted by the pouring tumult. Unblinking glares of primal hatred beamed from statuesque perches, their feral glowing stares fixated upon the mouth of the cavern, watching the agents positioned within the shadows and rocks.

Leave George be. He's too far gone, Artemis thought. *The vector, it's doing something to him. Just keep it together and get him and Corwin the hell out of here.*

Rivers remained staring at earthen walls, his body locked, save for the faint movements of shallow breathing. His dilated pupils remained forward and unflinching while droplets of water rolled from his soaked brow. Rodriguez waved her hand in front of his face. Rivers' stare remained fixed.

"Azazel," Artemis whispered to her twin. "Where have I heard that name before?"

"I see you've been neglecting your occult studies, sis." Aristotle jeered. "When are you agents ever going to realize that it takes more than courage and gunfire to win this? You would've made a stronger scryer than I. If only you embraced our family's latent gifts—"

"Now is not the time for your lectures, Aris. I didn't understand half that malarkey Rivers—that thing was spewing, despite the gravity it rang with. Azazel... that name, it resonates deep with me—"

"In a sense of dread?"

"Yeah... but I don't fear anything."

"I know."

"This bothers me because those words weren't for Raptor."

Aristotle nodded. "I sensed it, too. Those threats were meant for you."

"I can't help but feel a deepening sense, there's too much happening in the unseen. This demon's intent isn't superficial death and destruction. This, our most arduous mission ever, has grown into a nightmare."

"He's no demon."

"Then what?"

"An angel."

"A what? No, are you sure it's just not a greater demon? AD Howler warned us that the enemy was trying to bring them through. Ghost Team had fallen because of their battle with the dark sorcerer that brought over the demon prince. Perhaps this is one of them? Something we didn't catch?"

"No, Arty. Listen to me. I love your assertiveness, your decisiveness. But listen to me. This isn't a demon. Its power is beyond any of the infernal servants, that much is evident. It changes the environment, manipulates what we see, feel, and hear? All of us at once? No demon is that strong."

Artemis sighed.

"Azazel is the name of a fallen angel from the books scrubbed by the corrupted church, Arty. One of the worst from the Order of Watchers. So terrible, so twisted, so depraved that God tasked one of the highest archangels, Raphael, to personally imprison him in the earth. Fortunately, the watchers are of the lowest order, but the power this one displays makes me wonder..."

"There's more at stake here than just our lives. We've stumbled on to something apocalyptic. This fiend knows it. There's something hidden, a factor that he doesn't want us discovering."

"Therein lies the test. I'll do my best to figure it out, Arty. Just keep your people alive."

Artemis nodded. She took a kneeling position behind Milton. The heavy weapons specialist held the machine gun's stock tight into his shoulder. His aim traced over the enemy location.

"They're surrounding us," Milton announced. Artemis followed his vision to the menace in the horizon. "We've no way out of this. We'll never make it."

Tapping on Artemis' shoulder diverted her attention. Aristotle was next to her, worry weighing heavy on his brow as he sighed. His arm rose, slowed by reluctance that shook from it and into his core. Into the depths he pointed, where the darkness grew thicker along with the heavy odor of dirt lingering upon the tepid air.

"Out there is certain death." Aristotle spoke in monotone, his intentions channeling through a solemn meditative state. "It closes upon us. I can feel something approaching. Its power is unlike anything I've ever felt. I think it's the vector. The energy is similar. Images of two golden hands keep intruding upon my thoughts. There's a benevolence ringing from them. They are urging us back further into the depths. That's our only chance."

"There's so many of them out there, Actual." Milton paused. "Artemis... I want you to know... I never told you this although... I've felt it... since our first time together. But if we don't make it out—"

I need your head in this fight, big guy. She placed a finger over his lips, shaking her head. "Don't say it or think it yet. You can tell me the next time we're alone."

Milton nodded.

"We're moving, Raptor," Artemis announced. "Get ready to pick it up."

"Actual, are you talking about going to face them by cutting a path of fire from here?" Corwin groaned. "Just leave me. I'll slow you down—"

"No! We're not leaving you." Artemis pointed behind them, to the depths of shadows descending into the earth. "We're moving deeper."

Rodriguez slapped Corwin on the back of his head.

"Ow, Patty! I'm wounded here!" The fierce countenance of his snap faded when his eyes connected with hers. Rodriguez swelled with tears threatening to stream down her sandy cheeks.

"You're giving up, but you promised!"

Corwin took Pattie's hand, hoisting to his feet. Wincing brought an involuntary grimace, as agony trembled from his wound. Pressure formed on the deep gashes remaining sealed by stitches binding his flesh. He looked to Rodriguez, tightening his grip on her hand and nodding.

"I'm not giving up on us."

"That's a damn good idea, Actual," Rodriguez said, turning to Artemis. "This has to be a mine we're in, right? They usually have another way out. We'll find it."

"Agreed. Eyes open for another way. We're moving, Raptor!" Artemis ordered.

Milton rose from his cover, his hawkish glower never leaving those that stared back from the distance.

Artemis led with her rifle, the green tint of their NODs peeling away the darkness.

"Mira!' Rodriguez called out. "Pinche Rivers is still standing back at the entrance, mouth breathing and shit."

Aristotle pointed to the agent remaining motionless in his haze, save for the breaths of fog expelling from his nostrils.

"Rivers, get your ass in gear!" Artemis snapped. "I'm not telling you again!"

"George, come on. What the fuck?" Milton scolded. "Hey man, we gotta go! This place is about to get swept by the enemy!"

A slow shift of his body brought Rivers' empty stare to his teammates. "I must... go... take care of them."

"Yeah, bud. We need you. I know you've been through some shit. Is that thing still in your head?"

Rivers paced by the heavy weapons agent, who shrugged before retaking a watchful sentry over their rear.

Artemis' brow rose.

"Watch that one, Arty," Aristotle warned. "That aura isn't his anymore."

CHAPTER 11
DESCENDING INTO PRISON

mbrace from the chilling air lifted from their skin as Raptor descended deeper into the mine. Mounds of dirt crumbled under their steps, canted with the jagged surface. Shadows grew around them when the last vestiges of moonlight could no longer reach from the entrance. The air grew stale, riddled with musty earthen odors weighing heavy.

Tapping along Artemis' shoulder drew her to Aristotle's concerned gaze, leading to Rivers walking in a coiled hunch. His heavy plodding steps crunched loud within the tunnel. Rattling came from his rifle as it dangled from the sling, slapping against his body. Wide sparkles of illumination beamed from his eyes, usurping Raptor Team's attention through the momentary wash of their night optic devices.

"Get your shit together, Rivers!" Artemis scolded through sharp whispers. "Put some new batteries in your NODs. We can't afford any fuck ups."

The agent continued with the sheen of his pupils focusing on the darkness ahead.

"Doesn't seem we're being followed anymore." Milton said, bringing up the rear. "I've been scanning the mouth. Oddly enough, they've all remained outside so far."

"Finally, some luck on our side," Corwin groaned.

Artemis stopped. "Agent Rivers. I have had about enough of your insubordination!"

Rivers' empty eyes lowered, acknowledging nothing until finding a spot on the ground. A tremble went through his bowing legs, rising into his chest, until his head twitched. A gasp escaped from the agent. A hard grimace brought his face scrunching together and eyes clamping shut. Rivers bared his teeth through locked jaws and face rippling tension.

"Agent Riv—" Artemis paused when Aristotle put his hand on her shoulder.

"He's suffering. That Marine Corps style of demanding discipline to overcome hardship isn't going to work here. I can sense a turmoil rising within his spirit. But I can't feel anything beyond that. There's a barrier, warm and crackling with energies. Kind of like visiting a place after a huge argument. I can't figure out what is happening..."

The team commander sighed, bringing her gaze upon Rivers. She rose from her tactical stance, bringing her weapon to the side and walking over.

"George." Artemis softened her voice, reaching out for his shoulder. "I know we're all going through something right now. I know you're hurting, and tired. I'm going to get us through this. I promise. I need you to put away your grief and be the outstanding agent I know you are. We need you."

"Yeah, Rivers," Rodriguez added. "You're freaking great when you're on it."

Milton nodded, patting his back. "I know we pride

ourselves on maintaining discipline and being more procedural than other teams, but we are still family."

"We're not giving up on you, George." Artemis continued. "So don't you give up on us, okay?"

"Actual..." George whimpered from quivering lips.

"Yes?"

"Kill... me..."

"What?"

"Do it... kill... me... please..."

"Oh, for fuck's sake!" Milton shook his head. "Rivers—"

"Do it!" Rivers pleaded. "I... can't..."

"You can't what?" Artemis asked.

"I can't..." Rivers hugged himself, with arms clamping tight around his shuddering body.

"Agent, I need you to get it together—"

George screamed, lurching forward and reaching for the release cord on his vest. One hard tug brought the long wire outboard, unweaving portions of his armor, and sending plates crashing to the ground. Another haggard and echoing cry left as he clutched his rattling M4 carbine with its M203 grenade launcher. The release on the later was pressed, bringing the feed tube forward and the 40 millimeter payload plopping into the dirt.

"Agent Rivers!" Artemis scolded. "Put your gear back on! And reload your weapon now!"

"Actual... I can't..."

"You can't what?" she snapped.

"I can't... fight... him... any longer..."

River's trigger finger reached for the magazine release button on his M4, failing when his hand seized in place. Veins pressed to the surface of his forehead. Muscles strained along his jaws, clamping tight. The agent's head rose, his mouth jutting open, releasing a scream into the shadows of the ceiling.

Echoes of his torment rang in their ears with the shrill cries. Rivers collapsed to his knees, body deflating and slumping over. With head hanging low, strings of saliva cascaded from his wheezing mouth, until his body went statuesque.

"What the hell?" Milton murmured, dropping his jaw, and lowering the machine gun tight in his clutches. "Rivers, what's goin' on with you, buddy? You fight that bullshit! You hear me? Please, tell us something coherent!"

"Artemis, his life energies are gone..." Aristotle said. "There's a light within the vessel. But not the same as before..."

"You love her, don't you?" Rivers asked Milton.

"I—I..." Milton paused. "Rivers, you've lost your shit, man. Yeah, I love Artemis. What's it to you?"

The barrel of his M4 raised, aligning the sight with Milton's chest.

"Rivers! What the fuck are you doi—"

A burst of fire slammed into Milton's chest sending the large agent reeling into the surrounding darkness as piercing lead ripped the material of his vest. Artemis stepped forward, delivering a vicious front kick to George's face. The cackling agent turned his gaze to her.

Streams of blood spilled from his mouth, smearing across his teeth with a myriad of pink and red hues. The cackles grew louder, pounding in their ears like thunder. Artemis reared back, delivering another kick. Rivers caught her foot, bounced up and hurled her body by the leg. With a thud and a groan, she collided into the earthen walls of the tunnel, rolling to the ground.

John! No! Glimpses raced through her mind's eye. Artemis

pulled her hand away from a smiling Milton when he reached for it during a summer training hike. Her hard stare meeting his big and loving eyes during a weapons inspection. Quickening images dissipated within the second they arrived. There was only the cave and the warmth of adrenaline racing through her body with the blistering pace of her beating heart. *Gone... just like that... and I took our time for granted...*

Rodriguez tried to raise her UMP45 submachine gun, heaving upward though the weight of Corwin slowed her draw. The weapon leveled to her hip, with a duo of shots landing in small explosions of dirt beyond Rivers. Corwin pushed Patty over as return fire streaked across their position. Debris rained upon them with bullets shredding the walls. Corwin winced as they crawled behind a large stone. Muzzle flashes washed out their NODs, projecting rounds overhead.

"I must commend you, tasty little morsels!" Rivers' voice resonated with sinister depth. "Despite your lack of intellect, these toys aren't useless. The poor engineering is evident in your choice of projectile weapons over energy. I see the children of El have forgotten everything I taught them about weapons-crafting. But I must say, I find the recoil of these primitive firearms to be most entertaining."

Flickers of light continued to expel from the barrel of the roaring weapon. Rodriguez and Corwin remained low while the twang of ricochet mixed with dirt popping impacts. The bolt of Rivers' M4 locked to the rear, exposing the smoking chamber of the upper receiver devoid of ammunition. He tossed the weapon, approaching Corwin and Rodriguez.

They peered from cover. Blood sprayed out the front of his head as he staggered forward. Artemis stood behind the mad agent. Her M14 was trained on his dome. Skull fragments and brain matter rained over their position, the next two shots removed the top of Rivers' head. George fell over before them. Pink cranial tissue sloshed from the exposed mess, spilling to the ground.

"No matter. I was finished with this vessel." Rivers cackled from the sloughed remains of his mouth. "The contest is just beginning, my dear Artemis. I would say I am up by three. See you at the Glowing."

"Actual!" Rivers bellowed and groaned. "Without... fear..."

Artemis dropped to her knees. Her head lowered. She reached out for Rivers' hand. "Without limits. Goodbye, my friend."

"Son... of... a bitch..." Milton grumbled.

The heavy weapons specialist staggered, kicking stones in his stuttering steps. Deep wheezing breaths flowed through his wincing face. Tugging hard at his release cord, shattered ballistic plates collapsed to the ground. Milton gasped with defiance, shaking his head, he reached into his vest to rub away the pain.

"John!" Artemis ran over, hugging her man.

"I'm good, Actual," Milton answered. "Plates took the hit, but damn... that still hurt like all hell."

Artemis chuckled, wiping away the moisture from her eyes. "I didn't know..."

"They can't take me down that easily." He peered over to Rivers' corpse. "I heard..."

Artemis nodded. "He was battling that thing from within the whole time."

"Rest in peace, Rivers," Corwin announced. "You will be remembered, friend."

"We can't leave him here like this," Milton announced, unslinging his machine gun.

"No." Artemis said, caressing his hand. "You cover our rear. I'll bury him."

"What about the wendigo?" Aristotle asked.

Milton examined the rear of the shaft. "Despite our optimism from earlier, we can't tell for certain if they stopped their pursuit, Actual. I'll do my best if they show up."

"I know." Artemis caressed his face with her hand. "I'll be quick about it. I know time is important and we can't stay long."

"I don't like this, Arty." Aristotle sighed.

Artemis removed the entrenchment tool from Milton's pack as he turned to lie in the prone, his weapon centered on the rear route. The team commander snapped the small shovel together and worked its sharp edge into the ground with hard thrusts.

I almost lost him... in that instant of gunfire, John could have been taken from me. I've already lost two other great agents. Casting judgment on Ghost Team was wrong. I always reprimanded the Steiners during joint missions, claiming they weren't disciplined. But now... oh, it's registering, all right. The moments we have are always special. Maybe it was my fear of dropping my guard, because of what happened so long ago.

Coldness swelled in her lungs with the deep breaths of sadness. She glanced over Rivers' corpse, her vision racing away and back to the hole. She stabbed at it again with the shovel. Artemis' face hardened.

George's last words... he wrestled control away from that thing... somehow.

Follow the north star. When all else fails, we follow its bright presence to orient us. Memories of army land navigation training repeated in Carver's mind. *Let the evening be your guide.*

Mechanisms whined above after Carver pressed a release button. The dragging light of a shooting star expanded across the dotted night sky, as the sunroof's lid shifted away, receding into truck's upper cabin. He looked upward, his vision tracing a line for the little dipper's handle to the brightest spot at its end. A sigh of relief deflated the agent.

"Huzzah!" *Polaris! There you are. That is the north. I have my cardinal direction. Focus on the star. The town on the map... okay, now I'm getting somewhere. If I turn this way, it'll be west. Back to civilization. I hope.*

Heavy tread from tires imprinted on the forest as Carver continued blazing his path. Tree trunks appeared in the radiance of the LED headlights. The agent wrestled with his steering wheel, guiding the truck's nose away from the dense foliage. His gaze shot rapid glances to the sky, locking on to Polaris.

"Gas is getting low. Please, God in heaven. I'm not a praying man. But Howler always says you're here for us if we need you. Right now, I need a little help..."

The visage of tree trunks grew sparse in view. Rumbling from the cabin's journey subsided when the earth began to smooth. Lights flickered in the distance, coming into view as Carver passed the thick body of a hemlock. Glowing brilliance from the town's gas station sign came and went during its struggled to function.

"Eureka! Hot damn! It worked! Thank you! I promise to attend church every..." Carver swallowed. "Easter!"

Jasper stood outside the door, shuffling through a jingling

set of keys. Purring from the agent's truck usurped his attention. Carver greeted with a frantic wave.

"Sir, you are a sight for sore eyes! I hope you aren't closed yet."

"Well, I was locking her up for the evenin'. I close at ten every day, Son. You're one of Artemis' boys?"

"You know Actual?"

"Yes, I do. For many years now. Okay, let's get you some fuel, young man."

"Thank you, sir."

Carver killed the engine, slamming the door to join Jasper. A few clicks and a forceful shove of the nozzle sent gasoline racing through intake, feeding the warm truck's belly. The agent's view scanned over the darkened woodline surrounding the town, beyond the moonlit road cutting through its center. Fingers tightened around the thick plastic pistol grip of Carver's M4 carbine. Heavy odor from discharged gunpowder and residual carbon clung to the agent.

"What's your name?"

"Agent Ned Carver, sir."

"Well, I'm Jasper. Listen, Agent Carver. I don't really know too much about how ya'll run your gig, but something ain't feelin' right. Where's the rest of your team?"

"I... I don't know." Carver's voice cracked, lowering his shaking head. "There was nothing but silence for most of the mission. Until Actual called me up to reinforce their position. Drove to that hovel of a town, where the rest of Raptor had gone looking for that girl—"

"You mean Cray Village?"

"That dump. But when I got there, none of my teammates were around. The radio just stopped working. I started patrolling and that's when they came out..."

"We know about them. Try to avoid any dealings with the Cray folk. I'm not a scientist or doctor, not sure how to describe it, but let's just say their blood ain't that diluted. If ya catchin' my drift?"

"Oh yeah. Those people—I can barely call them that. They seemed more like crazed animals."

"The history of that place ain't pleasant. They left our little town more than a century ago, over spiritual differences."

"I dropped a good number of them. But... I lost the rest of Raptor. I have no idea if they're lost or worse..."

"Well, it's dark, Son. I know you government types probably have your fancy gizmos for dealing with that. But you look dog tired. Tell you what. My home is just behind the station. Not much, just some cots, an old TV, and my whiskey cabinet. I'm going to toss some steaks on the grill and some beans in the pot. You come have a bite, grab some shut eye until mornin'. Then head on back out to look for the other agents."

"A steak and some Jack sound like heaven."

"Hold on now!" Jasper snapped. "I didn't offer you any of my stash."

Carver snickered and nodded. "Fair enough, sir. I shouldn't be having any on duty anyway."

Rifting shadows from the surrounding darkness whisked away Carver's attention. He stared out into morass of unintelligible shapes. Wind brushed over his face, filling his nostrils with cold from the wilderness. Lights from the station sign continued to flicker, bringing glimpses of momentary blindness to the horizon. Blackness in the distance continued distorting the shapes his view struggled to discern. The lights died, washing away his view. After moments of blinking and eye rubbing, Carver's vision adjusted.

Distorted shapes grew larger within the dark of the forest. Looming silhouettes formed amidst the trees towering around them. Their numbers grew, lining the horizon just in view with figures of hunched wide frames, possessing large, canted backs and muscled slabs for shoulders. Thick arms covered in wiry hair dragged along axes, clubs, and other bludgeoning instruments.

Several rifles bounced within the clutches of select members, thumbs cocking back the hammers along their rusted and antiquated receivers. Into the light of the most remote streetlamp, they crossed. Carver's accelerating heartbeat drummed through his entire frame as the details of glistening sweat came into view from the unwashed horde.

"This can't be happening! How are they here?"

"What? What you mean?" Jasper put the gas nozzle back into the pump before wiping his hands with a rag.

"Jasper! We have to warn the townspeople! I don't know if they followed me or something, but they're here and they mean business."

"What?" Jasper stepped out next to the agent. His mouth dropped. His eyes widened.

"Warn the others!" Carver ordered, grabbing his M4 from the truck's cabin. "The Cray villagers are attacking!"

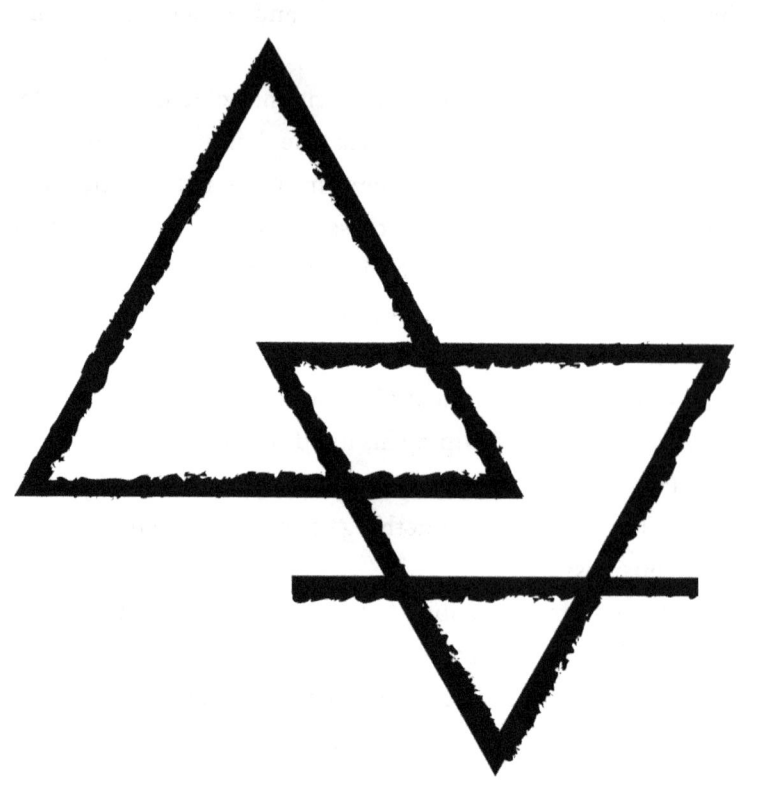

CHAPTER 12
USURPERS IN THE NIGHT

Tepid air ushered away the cold reach of the wilderness as Raptor Team descended further into the mineshaft. The narrowing passage tapered, funneling them into the darkness that lie ahead. Rusted carts and pickaxes with broken handles of dead wood became sparse in their presence. Rock crevices lined the tunnel, until remnants of the old mine were gone, as if the earth had swallowed them, leaving the team stuck in its gullet.

Milton trailed the others, his fierce gaze scanning their rear every few seconds. The agent's frown hardened, his finger poised on the machine gun's trigger. Apprehension slowed his steps, leaving his torso's attentions conflicted with ever-shifting position. Artemis carried the team from the front, guiding with the leveled muzzle of her rifle.

A gust of warmth blew across her face, blanketing over the team. Hot odor akin to rotting eggs and garlic invaded their nostrils, swelling into the pit of their stomachs with an unease. Coughs escaped within the group, save for Aristotle who patted his sister's back.

"Sulfur and phosphorus," the scryer warned. "Do you remember that smell from science class? When we burned those wretched elements, our clothes reeked like flatulence for days."

"Vaguely. You were always into the nerdy stuff. Enlighten me, again."

"Well, this is it, Arty. Just in larger quantity. Or there's a really large kitchen down there and someone doesn't know how to portion their ingredients. Once again thank you for dragging me out here." He nudged her with an elbow that was mirrored with quick retaliation and a weak smile.

I know what you're trying to do, Aris... thank you.

"And growing strong as hell," Aristotle continued. "The only reason we're able to breathe down here is most likely because of a large oxygen source."

"Raptor, be mindful of your gas masks, and ready to grab them should the environment worsen," Artemis ordered.

"Roger, Actual," Corwin acknowledged.

Raptor halted when Artemis stopped, raising her fist then pointing ahead. A large crack followed along the cascading trail ahead. The path continued between jagged rock precipices mirroring each other. Pickaxes remained strewn across the ground, with a few still plunged where they had been used. Cobwebs hung from the tools, which remained caked in rust that widened and distorted their shape.

"How old do you estimate this mine can be, Actual?" Corwin wondered.

"Judging by those tools, over a century."

"No sign of the enemy," Milton announced, joining them. "I was expecting them to hound us, but there's been zero contact. Not even so much as a visual."

Artemis nodded. "They want us to go this way."

"My suspicions exactly," Aristotle agreed.

"But why, Actual?" Milton asked.

Artemis reached out, touching his fingers. "I don't know. But something is telling me that we need to investigate down here. No matter the cost. This isn't just a search for missing civies or hunt for hostile vectors anymore."

A stiff-lipped nod was returned by Milton. "We're with you. Azazel, or whatever it wants to call itself, isn't getting away with this shit."

Avoiding the jagged rocks around them, they continued through the dark passage.

"Look at this!" Corwin exclaimed.

"Oye!" Rodriguez scolded. "You need to calm down and stop moving so much. Let me help!"

"Just look!" With a button's click, a laser shone from his brown PEQ15 advanced target pointer.

Raptors' sight followed the green illumination, highlighting deep gashes over the thick slabs of stone along their flanks. Six wide incisions were raked over the walls on each side. They aligned in a parallel trail, standing the height of the agents. Corwin brought his light behind them, highlighting the perimeter of the giant crack they entered through. The lacerations continued along the mouth's sides leaving the serrated imprints of its outline.

"Team, I don't think the miners dug this," Corwin said.

"Is that... no, it can't be," Milton murmured.

"Claw marks?" Artemis said.

The heavy weapons agent nodded. "But what the hell could be big enough to leave something like that?"

Flashes erupted from Carver's roaring M4. Recoil kicked in his grip, the weapon spewing hate with each trigger pull. Lead erupted across the street as a hail of fire ripped into the advancing Cray villagers. Their screams filled the night sky, mixing with the howls of retribution from their angered brethren that pressed forward.

Shit! Oh boy! Too many! Gotta think of something quick!

Feral eyes glared back at the agent poised behind the bed of his truck. Shell casings flew out from his flank, their fall to the street jingling as he continued with his carbine. The weapon's bolt snapped back, locking in the receiver's rear. Smoke drifted from the barren chamber. Hands moved with quickness, pressing the release that sent the empty magazine falling away. He lodged another in before slapping the forward latch, sending the bolt back into action.

Bodies dotted the ground as the villagers continued their advance. Rifle shots ricocheted off the ballistic-proof glass of the truck, forcing the twitching Carver to duck. Popping shots across the way spewed thick clouds of carbon into the air with return fire. Each shot followed the cock and pop of the levers feeding new rounds into their wood stock rifles.

Air churned with the quick movement of something heavy hurtling in the open. Carver dropped low, behind the walls of the truck bed. Whisking wind passed overhead followed by clanging echoes bouncing across the street. Carver turned, spotting a hatchet skipping away.

"Phew! That could've taken my head clean off. Those bastards!"

The agent opened the truck door, jumping in and bringing the engine to life. Headlights swelled over the area. Heavy steps plodded in the truck's bed, swaying the vehicle. Metal banged against the rear window with repeated wild swings. Their muffled cries of wild desperation carried into the cabin. Carver peeled out, slamming his palm into the horn that blared with the screeching of rubber along the road. Weight left the rear of the vehicle as the stowaways plummeted backward.

Carver slammed the brakes, putting it into reverse, looking over his shoulder. The truck's steel rear crashed into the villagers, sending them to the ground with a resounding thud. Tires went over them, the bulk of the vehicle crunching bone with horsepower that churned the wheels. Groans of agony soared to the stars. Carver brought the vehicle into drive, screeching forward again, the truck rumbling with each body it rolled over.

Impacts collided along the passenger side window, filling with more spider web indents from rifle fire. Air hissed around the truck, jostling about on canted weight. Carver bounced in his seat, attempting to focus on the new light appearing in the dash as a bright yellow circle with an exclamation point at its center.

Damn! My tires! They're out! I still have sixty miles left in them... and I'm going to use it running over scum! Enemies fled over the tracks left in Carver's wrath, stalking into the shadows behind the gas station before moving farther into town. *Shit! I can't contain them to only this front!*

The truck whipped around, with headlights exposing foes pouring from the woods. A stack of slender objects hurled into the air, bouncing underneath the vehicle's nose.

What the hell was tha—

Booming calamity erupted from below the truck, raising it into the air. Carver recoiled in the seat, covering his face when a bright flash consumed all vision. Choking smoke seeped inward, bringing the stench of expelled chemicals into Carver's lungs. He pressed the gas to no response. The vehicle convulsed in its final throes, a hiss rising from its grinding innards. Gone was the engine's purr, replaced with the screaming beeps of warning signals set alight over the dash.

Fighting through blurring vision, Carver shoved open the door and wobbled upon exiting the cabin. His worried gaze fell on the flames rising from beneath the bent hood, looking up to billowing clouds of smoke swelling to the sky. Shots bounced along the dead carcass of the truck, prompting Carver to drop behind it.

The agent shuffled to the tail end, peering over the horizon of the bed. Cray villagers sprinted forward, closing the distance between them. Sinister laughter grew louder in deep tones bellowing with low intellect and primal desire. Carver remained low, dishing away from the truck, and scurrying toward a dumpster. The agent peered around his new cover, observing wailing assailants opening the truck doors.

Carver's fingers rifled through his vest with a sigh. *Only six magazines left. I should've packed more like the others. Every shot needs to count. But damn it, these sturdy assholes don't go down easy!*

A tall figure walked from the distance. The brim of his wide straw hat carrying low as he approached his malformed brethren shuffling to make a path. Held tight in his clutches was an enormous rifle, with a long and wide barrel dwarfing those of his comrades'. Their beady eyes fixed on his steps. He glanced over the truck then scanned to the other buildings.

"What we do now, Papa Mathias?" a Cray minion asked.

"We do what High Priestess Sarai has commanded! We shall obey!" Mathias snarled, his curved and wart-covered finger pointing into the town. "This is the moment of retribution, why we have gathered our numbers so great in waiting. No mercy! Hail to the master!"

Hoarse roars of bestial fervor resounded and spread like wildfire as the contagion of bloodlust filled the eyes of the assailants. Carver broke into a sprint, racing for a building. Dozens of plodding steps clapped the pavement, their hounding laughter pulsing with his crawling skin.

Sweat streamed down Raptor Team's bodies, drenching their uniforms. Stains bled through, revealing deep saturation spreading underneath their armpits. Beads developed along their glistening faces, soaking into the pads of their helmets, and the buds of their communications gear. Their breaths grew deeper and stronger with lungs fighting the thick heat and dryness blanketing the area.

The decline leveled as their descent continued. Walls of earth and stone widened, the cavern growing with their journey. The left side of their path plummeted into a sheer cliff, covered in jutting sharp rocks. Artemis led their approach, peering over. A churning morass of fiery red, orange, and yellow hues blared from the eye of a pit that descended further into the depths. Towering pillars of thick steam and smoke rose, carrying over their heads into the ceiling far above.

"That pit is leading to hot magma from the inner earth," Aristotle said.

"This looks like something out of a science class," Corwin murmured.

"I hope this isn't a volcano or something," Patty agreed.

"There's a whole other world down here," Artemis noted. "Don't focus on the pit, but on what surrounds it."

The team leader's finger guided their attention along the bottom of the cavern, away from the glowing mouth of the pit to a thick canopy of trees stretching around the far-right hand side. Slabs of earth stood high, reaching to sharp points around an area of caves and flat ground with mottled detail. Milton turned the focusing knob on his night-vision goggles, shaking his head after several seconds.

"Can't make out what's surrounding all those caves and formations," the heavy weapons agent said, and sighed. "Anyone else?"

"Nada," Rodriguez shook her head.

"That's definitely out of range," Corwin added. "But I can tell what we're seeing doesn't occur in nature. This place is inhabited. Who the hell would be crazy enough live down here though?"

"Wendigo?"

"They don't arrange living accommodations. Despite their humanoid appearance, wendigo behave more like wild animals than humans."

Artemis' vision blurred until all colors she beheld meshed into a whirlpool of black, gray, and orange. Tension gripped on her shoulders with tingles that grounded into her feet. Energy reinvigorated her presence, erasing the throbbing sharp pains from blisters within her boots, the burning fatigue of overworked muscles, and weariness that gripped her mind.

Something washed over me. It cleansed me. But... what was that?

Light appeared in her psyche, pulsing in her mind's eye. Comfort came, withering away tension in every muscle of her body. Exhaustion seeped from her with a caress that ushered away the cavern's stagnant heat. Rushing water poured through Artemis' thoughts, clearing the remorseless apprehension that always gripped. Relief came like a flood, deflating the tough guard always ready within her. Worries had been cleansed, and Artemis stood upright, with Aristotle placing his hand on her shoulder. The twins exchanged glances in silent acknowledgement.

Their eyes closed, bringing their focus to the beyond. The radiance continued, flashing over a masculine figure from streaks expanding outboard of its back. Large black and unblinking eyes stared at Artemis. The being's hands were wide from the addition of an extra digit. In its grasps were a staff and a large fish he held upright.

"Finish it!" The instructions bellowed from the ether.

Odor from hot sulfur assaulted their nostrils with the return of darkness and the humming light of the pit. The twins looked to each other again. Their hands touched as they gazed down the path ahead.

"You good, Actual?" Milton asked. "Seems we lost you there for a second."

"We're heading in the right direction."

"Artemis." Milton leaned close for a whisper. "We can't continue like this. I'm not trying to undermine your authority, not because of rank or discipline but because I love you too much. But what we're seeing down there... that looks like a death trap."

"I know." Artemis checked the magazine in her M14, continuing the journey.

Milton nodded, following with the others in tow.

CHAPTER 13
DEATH GRIP

Deep panting laughter echoed around Carver with the desperate eagerness of unwholesome intentions. Hurried steps thumped in large quantity as hostiles crossed into the cement of the town roads. Glass shattered, with the swishing of liquid followed by the crackle of growing flames. The agent stared across the street to the large window displaying clothed mannequins behind the words 'Mortimer's Many Outfits'. Reflections of hunched figures appeared, with fires growing in their clutches, setting the contents ablaze.

Molotov cocktails. Those bastards...

A tower of smoke arose from the gas station, the growing fire consuming the building's charring husk. Air cracked with an explosion of whipping flames. The conflagration grew into a mountainous inferno, spreading in a slow pace. Mortimer's window smashed, breaking under a hard impact. Heart pounding exertion ran through the agent's trembling body. The shine of Carver's pupils reflected with orange, bearing witness to the rising firestorm.

The agent rushed out from cover, raising his M4. Optics came into view, highlighting over a fiend jumping and cheering at the handiwork of destruction. Shots popped with quick trigger pulls, sending 5.56 rounds puncturing the back of the tango's skull. The misshapen foe's eyes rolled into his forehead, his body crashing forward, thudding on the pavement. Snarling brethren turned, their tools of death rising after glancing over the drenched wounds of their comrade that spewed over the pavement.

Eyes trembled from the faces of roaring ferocity. They set upon the agent sprinting farther into town. Carbon spewed from the Cray villagers' rifles, sending shots punching into walls as the agent sped along. Carver dived, then grunted from a hard landing, crawling across the sidewalk to a small pick-up truck. He rose over the hood, the muzzle of his carbine barking retaliation that peppered the chest of an enemy in pursuit. The vehicle rattled with return fire burrowing into it, forcing the agent to take cover.

Remaining squat and low, Carver hurried beyond the automobile, heading into a boot pounding sprint as he rushed to the next. Howls trailed behind, climbing into the night sky with disappointment and rage. The assailants hounded down the street after the agent.

Gunshots erupted from the opposite direction. *No! Did these mindless slobs manage to flank the town? They're approaching from the—*

"Give Arty's boy some cover!" Jasper yelled.

Oh, thank God! The townspeople are here. But how are they going to stand against all this?

"We're coming, Agent!"

Jasper and two men in flannel ducked behind a car on the opposite side of the street. They rose with lethal intentions pointing from long barrels of a shotgun and a .308 Winchester rifle. The men bore down on the attackers with thunderous gunfire filling the street. Twelve-gauge shotguns belched swarms of pellets, slamming into an assailant. The first shot buckled the Cray villager's advance, while a follow-up caved his face into a bleeding pile of mangled flesh.

"Jasper, you're like an angel on my shoulder!" Carver called out.

"Didn't think we was tuckin' tail, did ya, Agent? Hell, we just had to get our huntin' equipment."

"Not at all."

Rounds sparked in both directions. The warm scent of gun smoke filled the street. Jasper spotted the flaming tail of a Molotov explosive soaring into the air. Glass shattered upon the vehicle they ducked behind, spreading bright rising flames, consuming all within its explosive radius.

"Gotta get from here," Jasper called out.

"Right, we're going to get swarmed at this rate. Let's fall back and get a better vantage point! Keep low, everyone!"

Growing fire consumed their vision with the brightness devouring the truck. Waves of heat rose, warping the view beyond their cover. Carver witnessed Jasper and the men fleeing. He sighed, dashing across the street. Pumping legs accompanied the pounding of his heart rising into his ears. Each step was joined by the loud cracking of gunfire trailing behind. A quick gaze to the Cray battlements brought attention to the new position the foes had taken behind the smoldering wreckage of his former vehicle. Their rusted rifle barrels aligned with Carver, tracing his movements with impending menace.

Flickers of a popping ricochet bounced along Carver's flank. Hot pain rang into his thigh with the next step. He grimaced, the agony soaring up his body, exiting in a yelp. Racing heartbeats sent a surge of adrenaline carrying him through the line of enemy fire as bullet impacts continued to erupt around him. The M4 dangled from the guide ring on his vest, clapping against his body with each step.

Carver's right hand clutched at the wound. Warm blood greased his fingers, spewing from the entry point with red meat swelling and curling around the small hole. The fragment shuddered in his flesh, its jagged metal presence continuing to stab the agent each time his foot touched down.

"I'm hit!" Carver announced. "Jasper, get your people the fuck out of here!"

"Ain't leaving you behind, Agent!"

The old gas attendant cocked his shotgun, releasing a blast that punched into an attacker's chest, sending it collapsing into a whimpering mess that folded over the pavement. Jasper rushed over, grabbing Carver's arm and hoisting underneath it.

"Hang in there, Agent!"

The townspeople returned fire from an alley, as Carter limped with Jasper to their position.

"Boy, do I owe you one."

"You owe me two, now." Jasper chuckled. "Let's get you over to the General Store. That's where the town meets for emergencies. We got the rest of the folk there, holed up with rifles."

The old man peered around the corner, ducking behind the building again as the wall erupted with enemy fire.

"Jasper, Agent Carver," one of their friends announced. "Let's slip out of the back and get going before that wound gets any worse. We got you covered. We'll be right behind you."

Carter nodded, limping away. *Where is the rest of Raptor? These people can't hold against this much longer...*

Whining from the bay doors competed with the screaming engines of the C160. Metal pulled away from the rear of the aircraft. Coldness rushed inward, bringing a chill over Team HoneyBadger's members lining the compartment's netted bucket seats. Moonlight reflected in the glare of Agent Hector Rodrigo's wide faced goggles. He gazed into the vastness of mottled shadows from the imagery below. He inhaled deep from the oxygen fed into his TMC mask, suppressing the nitrogen in his system.

"How is everyone feeling?" Hector asked his team through the integrated microphone. Thumbs up were returned from the dozen agents clad in full battle gear. "I appreciate those of you who volunteered for this. I know it's asking a lot seeing what we just completed. There're families waiting at home that are going to wait longer because of your selflessness. I thank them too for their sacrifices."

"Evil never takes a day off, Actual," Agent Rosemary Pierce responded.

"That it doesn't."

"We are two mikes from the infil point, Badger Actual," the flight master announced. "The crew are getting a lot of activity on visuals. Thermals have spotted large fires and multiple contacts maneuvering through the sector. All of it is among civilian assets, so Close Air Support isn't an option from here."

"Roger, I acknowledge. Everyone have a battle buddy look them over to make sure their jump gear is green?"

"We're green to green, Actual," Pierce responded.

HoneyBadger rose from their seats, shuffling to the wide mouth of the rear hatch. Freezing wind tightened its embrace on the agents. Hector approached the edge, halted, and looked to the jump master positioned at the door. With a nod of approval, Badger Actual took a thirty-inch step into the open skies.

Steel walls of the cargo compartment raced away from his peripheral sight. Movement forward became a plummet into the cold of night. Hector's body leveled with the horizon, relaxed, but poised against the friction pressing him. The engine's rumble faded with the growing distance, until only loud rifts of wind remained flooding in his ears.

Control your heart rate, Hector. Disciplined self-reminders rattled amidst his inner dialogue. *Relaxed and composed. Preserve the oxygen until touchdown.*

The ground below faded from view. Into the mind's eye hues of pink and white returned, lining the walls of a bedroom. Rays of light entered from windows bordered in frilled white curtains. A young girl sat on one of the beds, her face remaining statuesque with her lips sealed from prolonged closure. Delicate brown eyes from her long stare etched the heart patterns along the floor. Hector unfolded his arms from the doorway, approaching with slow steps, mouth compressing before clearing his throat.

"My girls liked pink," Hector announced. "You don't strike me as the type that likes this style."

"No, sir."

"You don't have to call me that. You're a guest here, Artemis. By the way, there's another girl that lives a few houses down. Her name is Patricia. That one has a foul mouth, but she wants to be a marine someday. I'll introduce you, so there's someone your age to talk with."

Longing eyes heavy with moisture met with Hector. She nodded.

"You make yourself comfortable, pick whichever of the two beds here that you want. We can repaint it if you'd like—"

"I'll be fine. Thank you."

"If you need anything at all just come get one of us. You're not a bother. Cena is every day at five."

"Cena?"

"Dinner. You're going to learn some Spanish while you're here." Hector smiled, turning to leave.

"Hector," Artemis called out.

"Yes?"

"Why did you volunteer to foster me?"

"We'll talk about that during dinner. But for now, just know that as an agent, in my line of work, I know what you're going through. The Agency pulled strings to look after you. We felt it best that you're around people that understand."

"So, I'm just a mission for you?"

"Everything in life is a mission, mija."

The parachute's pull dragged his body upward, ripping awareness from the stream of consciousness usurped by memories. Hector's descent straightened, his legs dangling, while he clung to the steering lines, guiding the path for HoneyBadger. Light and warmth morphed back to the tinted green of night-vision goggles outlining the mountainous regions surrounding their trajectory. Fluctuating masses rose in the distance, forming growing fires the closer he drew to the landing zone.

Tracer rounds sparked out in momentary streaks of

brightness racing across the buildings coming into view, striking into multiple tangoes maneuvering on the opposite side of town. Popping from 5.56 rounds competed with the wind for Hector's ears. *That's familiar, must be Arty's team. Tracers put their position to the opposite end of our LZ.*

Booming stretched a field, bringing thick clouds of carbon spewing up into the night sky. *That's a caliber I don't recognize. Each shot sounds heavy and different, likely from unmeasured primer.* Hector's focus shifted to sparse trees and covered in tall grass. He turned steering with all his might. Screams rang in the distance, mixing with cries of unintelligible words.

Hang tight, mija. I'm coming.

CHAPTER 14
DUDAEL

The trail leveled into a colossal cavern floor. Raptor Team went into the radiating light, traveling closer to the nexus of its pulsating reach. They moved behind a towering bastion of stone, peering from behind its girth. Images took shape in the distance among the illumination from multiple campfires revealing dozens of buildings. The makeshift city was composed of brown and tan tones from the various animal hides used in its construction. Crackles filled the air from a blazing wood pile, towering at the compound's center. A wall of earth and rock loomed behind it, riddled with massive holes.

"There's people down here?" Milton gasped. "What the fuc—"

"Shh." Artemis narrowed her eyes before answering in a whisper. "We're exercising noise discipline. Whispers only when we need them."

"Roger," the machine gunner murmured.

"There must be close to a thousand people living here."

"Arty, do you hear that?" Aristotle asked.

Chants resonated with a slow and deep rhythm, birthed in diaphragms, and rising into the throats of those calling out together. "Levrih nov mishovchorrim michvil h'rtz."

Artemis led with soft steps, weaving between the tents. Each foot placement landed among stakes and ropes, being gentle and measured in tempo. With the barrel of her rifle leading, Artemis peeled away the flap serving as an entrance, peering inside with her finger composed on the trigger. Clay bowls lined the floor of the domicile, filled with leaf flakes and brown powder underneath large stones. Furry piles of animal hides were stacked around the main support beam.

"Nothing in here, but it's definitely living quarters." Artemis whispered.

"Same in this one," Corwin answered, pulling away to rejoin the others.

"You're doing better," Milton noted.

"He doesn't listen." Rodriguez gave Corwin a hushed snap.

"Yeah, I think it's the pain killers and adrenaline. Maybe a bit of wonderment taking over after discovering such a place. I still feel like shit to be honest."

"Well... I found something..." Milton said.

The large agent closed with the others. In his clutches was a spherical object, its smooth round shape illuminated by the encompassing glow of orange and yellow that blanketed them. Milton swallowed deep, presenting it to the team.

Sighs of frustration escaped from shaking heads as they scanned over the missing mandible, to the cracked ridge where a nose had once been, over to the dark and empty eye sockets, and along cranial sutures lining through it.

"A skull?" Corwin sneered.

"Mira, look at the size of it, so small!" Rodriguez exclaimed. "That belonged to a child."

Milton nodded, his long and grim face matching Patty's.

"Could be the child of a missing camping party," Artemis surmised. "A lot of these groups lose folks, too. That confirms it. Whoever is dwelling down here is to be considered hostile—"

The others nodded. She continued.

"Maintain noise discipline. Do not engage unless necessary. Judging by our surroundings we are outnumbered. Things can go south real fast being trapped down here, with supplies running low and no means to fall back."

"Roger, Actual." Hushed acknowledgement spread.

Deep rhythmic chants resumed, whisking their attention toward the far side of the encampment. Glances and sighs of anticipation were exchanged. Artemis continued leading Raptor among the buildings. She raised her fist, halting the team who hid behind the domiciles.

Beyond their position, over a stretched mass of gravel riddled land, stood a crowd of individuals. Their bodies, decked in animal skins, swayed with a lazy flow in unison. Figures primed with slabs of muscle composed the majority of the horde, their towering size imposing even to Milton. Thick curling manes of mottled brown hair draped over their shoulders and wide backs.

Scorching bonfires crackled on the flanks of a large stone platform where the mass congregated. Ripples of heat rose, twisting and blending with rising gray pillars of smoke. Goat skulls lined the perimeter of the makeshift stage, their blackened, curved horns stretching outboard. A woman stood at the apex of the stage by a basin of stone layered in dried brown residue. Plump globular flies darted around the area, buzzing as the woman approach the large bowl, laying candles around its wide mouth.

She turned to the crowd, her near naked flawless russet skin glistening with sweat in the fluctuating lights. Rattling came from the bones woven into a shirt over her rippling abdominals that tapered into a tiny waist. Ribs extended from a necklace, draping over her thin shoulders and toned arms. From her scalp hung a cluster of unkempt raven curls that flowed from a crown of bone and gems. Within the middle of her forehead came sparkles from a large green stone, exuding brilliance whenever the angles of light changed.

"Arty..." Milton whispered. His face scrunched with visible confusion. "She looks—"

"Just like me." *It can't be... I thought she died... no... what have they done to you?*

"Persephone?" Aristotle gasped. "She's alive? Her aura has completely changed. It radiates with tremendous negative energies."

Cries rang out into the night, urging with desperation that carried with its echoes through the vast cavern. A petite figure struggled within the grasp of a large male, her grunts escalating. With big doe-like eyes she peered around, tears streaming down her thin cheeks.

"Neh! Neh!" She screamed at the priestess on the podium. "Neh, we allae canta ti wan! Neh!"

"You are correct." The priestess nodded with a long and grim countenance. "Indeed, the tribe has already given to our king his quarterly demand for a soul of innocence. One that was well expended bringing over another of the ravenous from the void. But more has been asked of us."

"Wantu ajuni un hagada! Ido hun turik?" the woman spat, her glare falling upon the long and thick cesarean scar running over the priestess' lower abdomen. "Emshi un gala, Persephone!"

Hurried stomps brought the priestess rushing down the steps, increasing to a dash that culminated with a fierce echoing slap to the woman. Teeth-baring growls were exchanged between them. The crying woman bucked in the tight grip of her restrainers, butting at another with the tiny sharp protrusions extending from her forehead. A mighty blow clapped on the back of her skull, sending her chin dropping into her chest. The woman dangled in their grasp, her eyes closing with fading consciousness.

"And more we shall give." The priestess smirked. "For our place is to serve his wondrous risen glory, not to question. Your giftless child was chosen because of your failures to carry the mark into it. You have brought forth the image of our great enemy instead of that which our master endeavored to reshape before the great deluge. Pray that this insolence will not cost you more, Pippa. You shall find yourself wandering the undergrowth soon, crying alone, and begging for forgiveness that will never come."

The priestess pulled away, returning to the platform. Footsteps along a staircase of stone brought forth another being.

They're not human. Artemis sneered at the twisted hind legs of the individual, clopping with each step through a kilt of tanned leather hides. The hulking figure stood well above the others, with thick curling horns that sprouted from his head. Cradled in his wide and hairy arms was a bundle of cloths. He presented it while lowering himself before the priestess and bowing with his face to the ground.

Cooing came from the cloths as an infant was unveiled. The priestess raised the naked child for the audience to behold, her arms locking out with the tiny baby's soft and chubby legs kicking at the air.

"We bind the universe and its energies to our will, which is that of the Master's!" the priestess bellowed. "Let the weakness of Adam Ha Rishon bring forth the strength of our kin! From this moment, from those before it, and those yet to come. As it was, so shall it return!"

"Ahoon!" The crowd called back to the priestess. "Mavet at Ha Rishon!"

Aristotle leaned closer to his sister. "Arty, I have no idea what language the others are speaking. Sounds close to Hebrew or Arabic, but also others..."

Artemis nodded.

The priestess walked to the basin, presenting the child for all to behold.

"Mavet, at Ha Rishon!" The chants continued, hands rising upward from the crowd with outstretched fingers.

Into the mouth of the large bowl the child was laid. After reaching behind herself, the priestess' hands returned, carrying forth a glinting object. A curved and sharp dagger was revealed in her tight clutches.

"Neh!" The woman's cries resumed, her body rattling with defiance. "Neh!"

The dagger rose. Artemis stared into the eyes of the priestess, a younger imitation of herself. Inside the blackness of her pupils were only dancing reflections of light from the raging infernos along her flanks. Artemis reached out, the coldness of loss that subsided but always remained, beginning to resonate once more. Missing within the priestess' gaze was the twinkle of a soul, replaced with an alien, unflinching, hollowness.

Persephone... Artemis winced, her breathing picking up pace despite efforts to swallow it. Redness grew with the watering of her eyes. *That look, like the most severe cases I saw when volunteering at the veteran's hospital. But even they still retained some of the daylight. What have they done to you, baby sister? If only I had arrived here sooner...*

The dagger lowered. Steel collided with the stone of the basin, the edge scraping loud after cleaving through soft and pliable meat. Shrill and infantile screams erupted from the tiny being. The shrieks rang out, pumping through each heaving breath the infant expelled from its small lungs. Chubby arms and legs kicked outward, flailing for reprieve. The child screamed through its crumpled face, mouth agape with unintelligible cries for mercy. The newborn searched, finding nothing save from the stagnant open air and the looming gaze of dark predatory eyes.

"Neh!" Pippa lunged forward, her cries joining with the infant's in a chorus of screams.

"Ahoon!" the crowd roared. "Mavet at Ha Rishon!"

"Yes, Pippa!" Persephone snarled, the dark globes of her eyes beaming on the grieving mother. "Marinate in your despair. Your energy shall feed him, too."

Cries from the basin rose as the blade sliced over the child's abdomen. Life fluids squirted across Persephone's glare. She remained unblinking, despite gore dripping from her brows. The harsh screams grew ever louder, clinging to the agents' psyches. Chills crawled up their goosebump riddled skin. Raptor Team looked to Artemis. Their leader shook her head with doubt, holding her fist aloft for them to see. *Hold position, everyone.* Reluctant nods were exchanged.

"Primitive ritual magicks." Aristotle shook his head. "They were used by these false gods to trick humanity into believing psionic abilities were gifted via their will, rather than the true source of creation."

Persephone's hands burrowed into the deep lacerations over the swollen red corpse. Blood greased her fingers, the entrails she reached for slipping from the first attempts to snatch them. The priestess removed her glistening red hands, placing the tiny liver next to the child's head. Squishing came from the dripping kidneys plopping next to them.

Within the blood-soaked stone bowl, the mangled remains lay strewn in the center, above the head locked in a flush grimace of agony. Sanguine fluid dripped off the priestess leaning over the circle of mutton she created. With an intense fervor, she gazed into the macabre sight, taking deep breaths, analyzing the structure and patterns. Her thin arms raised high into the air, bringing the crowd to silence.

"Our layers have been reestablished along with the gifts." Persephone scowled. "But they tell me that we are not alone, my people."

Members of the crowd turned, following the priestess' gaze to their homes. Raptor Team ducked behind the tents. Heartbeats raced along with profuse sweat soaking into their uniforms. The agents raised their weapons, locating barrels to sectors of fire and calming their breaths to find sight alignment.

"Shit," Milton whispered. "Do you think they saw us?"

"Interlopers from the surface have arrived as he predicted!" Persephone bellowed. "Death to the children of El!"

Roars mixed with the low growl of beasts and high pitch of men. Artemis peered over. Her gaze went beyond the pounding footsteps of the tall hairy figures closing, to the black eyes of her sister that met her own.

"Indeed, they are here!" Persephone yelled. "Tear them up! Their deaths shall feed our power within the layers!"

"Ahoon!"

"Shit!" Artemis said. "She saw me. She knew."

"Her psychic ability is powerful," Aristotle noted. "I can feel her influence along with a much stronger one, warping the layers with a masterful command! It's everywhere with this immense negative energy! We have to clear from here!"

"Too late!"

Rapid steps closed as a man leapt over their tent. The large being landed behind them, his hairy frame coiling like a cat. Sharp incisors bared from his shuddering growl. Artemis brought her M14 to the ready, aligning her sight with the creature. The beast man darted to the side, his quick pace bounding outside of her immediate sight. It closed on Artemis with hands of long, dirt covered nails leading a lunge forward.

Milton's machine gun roared into action, spitting fury at the being. Shots ripped into the beast, sending it careening and whining to the ground where it trembled in place before the strength of life spilled from its corpse. Hissing snatched away their attention, as the cover of their tent was removed with the pounding of large fists from tall figures. More of the beings forced their way through the collapsing support poles, stepping over fur piles, and ripping through the animal skin walls.

"Arty!" Aristotle cried out. "We don't have the advantage of open distance anymore!"

Buckshot sprayed out in a torrent of destruction. Rodriguez shredded the chest of the first tango in view. The creature roared, clenching its body. Patricia cocked the shotgun's forearm, before sending another blast that toppled the creature shrieking to the heavens. Over their fallen comrades, the bestial reinforcements entered the fray with growls of vengeance.

"They're too fast!" Rodriguez said. "There're so many!"

"Look away, everyone!" Corwin yelled. "Flash out!"

Raptor Team turned their scrunched faces when metal objects rang across the ground. Predatory eyes from the other side followed the bouncing objects. A momentary bright flash consumed the area along with the loud expulsion of sound, leaving the agents' ears ringing. The beastmen recoiled, squealing, and collapsing in place while covering their ears.

"Fall back!" Artemis ordered. "Double time!"

The agents dashed through the tent city. Corwin turned, hurling another flash bang behind them. Screams of agony followed. Raptor dashed through, rushing past buildings, and hurdling over small campfires. Howling followed the team, carrying closer with great speed. Another flash bang brought agonizing cries from their enemies.

Artemis pointed to the vast range of trees, draped in shadows from the canopy that loomed overhead. The others trailed as she led them into the wilderness. Darkness blanketed Raptor Team, with only spots of the glowing pit now able to reach them. Rodriguez and Corwin looked back, searching between the foliage and tree trunks.

Their enemy halted at the mouth of the woods. Beastmen left their coiled battle poises, rising upright. Trembling fury that once crawled through their bodies was replaced with a statuesque apprehension. A horde of hairy bestial folks gathered in number. One pointed into the depths of the forest, murmuring to the others who shook their heads with doubt, taking steps away from the perimeter. Heads lowered and the way was made for Persephone, the sea of hybrids parting for their priestess. Her long face shifted into a sneer, the bones rattling when she crossed her arms.

"They went into the undergrowth," Persephone snarled, examining the depths of shadow with the agents' silhouettes peering back. "So be it. Foolish warriors of El have no idea what awaits them. They're already dead."

CHAPTER 15
THE BRAVE AND THE DEAD

Jasper grunted, helping Carver as they hobbled along the pavement of the main road. Bullets cracked across the ground, shattering into fragments that ricocheted in the night. Loud pops from rifle fire thundered in the distance behind them, sending rounds sinking into a car they managed to get behind, before limping onward.

"We'll hold them, Jasper!" one of the townspeople announced. "You get your old behind and that wounded Fed back to the General Store!"

"You two trying to be a big hero today, Phil?" Jasper groaned, heaving the agent. "And you, Bob! Heck, I already know you're the shooting type."

"Just don't want your old carcass dying on me before I can collect on our card games," Phil snapped. "Now go on!"

"And here I thought you cared. Come on, Agent Carver. We're almost there. I'll pour some whiskey on that bullet bite of yours."

"I think I'm going to need that whiskey more than my wound."

Jasper chuckled.

The brave duo of townsfolk took to a crouch behind the car shaking with the punctures of enemy fire. Phil watched Jasper and Carver clear behind another vehicle, lowering themselves below its metal frame.

"Jasper!" Phil snapped. "Why in the heck are you stopping?"

"The agent is hurting! Just giving him a second!" Jasper's snarling retort was seen through the front and back windshield.

"Thought you government types was supposed to be strong?"

"I'm fit, sir. Not invincible."

"Fair 'nough."

Bob turned his blue and white baseball cap backward and rose from his crouch, delivering a wall of roaring buckshot that sprayed across the sidewalk, knocking back a screaming Cray villager. Shells echoed upon spilling to the floor, their empty red cases lingering with the smoke. Phil's attention was stolen from Jasper. He remained wide eyed and shaking with each loud blast.

"Will you let me know before you're about to go ham!" Phil snapped. "Damn you, Bob!"

"Just a little gunfire, Philly." Bob snickered. "We been together for seventeen damn years. You'd think you'd know when I'm about to go ham by now!"

Phil's eyes narrowed, shaking his head once again.

Jasper and Carver rose from their position, resuming their galloping limps. Bob continued pumping and firing his shotgun, until the smoking feed chamber was devoid of rounds. He dipped behind the car, plucking shells from his bandolier, and popping them into the weapon's feedtube.

Phil fired his rifle. A Cray villager's head snapped back. A gaping bullet hole erupted within the attacker's forehead, sending pink chunks of soft tissue darting into his comrades in tow. Hoarse cries of bestial retribution rang out with each foe they felled.

"How many of them bastards are there?" Bob asked, rising from his position again.

A wide callous-covered hand seized the hot barrel of his shotgun. Tremendous strength saw the weapon ripped from Bob's grasp, discarded along the sidewalk where it bounced and rattled. Saliva poured from a canted mouth during a bellow of anger, revealing crumbling yellow and brown nubbins of teeth. Warm clouds of breath gushed over Bob, overpowering him with a putrid stench, forcing a gag to rise against all resistance.

The obtuse slanted face glaring back at Bob held a countenance of malice, brought together in scrunched wrinkles from where his brows should have been. Their foe's body shook with brutish fervor to satiate the primal desire of his rage. Time slowed with each eager shudder in view, even as he raised the dull gray hammer.

The loud thud and crunch that followed signaled the caving of Bob's forehead. Floating followed, all sensation of grounding whisked away from his body. The throbbing sensation rang in Bob's skull, down his face and through his ears. Pain was fleeting, washed away with the mind's alarm calling out that something critical was wrong. Fading vision looked up to dotted lights of the night, a narrowing darkness enveloped all he beheld, until all thought ceased after a vicious successive blow.

Phil screamed, the bullets in his grasp rolling out of his shaking fingers and skipping underneath their cover. The vile twisted figure grabbed his love, preventing Bob from falling backward. Another violent stroke followed, bringing streams of red over the compacted visage of his prey. Phil grasped his rifle by the barrel, swinging the weapon with a wide arc. The wooden buttstock went into the face of the Cray minion, sending blood surging out his nostrils. The malformed man staggered. Phil reared back, clubbing his foe with another fierce crack. The villager whimpered, careening head-first into the car window.

Fierce eyes appeared in Phil's peripheral when another appeared on his flank. He swung again, but his arm was intercepted by a large grip of thick fingers. Screams of defiance from Phil caused Jasper and Carver to turn. Their friend spat in the face of his assailant, as another came from behind, driving the pointed metal of a pitchfork into his lower back.

Phil cried out to the heavens, his wailing spreading through the air, held aloft on the shaft of the tool. The warped villager displayed his strength, brimming from tree trunk like arms, waving his quarry upon the end of his weapon. The foe slammed Phil into the hard pavement, pinning him down. Deep cackles ringing with unhinged delight sounded off as others gathered around with weapons raised.

Jasper's breathing grew rapid, his frame heaving no longer from the strain of helping Carver, but from the growing horror that now spread to his watery red eyes. The old man swallowed hard, mouthing the words 'thank you' before continuing with Carver.

"I'm sorry," the agent groaned.

"Good folk know when to make the sacrifice for what's right." Jasper's voice cracked.

"Your friends won't be forgotten. When we make it out of

here, I will report back to the Agency and make sure they're given proper honors."

"If we make it out of here, Agent Carver."

Lights blared from broad windows reading 'High Mountain General Goods'. Within the brightness of the store were three individuals, shouldering long, wood stocked, bolt action hunting rifles. The flannel wearing individuals waved at them as they hobbled closer to their destination.

"What a relief," Agent Carver murmured. "We made it—"

A rifle shot roared from the double door entrance of the store. A man stood within the frame, aiming with his weapon, the barrel of which trained close to the fleeing duo. Another shot caused them to cringe from the muzzle flash expelled at them. The bullet hit its mark. A closing assailant screamed, toppling face first, writhing in the blood spilling from his chest and staining the pavement. The man in the doorway waved, urging them onward.

"Jasper, I can see them bastards behind you still coming!" their savior screamed. "Keep a move on!"

"Not out of it yet," the old man murmured.

Renewed vigor fueled by the rush of adrenaline and a rapid heart pushed them the rest of the way.

"Fine shooting, Fred!" Jasper greeted him. "Didn't even hear that one coming up behind us with all this commotion!"

Fred shouldered his rifle, reaching out to assist with Carver. "Ya'll rescued the agent, but what about..."

"They're gone." Jasper's eyes lowered. "Went down swinging while saving us."

"This is our fault," Carver said. "If we hadn't conducted this operation—"

"Don't go saying that. Them devilish Cray bastards have been asking for a fight, kidnapping children, and women, stealing things in the night. No, Agent. This reckoning was comin'. With or without ya'll."

Carver peered around, greeted by the arrival of a stern-faced woman, her hair wrapped up inside a thick wool cap that matched her black and green flannel shirt. Behind her followed a tall wide-eyed girl, mirroring her swarthy features and thick, unkempt brows. They unslung their rifles, the girl taking the doorway. Her weapon raised, aligning the iron sights with a Cray villager appearing among the vehicles. A controlled trigger pull sent forth a shot of lead hate that pierced through the target's face. The near human foe's body fell back, thudding loud in the street.

"Agent Carver, these two ladies are Wendy and her daughter Jessie Wonder."

"Nice to meet you, Ms. Wonder."

"No, no, dang it!" Wendy scowled. "Wonder is just a nickname we gave Jessie. Because it's a wonder if she'll ever be right."

"Mom!" Jessie snapped before firing again. "You should be thanking your lucky stars right about now, that Pa raised me not to be a pretty lil' princess. I could be huddled up like the rest of them doing absolutely effin nothin!"

She pointed off to the many women and children tucked away within the aisles of the store. In their shaking hands were baseball bats, hockey sticks, and axes.

Wendy rolled her eyes. "Agent Carver, you're a handsome young man with a job. Are you single? Would you like to marry my nineteen-year-old tomboy daughter? Make an honest and decent lady out of her? I'm going to warn you, she's difficult. As you can see."

"Mom! You're embarrassing me! I don't need to marry no man! I'm self-sufficient. Thank you very much!"

Carver smiled at Jessie. The young woman's freckled cheeks turned rosy, her full lips peeling back with a hesitant blush. They shared gentle blinking eye contact, before the agent's eyes shifted away, scanning throughout the store.

"They're coming!" Jessie announced, firing out into the street. "I'd say about fifty yards and closing!"

"I'm heading up the back way to the roof top," Fred announced, jogging away.

Jessie slammed the door shut, locking it before joining Wendy and Jasper behind the long checkout counter, overlooked by the main lobby's vast window. From the moonlight shining through the spotless glass surface, looming figures appeared crouching behind the cover of remaining vehicles. Additional tangoes hurried along the sidewalk hugging close to the buildings.

"Losin' their boldness," Jasper murmured. "We thinned their numbers real good out there."

"Still lookin' like a big ole gaggle though," Wendy murmured, topping off her rifle with rounds into the chamber. "Well, here goes nothing."

Carver fumbled through small white boxes located along the aisle with a large red cross above it. Elevating pain shot through his wound as the surge of adrenaline subsided. Each step and movement sent sharp agony climbing up his leg, into his lower back, where it dissipated into his shaking hands.

"Need something to clean it with for now," Carver stated, continuing his searching.

"Mister?" a little girl asked, her dirty-blonde pigtails swaying and a smile missing her two front teeth. "Mama said you goin' to need this."

In her grasp was a bottle of rubbing alcohol and iodine. A woman with long brown chocolate curls loomed in the front of the pharmacy desk, with a weak smile and a little boy clinging to her leg. Carver nodded to her, taking the help in both hands before raising them and nodding.

"Your mama is a brilliant woman. This is going to help a lot. Thank you so much."

"Yay!" The little girl's smile widened. "Goin' to help others, sir. Thank you for protecting us."

"Don't thank me yet, kiddo." Carver grimaced watching her scamper away. "We're still in the thick of it."

Thundering shots from rifles up front bored through the window. Shards of glass poured out from the cracking mass that gave under the next salvo, leaving jagged glimmering messes along the frame. Civilians cringed under the resounding tumult that carried through the building. Muzzle flashes spewed forth with clouds of vapor swelling the air with the hot scent of expended gunpowder. Hands worked quick, unlocking bolts, and rechambering new rounds of ammunition within the weapons before successive trigger pulls brought forth more roaring violence.

Carver hurried, the pain still humming through his leg, calling out into the back of his thoughts where he tried to stuff it away. Thick clouds of carbon spewed forth from across the way, bringing shots of heavy lead ripping into the store. Jasper and the ladies ducked behind the counter. Carver joined them crouching low. A grimace and heavy breathing came from the agent, his shaking hands fighting the urge to nurse the reverberation of anguish.

"What caliber you reckon they using, Mama?" Jessie asked.

"Dunno, heavy stuff though."

"Girls, admire the guns later," Jasper admonished with exasperation, rising from cover to fire back. "We make it out of here alive, I'll personally drive you to Cabela's for whatever you want."

"Mr. Jasper, I'm holding you to that!" Jessie exclaimed, dropping a foe sprinting for the front.

Flashes of gunfire erupted along the streets, peeling back the shadows that draped the uneven frames of the enemy horde. Grim faces scowled at them, bearing sneers of teeth chittering with hateful obscenities.

"What are you doing?" Mathias bellowed at his minions. "No mercy! Do not relent!"

Carver peered over the counter-top, seeing the tall figure wearing a wide straw hat, placing a large caliber rifle into his shoulder. Darkness peered back from the wide and long weapon barrel pointing at the agent and his comrades. The polished barrel contrasted under the lamp light, against the thick wooden stock lined with dark marks of wear.

What the hell... how did they get a Snider-Enfield? Carver's thoughts blared in his mind. Panic poured from his escalating heart. *They've been out of production for well over a hundred years!* "Get down!"

"We're taking cover already, Agent Carver!"

"No, faces to the ground! Now!"

Booming calamity screamed forth like lightning from the barrel. A huge .577 round punched through the checkout counter, caving its center with a deep hole. Carver rose, aiming down at the cloud of smoke, dissipating to reveal Mathias' wide grin bearing upon him. The Cray leader's thick wrinkles climbed around his unwavering maniacal stare locking with the agent.

The large figure's coat billowed as he maneuvered away with unnatural speed powering through his thick legs. Carver's return fire ripped across a car hood, the reticle of the agent's sight following the large figure. Trailing shots peppered over a Cray villager, the minion collapsing in the crossfire, with Carver still scanning for Mathias who dipped out of view into an alley.

"Good call," Jasper groaned, rising from the floor. "What the heck was that fella packing? A cannon?"

"Ma!" Jessie cried out, her lip quivering. "Mama!"

Carver looked down to a pool of red spreading toward the ridge of his boot. Wendy sat next to the counter, her forehead crinkling through the strain. The woman's eyes stared into nothingness as she rocked in place, clutching her side tight with both hands. Blood seeped through her shirt, spilling to the ground from the missing chunk of tissue, separated by the thick bullet fragment lodged in her. Jessie knelt beside her mother. The daughter's hand reached out, touching Wendy. All movement stopped in the woman's body. The spark of life extinguished from her pupils. Her head rolled back.

"No!" Jessie bellowed, rising from behind cover, firing a series of shots at their foes. "Damn you all to hell! Damn you!"

Mathias curved around the corner of the building from the alley. A moment of aim brought his shot upward. Screams rang from the roof top. Fred's heavy staggering steps rapped along overhead before he fell from above. His body smashed to the hard black concrete, leaving limbs jostled and his rifle bouncing on the ground.

Molotov cocktails bobbed in the grips of several Cray assailants closing the distance. High-pitched war cries echoed into the night. A slew of rifle shots came from the concerted aim of foes poised beyond the store. Sparks flew along Jessie's rifle as it buckled under a striking bullet. The girl screamed, dropping her firearm. She toppled over grasping her left eye.

"Move in on them!" Mathias barked. "Set them alight and let the survivors choke on the smoke of their roastin' kin!"

Carver grabbed the young woman, pulling her close to cover. Blood trickled between her fingers, her mouth agape with sobs. The agent reached into his medkit, drawing out gauze by the fistful. Jasper fired, dropping one of the charging assailants, who discarded the fiery cocktail to his feet. Flames exploded, forcing agonizing cries from the villager that cooked away his peeling skin and clothes in the middle of the street.

"Fragment got your eye when it hit your weapon," Carver said. "Please stay calm, Jessie. I know it hurts, but I'll take care of you."

The rest of the foe's number continued their sprint for the General Store. Jasper ducked back down, looking to the agent, with doubt shaking his long face. Relentless bursts of enemy fire sprayed their surroundings, until the footsteps clapping on pavement became apparent and close.

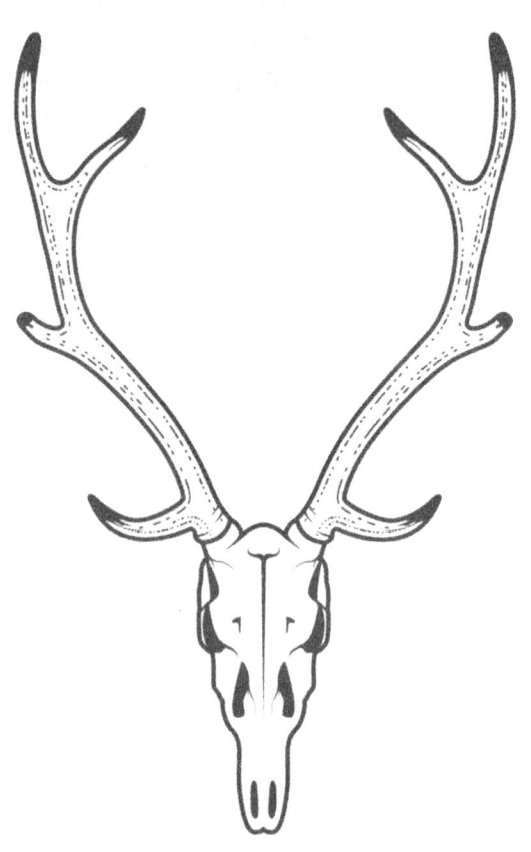

CHAPTER 16
A LITTLE TREE IN THE WOODS

You will find the answers you seek at the glowing mouth, Artemis Coleman, warrior daughter of Hawwah. Beyond the realm of even the lowest amalgamations, lies the gate. It is there you will receive the closure you seek.

Concerned looks fell on Artemis, nodding to invading thoughts. Raptor Team's footsteps crunched along the brown and green leaves strewn over the forest floor. Orange illumination continued around them, spreading through the breaks in the canopy of trees. The glow remained a lazy haze, bringing detail to the ocean of blackness washing over their view.

"The enemy has ceased their pursuit, Actual," Corwin announced through heavy breaths.

"At ease, Raptor," Artemis ordered.

The agents positioned by a tree. Artemis snapped her night optics into place, bringing a tint of green into view, formulating lush hanging foliage, and the tall tree trunks that bore it. She gazed around to globular bushes, bristling with spiked protrusions. Bladed leaves rose from ferns, with thick vine-like extensions stretching below their bodies.

Decisions are all that you have left. You've been immersed beyond my reach. Efficacy is your only weapon now, against the Dark Archon. Let it and the factors beholden within, guide your efforts. Now I must attend the courage of another. Atah, Malkoot, Vegeburah, Vegedulah, Leolahm, Ahman.

What the hell was all that?

Whining came from Artemis' NODs, before a loud hiss. A pop went off, followed by a small cloud of white smoke that rose from its sizzling innards. The jungle zipped out of her vision, ushering forth the darkness. Stink from burning metal and plastic hovered over her face with sharp bursts from the receding smoke. Artemis coughed, waving the stench away before fighting with the activation knob to no avail. Corwin snickered behind her, the pitch of his laughter growing in her ears.

"What's so funny, Agent?" Artemis turned and snapped.

Corwin and the others looked to their commander with a raised brow. "Come again, Actual?"

Artemis shook her head turning to the broken device, stuffing it back into the pouch on her vest while glaring at Corwin.

"My NODs are dead," Artemis announced.

"Mine, too," Rodriguez replied. "Just poof and they stopped working."

"We have to circle back. Something is telling me that glowing pit is where we need to be."

"Arty," Aristotle interrupted. "I don't think that's a good idea. We need to get the heck out of this place and refit your team, then come back with reinforcements. We're in over our heads here. That entire city of fiends just collapsed on us. Why they haven't pursued is a mystery. All of us should be dead right now."

Artemis shook her head. "No. We have to get to that pit we saw from the overlook, the one just beyond that podium."

"You want us to trek through that city again, wading through numbers we can't contend with?"

"It's the only way out. Trust me."

"Sounds like you're devising something," Corwin said. "We'll let you think it over, Actual. I think we should break open an MRE."

"Yeah, chow sounds good. Gather our strength, recharge a bit, and refocus during this respite," Milton agreed.

Packs unzipped with hands rifling through them for the plastic containers labeled 'Meal-Ready-to-Eat.' Corwin grinned, plopping down by a tree next to a small bush. His fingers ran through, opening the contents of cardboard boxes and smaller plastic packages, containing a parody of lasagna, with a strong wax aftertaste. Flapping in his hands was a small, thin plastic green pouch with the words 'FRH - Flameless Ration Heater', sliding the package of his main course inside. The agent added a few ounces from his canteen, folding over the mouth of the pouch before placing it into the original cardboard container of his meal.

"Stand still," Rodriguez slapped Corwin's shoulder. "I'm trying to look at your wound but you're moving too much. All you care about is stuffing your face when I'm trying to check on you, estúpido."

"Sorry. I'm just so hungry. I'm surprised you aren't cooking one."

"Blah, you're always hungry! But yeah, I will after I know you're good."

Their eyes met, his hand covering hers and bringing it to a

stop. Rodriguez's big brown eyes were apparent in the proximity, exuding concern through her thick brows. The agent's full lips wanted to drop into a frown of disapproval, but Corwin's boyish smile warded it off. She reached out, caressing his cheek.

"Idiota guapo." Patty shook her head and smirked. "What am I going to do with you?"

"I still have that beef jerky if you want some."

"Yep, you're definitely feeling better. The wound looks fine, too. Still clean with no signs of infection. I just gave you another shot to keep it numb. Now, I'm going to make my dinner."

"Suit yourself. Let me know if you change your mind."

"I'll take some of that." Milton rose approaching with his hands out as Corwin obliged.

"Why are you acting so rambunctious?" Rodriguez asked. "You trying to keep your mind occupied, huh?"

Corwin looked down, stuffing a handful of jerky into his mouth before giving a reluctant nod.

"You can't blame yourself for what happened to her." She placed a hand on his shoulder. "We do our best, but we can't save everyone. I wish it weren't that way though."

Corwin's blank stare rose to the distance.

Rodriguez sighed.

Artemis peered around. Darkness immersed their position, keeping the details of their surroundings low with the fading orange residual hue of the pit. The pulsing glow stirred the shadows, fluctuating in her peripherals. When she turned her gaze, it was met with only the shapes of the forest. Leaves, branches, bushes, and ferns materialized after passing seconds of discernment. The team leader shook her head, before removing her combat gloves to rub her eyes.

"Perhaps Corwin has the right idea." Artemis murmured. "Let's just eat and recharge. Even after whatever happened earlier, there's still the desire for normalcy."

"I know what you mean." Aristotle agreed, rifling through his pack as he plopped down by a tree.

Artemis unslung her pack, kneeling to open its mouth and dig for rations. Movement flicked through the corner of her eye. Her head snapped, sending her vision racing after rifts in the darkness. A long stare brought outlines of low hanging branches into view, the many thick leaves riddled along their length, distorting the shape under hues of weak light, pulsating like a heartbeat.

This is going to be trying with my nerves, Artemis thought with a sigh. She peered over to Milton, his tall and wide frame clear and visible while he kept sentry over their rear. *John is watching our six. This shouldn't be a problem. Don't micromanage. That irritation is the last thing they need right now.*

A few minutes passed, and the warm vapors from FRHs billowed through packages that were opened by eager hands. Plastic spoons dug into the containers of hot food, shoveling into the agents' mouths with eager abandon. Crinkles came from the wrappers of peanut butter tubes, spread over thick crackers more akin to cardboard than bread. A few bites later found agents' teeth full of a condensed mess that sucked the saliva dry from their mouths.

"I—" Corwin took a deep gulp from his canteen washing it all down with a hard swallow. "I never thought an MRE could taste so good. Oh wait, I forgot about the Crucible. Those three days of hell. That's another time they tasted this damn good! Funny how they seem to get better the longer you're in the field."

Milton nodded, taking another scoop from his package. A

vibration in his peripheral vision brought his attention away from the aroma of imitation tomato paste and noodles. He paused, losing track of his fellow agent's words. The grumble of his stomach went without notice. Milton gazed into the mess of shadows where long images hummed with the fading presence of orange. His straining eyes formed the images of leaf clusters from the dangling branches. Trunks from other trees began encircling them, varying in width. The agent shook his head before digging back into his entrée.

"Trade you my ranger bar for your poundcake, Patty." Corwin winked.

"You think I'm loca? Pfft!" Rodriguez snapped before chuckling. "No deal! I don't care how cute you are."

"Milton, you all right?"

"Yeah, just the shadows doing what they do. You know. Damn I wish the NODs hadn't died on us."

Corwin's attention shot over to a shifting patch of darkness. His eyes narrowed on a black silhouette of a small tree standing between a pair of its towering brethren. From its head sprouted long branches ending with multiple sharp points. The scent of warm cheese and noodles pulled him away from monitoring the trees, returning to his dinner.

"Let's finish this meal quick," Corwin agreed. "We've been indulging a bit much."

Aristotle bumped his sister as she went for a bite. A frown was returned, before a sharp elbow was given into his side.

"Okay, easy!" Aristotle pleaded. "I just wanted to talk to you about something. I should've known better than to bother you during a meal."

"Spill it," the munching Artemis demanded.

"I'm getting vibes. Like we're not alone. Feeling something in the etheric layers, despite how messed up they are down here. There's something about this place in particular."

"Agreed." Artemis called out to the others, "Raptor Team, finish up chow. We move in a few mikes."

"Roger, Actual," Corwin replied.

"You all know the plan. We need to finish investigating down here. The Agency is going to require a full report of all the new vectors we've encountered and their operations. I—" *Movement!*

Artemis paused. She gazed into the morass of shadows, finding only the outline of a nine- foot tree standing dwarfed by the gargantuan flora around it. Spike-like branches rose from the flanks of the uppermost portions of its thin trunk. She reached down, grabbing the stock of her M14 rifle, raising it slow into her shoulder. The sight reticle centered on the tree, magnifying her view, yet the details remained draped in the dark.

"What the hell?!" Corwin screamed out.

The agent struggled to stand upright, his leg fighting to move forward but to no avail. The tight grasp of vine-like tentacles wrapped around his calves. Corwin unclipped a nine-inch combat knife sheath from his vest, sliding out the black carbon steel weapon whose edge shone in the gloom. Shrieking expelled from the tree's foot, where the agent had enjoyed his supper. Bladed leaves rose, shuddering with each high piercing scream that chimed over the area.

Limbs grew cold, slowing as the thumping vibration of pain rose into Corwin's skull. The shrieking escalated in pitch and volume. Corwin's bones reverberated with a wilting resonance. Quaking agony continued pushing through his body.

"Ca...ca...can't... move..." The agent whimpered.

"Mira, get away from it!" Rodriguez screamed.

She leapt upward, spinning around with her shotgun and blasting into the wailing fern. The screeches continued from the frayed bundle of leaves, more tentacles pulled from the dirt, ripping up through the earth by the dozens. Outward they stretched, racing for Corwin with their constricting embrace.

The agent's fingers loosened on the knife handle. The sharp steel sharp from his hands. Corwin's head bobbled, and his bent legs staggered as he tried leaning away. The tight pull drew him closer, toward the fern. Its leaves flapped with the endless screams, shaking even at its foundations of dirt. The brown frame pulled from the moist soil, raising small mouths upon spherical pods into view at its base. The agent's eyes widened as several barbed stingers slid forward, readying their aim in his direction. Brown ooze dripped from its barbs with a noxious fume that muddied the agent's vision.

"Get it off me!" Corwin pleaded.

Milton fired a burst from his machine gun into the foliage. Artemis pulled the trigger, a controlled pair pierced the vector. Rounds sank into the plant, ripping its leaves. The shuddering and screams continued. Corwin's eyes widened at a large maw rising from the ground. Dirt rained off its many fangs, drooping from the roof of its mouth. Warm breath reeked like the stench of spoiled milk, pushed from its slimy innards with a vicious hiss aimed at Corwin.

"Guys! Help!" The agent fell over, drawing close. A bite crunched down on his helm, struggling to pierce its prey.

"Corwin!" Artemis yelled. "I'm going to drop a pyro on this vector. Get ready to fucking move!"

Artemis stepped close, watching the ground as she closed the distance. From her vest she withdrew the bright red cylinder case of the AN-M14 incendiary grenade. The pin popped and away the grenade went, landing into the bushel of shrubbery forming the creature's body.

Brightness expanded with a streaming cloud of smoke that billowed into the canopy. Burning shards crackled from the explosive, withering the foliage into curled blackening husks. Milton and Rodriguez grabbed Corwin, tugging against the tentacles that lost their grip and gave under its fizzling death throes. The creature shuddered, its entire being devoured by racing flames. Black flakes spewed from the vector's convulsions, littering around them with the musty reek of char. Artemis drew close, her weapon at the ready, trailed by a cringing Aristotle. Movement ceased from the seared husk of the creature's body.

"What the hell was that?!" Milton exclaimed, reaching for Corwin's arm to hoist him off the ground. "Cor, you okay?"

"Something went into my body... the vibrations... they paralyzed me!"

"You are getting busted up this hop," the large operator patted his friend. "You seem the worse for wear, but everything still looks in place... for now."

"What's that supposed to mean?" Corwin's eyes widened.

"I mean it's a new vector, we don't know what kind of poison it may ha—"

"What?"

"I'm sure you're fine. Doesn't look like it broke skin or anything."

"Stop freaking me out, Milty!"

"Pendejo!" Rodriguez kicked Corwin's shin, sending the agent clutching the bruise and hopping on his good leg. "You need to be more careful!"

"Patty... I—"

"I've almost lost you twice already!"

Corwin nodded. The short woman slipped her arms underneath his while bringing her head to his chest. He wrapped around her and sighed.

"We haven't even been on our first date yet..."

"You're right. I'm sorry. I was careless."

Aristotle knelt close to the smoldering and wilted mess. His head shifted, examining the ashen tentacles, and sacs hanging along its bottom. The mouth remained jutted open, petrified in the cries of its last moment. The scryer's lip sneered in disgust at the long humanoid tongue lying between rows of flat incisors that trailed back into wide molars.

"Don't get too close!" Artemis warned.

"Good call, Actual," Milton stated. "Don't know if it's permanently out of commission or not. You never can tell with these new vectors."

"This plant seems to have hybrid characteristics," Aristotle announced. "I've never seen anything like this in all my studies of cryptozoology. There're plant, insect, and human traits."

Artemis peered to the other ferns and bushes within their surroundings. The others followed the direction of her gaze. Stillness and silence overcame the team, their eyes scrutinizing everything they beheld in the long passing seconds. Raptors' hands wrapped tight around weapon grips. Tension from readiness hummed through their muscles, still surging with adrenaline. They shifted, facing outboard, scanning the numerous articles of wilderness with firm brows and lip-biting ruminations.

"Who knows what could be around us... just waiting..." Rodriguez uttered.

"I'm sure it's deceased, Arty," Aristotle continued. "I think it's of the utmost importance that we take a sample of this vector back to headquarters."

"I'll see what I can salvage of this mess."

The crisp slide of a knife's edge focused everyone's attention. Artemis slung her rifle, now wielding twelve inches of glinting sharp steel. Her brow firmed over her long face, eyes searching for the stingers. She removed a large plastic bag from a miscellaneous pouch on the lower end of her vest, fluffing it open with a wave.

"No... Actual... don't..." Corwin pleaded.

The blade sliced through a cluster of leaves, and she stuffed the sample into the sack. A barbed stinger lowered, twitching, and leaning closer to her hand. Weapon barrels rose from the other agents with buttstocks popping into shoulders, their sights aligning with the corpse's black husk.

"Posthumous reflexes like when a dead snake bites someone," Aristotle noted. "Perhaps it's best to approach without your usual cocksure swagger, Arty?"

Rapid swings of Artemis' hand brought the knife cutting into a low grasp at the base of a stinger. Black flakes covered the palms of her leather gloves as the outer layer of the creature's skin peeled and crumbled. From underneath its uppermost crust oozed a translucent yellowish liquid that rolled down its body. A quick swipe removed the appendage, bringing the other stingers upward into a ready position. Sharp points aimed at Artemis, who lowered her posture, scanning the impending threats.

"Watch out!" Aristotle exclaimed. "I told you to be cautious!"

The coiled tension faded from the corpse, lowering the stingers back into the leafy body. Brother and sister sighed together with relief.

"You're always worrying me!" Aristotle snapped. "Will you freaking acknowledge me for once when I try to advise you! If

I'm going to be dragged into what looked like the actual Hell, the least I can get is some reciprocation of my advice!"

"This sample should suffice for getting DNA testing." Artemis stuffed away the stinger along with its oozing meaty base.

Aristotle shook his head.

Shadows shifted through the edge of sight. The agents spun around, finding only the surrounding darkness. Artemis sheathed her knife, taking position next to Milton with her M14 pointing into the distance. Grim frowns and nods were exchanged in quick glances to each other, with the silent acknowledgement of imminent danger.

"I saw that now!" Milton said.

"Yeah, not just the shadows playing tricks this time." Rodriguez cocked her shotgun.

Wide black silhouettes of tree trunks streaked over their view. Milton's glowing reticle went over a fern, pausing for a moment, searching around it, before shifting farther left. A plump and fluffy bush came into view, its flowing greenery between the bulk of two trees. His vision lifted, spotting a smaller tree behind it. From the peak of its nine-foot stature, two large branches extended with a cluster of smaller limbs. Its barren appendages revealed several sharp points due to the lack of foliage, in comparison to its larger brethren.

Milton continued the scan until movement brought his tracking back to the bush. Echoes of the plant-creature's ringing attacks played back in his memory. Nothing appeared in the reticle. He sighed and shook his head. The shadows peeled away. A presence drew closer behind the plump article of foliage.

The small tree stepped forward, until the glow of orange hummed over its snarling yet emaciated visage. Spiked teeth lined its opened jaws, reaching over its upper lip. Antlers extended from its large skull, covered in a dark mottled gray like the rest of its gaunt frame that flexed with rib bones pushing through its tight flesh.

There was only a blur of horns and long blackened claws that sprouted from craggy knuckles. It pounced on Milton. The large agent bellowed, toppling over, his machine gun roaring blind shots into the canopy. In a thudding slam, his back hit the ground. Breath from the creature felt like blanketing clouds of freezing mist. The others turned, their guns aiming to the unknown vector as it raised claws for the kill strike.

CHAPTER 17
DIGGING DEEP

Jasper rose from behind the counter, his rifle barking off two rounds that punched into the hearts of charging Cray villagers. The foes buckled in their path, dropping their Molotov cocktails. A conflagration of flame rose beneath their corpses, searing the pavement in its reach. A wall of smoke rose into view. Jasper aligned the rear aperture of his weapon with the front sight tip. His arms hugged the rifle close to his body, the buttstock snug in his shoulder. The rapid beat of his heart pulsed through the palms of his sweaty hands. His stone-faced glare held back the urge to rattle with inundating fear crawling through his spine.

"Whooo!" hollers from Cray reinforcements called through the night air.

"Agent Carver," Jasper called back. "We're done for here. Lead the others out the back."

"We have to hold! Jessie is in no condition to move right now; she's in shock and bleeding profusely!"

Close war cries swept away Jasper and Carver's attention. Foes leapt through the walls of smoke and fire. The first Cray villager landed with stuttering steps catching his fall, continuing his breakneck stride for the General Store. Jasper's shot felled the first, but several more bounded on the scene closing the distance.

Cocktails soared. Glass shattered at the front of the store, sending a bastion of fire and smoke rising along their view. Grunts of effort followed more bottles hurtling through the main window. Carver and Jasper cringed behind the counter. Shards of debris jettisoned around them, crashing among the growing blaze. Sweltering heat blanketed them in moments, bringing the hot sting of pain and discomfort over their bodies. Choking coughs expelled from their lungs with an involuntary racking force.

"No mercy!" Mathias roared from outside. "Slaughter the menfolk and we shall devour the flesh! Capture whatever children and women are available!"

"Retreat!" Carver screamed to the others, watching them pile out the back door before turning to Jessie. "You have to get up, Jessie. I know you're hurting, but we must go."

"Leave me here with a gun…"

"No!"

Agonizing groans escaped from Jessie as Carver pulled her up. The young woman staggered to remain afoot with one hand clutching the soaked gauze, while the other clung to Carver with a cemented grip. The agent held her upright, supporting her weight on his shoulder with her arm over his neck. They took a few steps before the cackles of nearing foes resonated in their ears. Carver turned, finding hunched silhouettes pacing among the shifting light of flames and the thick gray clouds gathered. With one hand, he drew his M4 by the pistol grip, the buttstock tucked underneath his armpit, firing in slow succession against the recoil that pulled his aim away with each shot.

Howls of anger rose among the teeming foes. From the darkness leapt a countenance shaped like a sack of potatoes, bearing an open mouth of withered teeth, where globules of saliva jettisoned from a trembling growl. The glint of a hatchet bobbed in the adversary's grasp, rising with its menacing frayed edge coming into view before a fast swing. Carver's M4 rose to hip level, his finger giving rapid tugs to the trigger, only to find the weapon's bolt locked back, and the magazine's payload depleted.

The sweeping attack struck Carver in the shoulder, its sharp edge biting through uniform fabric and the meat of his arm. A yelp expelled from the agent's lungs. He cried to the ceiling before toppling over with Jessie. Wide swathes of pain roiled down his limb, channeling through his body with a paralyzing grip. All thought was ruptured by the blaring sense of urgency reverberating through him, wilting his core. Warm blood showered down his sleeve, streaming over this fingers that twitched with flooding impulses of anguish.

"Agent Carver," Jessie screamed. "Get up! Please! I can't see anything!"

Tremors rose into Carver's cheeks. He grimaced with squinting eyes that wanted to close. The presence of his attacker loomed closer with each step. Deep breathy laughter shot through the Cray villager's wide mouth and nostrils. Carver rolled away, drawing his nine millimeter Beretta side arm from its holster. He canted his arm upward, double tapping the trigger. Two loud popping rounds sank into the squealing foe's abdomen, sending him lurching back into the smoking reaches of the room.

"That's my hand." Carver helped Jessie back to her feet. "Jasper!"

"Come on, you bastards!" Jasper mocked, firing his rifle until expended.

Carver staggered through the smoke with Jessie. Jasper cried out. Wind flooded through, pushing away the smoke. The old man was on his back, hands rising to protect in vain as a knife rose, gathering the momentum of a kill shot from the Cray villager upon him.

The Beretta rose in the agent's shaking hand. Sights aligned on the enemy's chest, following a slow and controlled trigger pull. The stout nine millimeter round slammed into the assailant's torso, sending the wailing enemy folding over, his knife ringing upon the floor and bouncing away. Carver hurried, grabbing his friend from the ground.

"Looks like I owe you one." Jasper smiled.

"Well, I guess we can take it off the ones I owe you." Carver winked.

"Let's get out the back!"

"Yeah, seems the civilians already went—"

Splinters of resin erupted from his chest as an impossible force propelled Agent Carver across the floor. Material within the center of his vest frayed from a gaping hole, leading to a massive dent in his bullet-resistant plates, crumbling into shards. A tremendous ache pulsed through Carver's sternum. Struggling gasps rose from his lungs, fighting claim oxygen.

"Agent Carver!" Jessie screamed.

The tall silhouette of Mathias stepped over the shattered remnants of the window, his long coat swaying with each step. A grin stretched through his long gray whiskers, with matching brows twitching in maniacal fervor above his lengthy corkscrew nose. He tossed the large rifle to the ground.

From his jacket, he unsheathed the long steel of a sharp knife, while drawing up a sledgehammer caked in brown corrosion.

"Guess I gotta slaughter the piggies the old-fashioned way," Mathias declared, in hissing contempt. "Good. Guns take all the fun out of it. Something about beating and slicing a living being just feels... right."

The large foe turned. He bounded forward, swinging his hammer at Jasper. Loud thuds came from the old man's arms as he brought them up to shield his head. A loud crack followed, with Jasper wailing. His left arm went limp over his torso, drooping with the shattered fragments inside. Jasper hobbled, yelping before toppling to the floor. Writhing followed from the pain coursing through him, as he grimaced and folded into a fetal position.

Mathias grinned, parading upright with a saunter to the fallen man. "Your cries are my music. Your pain is my bread. Your blood is my water. Only now in your final moments of futility do you wonder... where is your God?"

The nine millimeter pistol blared in Jessie's hands. Redness surrounded her vision. Blurs appeared instead of shapes, distorted by the suffering resonating through her face and throbbing into her skull. Mathias turned his grin to Jessie.

"Depth perception lacking there ain't it, girl? Bet you're finding it kinda hard to aim." Mathias rushed toward her, the sharp tip of his knife leading the charge. "You think you're sufferin' now? Wait until you feel what me and the kin have planned for you."

Blurs of brown and black flared in Jessie's vision, growing larger. Her eye struggled through the rapid twitches, and steady pulses of grief. Sounds from his steps across the floor betrayed the distance she beheld of him. The angle seemed to her right; she led with only the front-sight tip of the barrel.

Two shots chimed off, loud and echoing into the empty store. The second bullet snapped the bolt with authority.

Mathias snarled, careening before dropping to a knee next the girl. Clanging from his knife resounded as it escaped his grasp, sliding across the floor. He nursed the two holes leaking from his abdomen. Jessie raised the Berretta, leveling the smoking barrel with Mathias' head.

"This is for my mother and my eye, you bastard!" the young woman roared.

Jessie pulled the trigger to no response. She pulled it again, jerking the weapon and shaking her head. There was only the clicking of metal.

"No," she murmured. "Not now..." after drawing the pistol close, her blurred vision inspected the weapon's slide, locked to rear and empty.

A mighty blow struck her kneecap, caving it inward so that it bowed, until popping under the pressure. Jessie screamed, piling to the floor, where she wailed and rolled. Her calf and foot flopped from the cherry red stump of her thigh, among the folding skin and stretched ligaments. Mathias' grin returned. He rose upright and reset his hammer for another swing.

"Hurts doesn't it, bitch? Where's all that heavy language of yours now?"

Jessie's cries resounded into the night.

"That's what I thought. A little stress and you sorry-ass Christians fold like paper. Ya ain't nothin' when you ain't got the numbers, huh? You think we just forgave and forgot about what your ancestors did? This was a long time comin'. And you wonder why even your own pathetic book said this world is gunna be ours again?"

Light reflected from the shine of metal in the corner of Mathias' view. His head shifted, greeted by the point of a nine-inch Ka-bar knife. Carver lunged forward, bellowing with the strength of rising anger. The leather-handled combat tool's wide head narrowed into a slick point that pierced through coat and shirt, sinking between Mathias' rib cage.

The cult leader's body seized in place, save for his head that jerked back as his wailing mouth opened. Both of his wide hands reached for the blade, only for Carver to withdraw, and thrust once more. The knife sliced through the fingers of Mathias' attempts, finding its mark in a new section of his abdomen. The tall fiend turned, swinging with his mighty hammer. He staggered, from the weight of Carver leaping on his back. The agent stabbed again, grunting loud with each successive puncture. Blood spilled over his hand, greasing his grip on the knife that slipped from his grasp.

Mathias collapsed, with Carver spilling on the floor next to him. The agent stared to the ceiling, at the dead bulbs and those that flickered, fighting to stay alight. He looked to the light of flames around them, fluctuating against the creeping darkness of the night, and the smoke thickening in his gasping breaths.

"Jessie... Jasper..." Carver pleaded. "Please tell me..."

"I'm alive..." Jasper groaned. "Comin'... just give me a sec... them bastards..."

"They killed our father!" a deep, drawn voice ringing with low intellect bellowed in distress.

Urgency pumped through Carver's body, sizzling in his mind with alarm. He rushed to his feet. Shards of glass, splinters of wood, and char riddled the floor. Carver scoured for a firearm. The cries of rage and sorrow drew closer, as remnants of Cray villagers surrounded the window. One of the foes leapt inside, his face twisted in grief with tears pouring from his warped eyes. A half growl and cry left his trembling mouth, sneering at Carver.

The agent held firm to the knife, his hands squeezing it through the warmth of his foe's blood. Carver brought his weapon to the ready with its sharp point aiming at the hunched challenger. Pain channeled from the aching bruises that covered his body, along with the rigidity of fatigue drumming in his muscles. Carver remained firm, legs bent and shoulder width apart, his freehand elevated to the guard, with his frame cocked away poised to strike.

"Here I thought all this McMAP training was a waste of time," Carver murmured before roaring back. "Come on! You gotta earn this meal!"

The Cray villager stormed forward, screaming his rage to the heavens through his quaking lungs. Gunshots rang in the distance in staccato bursts. Warm red mist sprayed from the assailant's head, obscuring Carver's view. Controlled shots continued in pairs, striking center mass at the villagers' ranks. The tangoes dropped, some writhing in pain, shouting before a round to the forehead silenced their woes.

Carver's forearm wiped away the mess over his face, returning his view of the battlefield. A few Cray villagers were fleeing, while the majority remained piled on the floor. Figures approached from shadows in the distance, down the middle of the two-lane street. The first approached with his M4 carbine at the ready, shifting and scanning the area with his night-vision goggles. Others followed along his flank, drifting behind in a wedge formation with a sector of fire that overlapped from the front, stretching along their outboard sides.

"Please be friendlies..." Carver gulped.

When their point person in the formation came into range, Carver dropped his knife and sighed with relief upon reading the words 'Unholy Slaying Agency' next to the name 'Sellers'. The other agent raised his fist, bringing the formation to a halt.

"Stand down, Raptor6India," Hector ordered, approaching past the formation. "We've come to reinforce and refit your team."

"HoneyBadger!" Carver exclaimed. "Commander Rodrigo, I could cry right now. It's been a trying hour, sir."

"We got here as fast as we could."

"Better late than never." Carver chuckled. "We have many civilians that are still—"

"The second element is already securing them on the south side. Medics up, we have a young female over here that needs immediate attention!"

A Badger member jogged past Carver, who noted the large cross along the back side of her bouncing oversized pack. The medic took a knee near Jessie before placing a hand on her shoulder to keep her from getting up. She plopped the large pack on the ground next to the wounded woman, her hands rummaging with practiced precision.

"Ma'am, please do not move," the agent instructed as she withdrew a syringe and gauze from her pack.

"Are you an angel?" Jessie wondered.

"No ma'am."

"My friend Jasper is also in need of medical attention." Carver murmured. "He's somewhere... over there... probably passed out."

Fingers weakened in Carver's grip on the knife. It slipped from his hand, clanging on the ground. The agent wobbled in place, before Rodrigo rushed to catch him.

"Easy there, Carver! Have a seat."

"Sir—"

"Hey, I'll tend your wounds." Rodrigo looked to the rest of

the team. "Secure the area, tend to the civilians. Patch up every single wound you see on them. Give me three squad leaders to clear and mop up any tangoes that may still be within the town. Every building, room, even closet, gets cleared before we allow the civilians to return to their homes. Call in rotary wing CASEVAC for those that require anything deemed beyond our trauma medics' capabilities. Codify reports from each household immediately afterward."

"No foe too mighty, no task too great!" The chorus of response came from the dozens of agents scrambling into action.

"Carver, you did damn good, Son," Rodrigo said. "But tell me, what's the status on the rest of your team? Where is Artemis?"

"I don't know, sir. We got separated. I haven't seen my team in almost two days. I can't even confirm if they're still alive. This place... it's playing tricks. There's something more going on here than just a cultist or wendigo hunt."

"Yeah, Curmudgeon had strong suspicions. I guess this confirms it. Something more going on here, like what?"

"Evil beyond our reckoning. Something more powerful than anything we've ever encountered before. It..." Carver glanced away and sighed.

"It what?"

"Whatever this vector is... it scares me..."

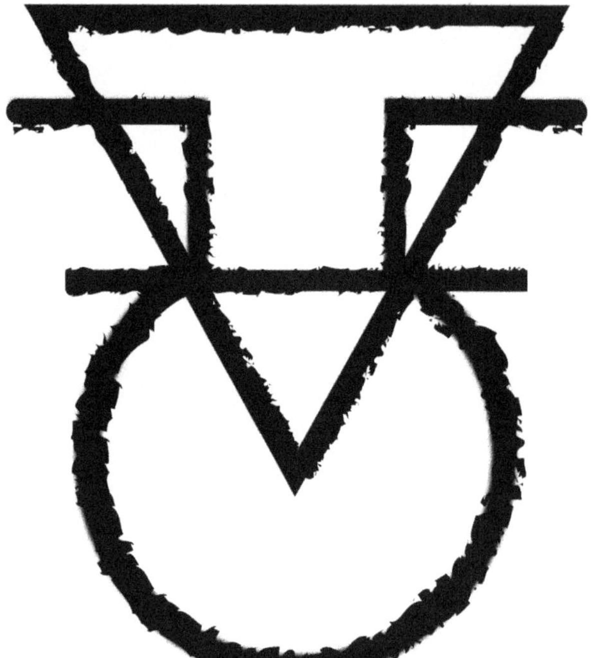

CHAPTER 18
APEX

Smoke and carbon spewed from weapons dealing Raptor Team's fury into their foe. Milton's anguish bellowed between shots. Blazing incendiary rounds gathered along the creature's back that extended with wide muscles like a cobra's hood. It turned, snarling, the large agent's blood dripping from the tip of its arched claws.

The vector's undulating mouth propelled a scream through the area. Thousands of shrill voices rang into their ears with pulsing cries booming into their heads. The pain escalated, leaving the balking agents staggering, their quaking arms fighting to keep their weapons trained on the menace. Cold raced through their bodies, pounding with the call of rage that reverberated around them. Currents of distortion erupted in their vision, blending the colors they beheld.

"What the..." Corwin groaned.

"The scream..." Rodriguez keeled over to her knees.

"It's like the... plant but... much more..." Artemis managed to grunt the words through clenched teeth.

The scream whisked away, into the depths of shadows, still

echoing around them from every direction. Their sight steadied, leaves and branches reformed, the quaking slowed, until stillness resumed around them. Weapons retrained on Milton's position only to find no sign of the large operator.

"The hell?!" Corwin cried out. "That thing just carried big Milton off like an action figure!"

No! John... bearing, discipline, courage, like the corps taught me. Do not panic. Do not let the stressors of combat overcome you. Check the team. Do not rush blindly. Assess the new variables of combat. "Get ahold of yourselves. Give me a status," Artemis ordered.

"My head feels like it's been bounced like a basketball, Actual," Rodriguez replied. "But I'm ready to Charlie Mike."

"I'm good, Actual. We can't let that thing get away with Milty."

"And we won't. But I have no idea where to start looking in this place."

"I think I saw it heading that way." Corwin pointed into the darkness. "It moves like the shadows, faster than the smaller ones."

"We hurt it," Artemis said. "That's why it fled. That means we can kill it. I want close movement, no cowboy or hero shit. We maneuver lined up and within arms' reach of each other at all times. I don't want to lose anyone else down here. We know how the lesser variants of this vector hunts. Follow the same protocols for now."

The others nodded.

Shining orbs were caught through the corner of a glance. Artemis spun to her right flank. Her M14's sights highlighted morphing shadows that ducked behind a bush. Rodriguez and Corwin's point of aim followed as they took positions beside their team commander, with Aristotle crouching behind them.

"We got contact, Actual?" Corwin asked.

"I don't know, but something else is here..." Artemis murmured.

"Neh, ajuani lenu!" a feminine voice called out.

Tiny hands rose from the rustling bush. A petite figure stepped out. Big doe eyes stared at the agents, gleaming with a luminescence akin to a nocturnal predator. Small horns sprouted from the cranium of the short woman, rising two inches above her mane of curling auburn locks. Heavy bags swelled under her eyes, glistening with fresh tears.

"Don't shoot!" Aristotle exclaimed. "It's that Pippa woman that was fighting with the inhabitants."

"Stand down, Raptor," Artemis instructed.

"Actual, are you sure? I mean, look at it!" Corwin scoffed.

"I'm sure. Go to the alert."

"Roger," Rodriguez acknowledged.

Slow reluctance saw the barrels of their weapons pointing to the dirt, remaining poised in their grip.

"Make one move on Actual and we'll light your ass up," Rodriguez barked.

Pippa's lip quivered, taking a slow step back.

"Patty, stand down," Artemis ordered. "You're going to scare her off."

The team commander smiled at the strange woman, removing her hands from her rifle, and allowing it to dangle from the D-ring on her vest. Artemis stepped forward, waving slow and calm. Pippa stopped in place, her head shifting with rapid examination.

"Ankleh omhadi mon?"

"I'm sorry but we don't understand you."

Pippa sighed, scratching her head.

"But you seem to understand us."

The woman nodded. "Len ottani. Neh, comi an dar."

Aristotle stepped out from behind his sister. "I can feel her energies and despite her outward appearance, it's not negative."

Pippa's eyes connected with the scryer. "Len, yuilini wa eh!"

The woman folded her hands together, lowering her gaze to the grass. Her breathing grew deep and relaxed. Pippa's aura expanded, connecting with Aristotle's. The cord was set between their minds.

"She's gifted, like me, knowing how to use the telepathic frequencies."

Artemis nodded. "We do not mean her harm, but we must find John."

Aristotle clasped hands with Artemis, his gaze falling into the big shining brown irises that peered through a stream of tears. Vision warped into the fields of rifting currents fluctuating around the pair, bringing into view the energies that formulated reality. Hot flashes consumed their perceptions, pouring over them with tingles. A shield of light expanded from the figure next to her, illuminating the countenance of Aristotle and holding back the ocean of crimson.

I don't want to be here. We shouldn't be here. What is this that surrounds us? It's so uncomfortable, I want to leave but I can't. It's as if we're about to drown, but my breaths continue. At least that's the best way I can explain it.

"*The ruinous energies of this area are beyond anything I've ever encountered or even studied from the Librarians of the order. Stay near me during this. My psionic shield will protect you.*"

My brother... I forget how talented he is. The scryers are truly incredible agents.

Pippa stepped into view, her aura radiating a dark gray presence, contrasting with the light of Aristotle blaring around her.

"Her aura is devoid of the breath."

What does that mean? I've heard scryers mention that about other vectors.

"I'm not sensing hostility, but deep sadness."

She mourns the child that was murdered.

A seam above Pippa's brow widened and currents flowed from the opening. A soft round newborn's face appeared, outlined with a rosy pink that culminated at his cheeks. Tiny lips glistened with saliva, eager to suckle at the nipple Pippa presented. She held the child in both arms, smiling at the gentle face feeding from the nourishment provided.

"Her child was flawless, human like us..."

The mind's eye shifted, bringing a quick glance to the entryway flapping from the bursting intrusion of a large figure. The being's horns curved upward, from his muscled forehead riddled with tufts of dark brown fur. He was on top of the mother before she could turn away. His thick arms snatched the child from Pippa's grasp. She rose, her limbs still warm from the child's presence, reaching for what was hers, the little being she brought into this world. A hard blow came from an angle unseen, bringing her view crashing backward, until there was only the ceiling. A slow extension of her arms reached out, searching for the infant's cries that faded as the invading presence left.

"These vectors sacrifice the children that are born human and retain the breath."

"She was unarmed and tossed to this area to be eaten by the things that dwell within it?" Artemis asked. *"This is why she's*

seeking us for help. Does she know where that giant wendigo took John?"

"*Let me search her mind.*" Aristotle replied.

Branches and leaves brushed into Artemis' vision, as it raced through the dark wilderness. Beyond where the land dipped into lush thickets, stretched the mouth of a cave. Cries echoed from the entrance, the wailing of which crawled through their skin. Teeth gnashed with heavy breaths expelling clouds from the sneering mouth of hunger. Eager chomps clamped upon the shuddering victims beneath it. The agent's slow steps brought them closer, peering within the entrance leading to darkness.

A pale figure lay on the ground, its gaunt body writhing. Dark life fluids spilled from the gaping tear across its throat. A flap of skin hung over its exposed chest where portions of flesh had been chewed away. The hairless figure's claws dug into the ground, its eyes staring into the impending arrival of certain death. It shuddered, until its head rolled away from the shoulders, hanging by the tendons of its neck.

That's one of them! What could've torn a wendigo apart in such a manner?

More claws reached from depths of what could not be seen. The curved nails scratched into the ground of the cave floor, ripping at the grass, and digging into the dirt. Handfuls of earth lifted away into its tight clutches, the length of its arm quivering with another salivating bite. Strain ran through its body with a whimper. The desperate victim was dragged further into the darkness.

High above the shadowed outline of its brutalized corpse flashed a set of large yellow eyes. Wailing expelled from the cave, brushing across a young Pippa's face with the chilling embrace of winter's wind.

Rapid steps brought her backward, fear keeping her view locked on the cave. A massive arm reached out with claws unfolding, grabbing the other corpse. It dragged its prize into the shadows with ease. Pippa turned, her view bouncing as she ran, the heavy breaths of her quaking lungs swelling in her ears.

"*Devoured its own kin...*" Artemis pondered in disgust.

"*An evolved form of the vector, but how did this happen?*" Aristotle wondered.

"*It doesn't matter! That thing has John. So that's where we are going. We've wasted too much time. Ask Pippa if she can guide us to its lair.*"

Green swaying leaves returned into view, with the plethora of tree trunks lining their vision once again. Corwin stood in front of Artemis waving his hand, searching for eye contact with his commander. She looked at him and raised a brow.

"Sorry, Actual." Corwin took off his helm to scratch his head. "Just checking. You went radio silent for several seconds there."

"So, what's the plan, boss lady?" Rodriguez asked. "I don't like this."

"We can trust her. She's not like the others," Artemis replied.

"Okay, if you say so. But I'm keeping watch on her. Any funny business and I'm going to smoke this puta."

Lingering thoughts flooded from the residual connection. A view of young Artemis manifested, where she stood near the entrance of the mine that brought them to the kingdom. Next to her was Aristotle, the three of them exchanging a flash of eye contact before Pippa raced back into the depths. The hope for more had been dashed, overcome by the fear of those that looked so different.

"We've met before," Artemis said.

Pippa nodded. "Yeek, en yuli."

"Can you take us to its lair?"

Pippa lowered her head, shaking with doubt. Trembles crawled up her back. The woman's bosom expanded through her brown leather shirt, her breaths growing heavy.

"You've nothing to fear. We will protect you, Pippa. Please, show us where it has taken John."

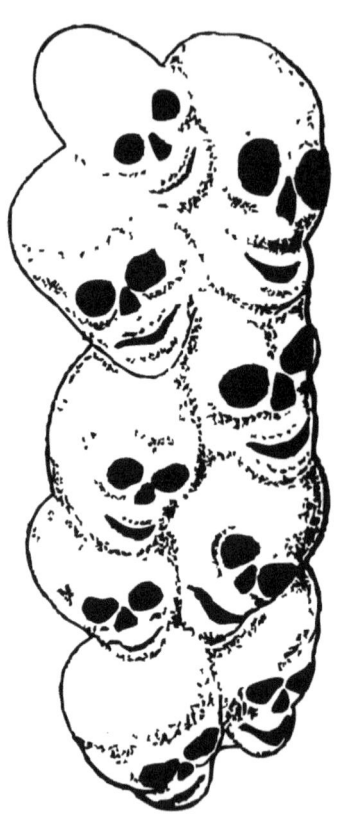

CHAPTER 19
LAMENT AND VICTORY

My John, with his kind heart and big smile. Even when I thought I had learned my lesson earlier, it didn't hit home until now. How fleeting are the moments of life that we take for granted. In this moment, I've only regret for the walls that I've put up in the name of discipline, forgetting or just not knowing how to be both a woman and an agent. I've lost so much. I won't lose you, too...

Artemis spearheaded Raptor's quick pace between the trees with Pippa at her side, guiding with the urgent direction of her slender hands. Watchful scans came from the agent's rapid gazes in a constant shift between the foliage, divots in the uneven earth, and the horizon of shadows forming a cage of obscurity. Artemis glanced back to the dour faces of her team, their firm-browed gazes glowering hard at Pippa, then back at her to shake their heads.

They don't trust her. I can't say I do either, but she's our only hope.

"I don't like it," Rodriguez whispered. "We could be led into an ambush."

"Me either," Corwin replied. "But we have to rescue Milty."

"Fine, but I'm not taking my eyes off her. You watch Actual's six because my full attention is going to be on this cochina."

The two agents shared a nod. Rodriguez broke the tension with a smile and a wink. Corwin blew a kiss before they stuttered in their steps behind a halted Artemis. Their team commander stared into the depths of the wilderness, the earth rising with small rolling hills, and thick trees of massive width, possessing height beyond their vision. The Glowing's reach was minimal in the density of branches and hanging lush, its orange tint becoming a mere trace in their mottled vision of blackness.

"I want everyone to keep close," Artemis instructed. "This low visibility can cause friendly fire if we aren't careful."

"Acknowledged, Actual," Corwin responded.

Howling flowed over them, carrying with the winter's wind, their ears ringing with dozens of simultaneous voices crying out in high pitch. The agents' vision guided their weapons as they turned about, searching through glimmers of detail in the ever-changing quagmire. Cold vibrations flooded over them, clutching at their limbs with the stillness of hesitation.

A hand reached out, grabbing Corwin's shoulder with strength and authority. The agent spun around, the reticle of his rifle hovering over Artemis.

"Stand down!" she ordered. "It's just me, Agent. We're going old school, like the days of basic training at the depot and the island."

"Ah, gotcha. Reaching out and touching each other to keep it tight, Actual?"

"Yes." Artemis peered around. "Do not rush it. Stay with me. We're moving."

"It's playing tricks," Rodriguez noted. "It knows we're coming."

"This place is saturated with negative energy, Arty," Aristotle noted. "I can't track a presence beyond our immediate area. The farther out I try to reach, the worse it gets. Like swimming in the ocean during a storm."

Artemis nodded. "Careful where you aim. We don't want to hit John."

Leaves rustled in the distance, the crinkling noise carrying from outside their peripherals. Their vision struggled to track it, until the snapping and crumbling became only small crackles. A warm breeze pushed into their ears, reminding them of the voices it once carried. They spun about again, searching for the gentle circling patters that faded and returned across the grass.

Weapon barrels rose, training sights on the slight crackles spotting around them. Tension coursed through their bodies into their twitching muscles poised and ready. Fingers remained touched upon triggers. Breathing escalated with the burn of fatigue beginning its slow rise through their locked bodies, culminating in their shoulders and arms that swelled hot from growing exhaustion.

"Sounds like it's all around us!" Corwin exclaimed.

"Wahum!" Pippa pointing ahead. "Ick bey wahum!"

A shrill scream rose in the distance. "Help," John sobbed, continuing a throat rattling yell.

"That's Milty!" Rodriguez said. "That damn thing must be trying to eat him!"

"Neh!" Pippa snapped. "Neh, uj so wahum!"

"Cállate, puta! Actual, we have to do something!"

"We continue moving—"

"Help me!" Milton screamed for an elongated period, his voice propelled with a haggard urgency.

"That damn thing is trying to eat him!" Corwin yelled.

"Neh! Wahum!" Pippa urged.

"Silence!" Artemis snapped. *John...* "We're moving quick! Keep close! Double time it, Raptor!"

"Neh!"

Another scream drew Artemis ever closer. The agent escalated her pace until at a full sprint. Her eyes skipped over the landscape of shadows, sidestepping a bush that she gave keen attention toward before speeding around it.

"Neh!" Pippa continued her protest, keeping behind Artemis.

Wind brushed against Rodriguez, calling her focus to their left flank. Bouncing jarred her vision, blurring the manipulation of shadows that morphed around their travels. She slowed, her glower straining in the hunt for images to recognize.

Throat wrenching screams continued. Artemis leapt over a bush, landing with her rifle aimed on the source. Slow steps brought her forward, the heavy breaths of fatigue raking over the silence that surrounded them. Trees were sparse, the majority surrounding the small field of grass before them. A break in the canopy allowed for illumination where the pulsing orange battled with the creeping shadows. At the forest opening, the earth arched over in a wide entrance, with a gradual drop.

This is it. The cave from the images of Pippa's link with Aris.

"Patty!" Corwin called back.

"I lost sight of her, too," Aristotle said. "She slowed for some reason."

"Neh, oka wati!" Pippa pointed at the cave, backing away to the cover of the trees that lined the area.

Artemis approached the mouth, the red reticle of her optics scanning over the crevices of stone and dirt walls. Motions shifted in the darkness on the ground. Artemis lowered her weapon, leveling with the object, keeping her stance and approach slow and steady. Unintelligible murmurs came from a figure shuddering in the fetal position. She gasped, recognizing who lay before her. Lowering the rifle's aim, she took to a knee near the body of her beloved.

"John," Artemis whispered with sharp urgency. She scanned over him, her hands in a gentle touch over his body, searching for any signs of injury. "I'm here. Are you hurt?"

"Arty..." Milton shifted upright into a sitting position. "Oh... my head is killing me... but other than that, I'm good... just need a minute..."

Artemis smiled, leaning in to kiss her man. "Your screams had us worried that it was eating you."

"I wasn't screaming... I've been unconscious until now..."

The joy drained from Artemis' face as she peered back to the entrance. "It led us here..."

On wobbling legs, Milton rose from the ground. A bruise over his right thigh resounded with trembling urgency from the pressure of each step. Memories appeared in fleeting glimpses within his mind's eye, the agent remembering how his equipment bounced against him while in the creature's clutches.

"Damn... my girl and I took a beating," John announced. "Let me make sure she's still in this fight."

Artemis nodded. "Take the time you need to gather yourself."

Milton's hand traced along the cord from his machine

gun's stock to the guide ring on his vest that kept it secure. His hand motioned over the weapon, opening its cover, and clearing the belt of rounds from the feed tray. He pulled the charging handle to the rear, before switching the selector to safe. Pulling the trigger, the weapon's safety held the bolt in place. Milton then placed the weapon on fire and the bolt drove forward, guided by the charging handle. A quick shuffle of his hands brought the belt of rounds back into the feed tray. He cocked the weapon one last time, preparing it for battle.

"She's still in this. I can Charlie Mike, Actual. My gear is still attached and functional."

Artemis reached, their fingers stroking with tenderness as she peered into his eyes. Foreheads came together when they faced each other, with small sighs of relief deflating the tension roiling through their shoulders. *This is far from over...*

Artemis turned away, her rifle shouldering back into the low alert position, with her hands poised over the stock. When the cave walls peeled away from their view, the orange glow washed over their vision. Details of the forest realigned within their squinting eyes. A form grew larger between the trees. Artemis' hard stare focused. She stepped forward, her rifle rising, and breaths growing faster.

Grass crunched beneath closing steps. A petite form caused Artemis and the rest of Raptor to lower their guard.

"Mira, two friendlies approaching." Rodriguez announced with Pippa in tow. "Be cool."

"Stand down." Artemis ordered. "Patty, you had us worried back there."

"Sorry, Actual. I thought I saw something. I didn't want it to flank us so I thought I could hold position and let it maneuver for me to counter."

"That was dangerous but clever thinking. And what if it didn't work?"

"I'd be the next snack I guess." Rodriguez shrugged.

"Not cool," Corwin snapped.

"No heroics, Rod," Artemis said.

"I know but—"

"But you've always been a selfless warrior." The two women exchanged smiles of respect. "That's why you're my go to agent for the difficult moments. No one digs harder than you when we're in the trenches, Patty. Always thinking of others before yourself."

"Wow, Arty. You're really thawing out on this hop," Aristotle noted.

The wind rose, and its cold stinging bite upon their cheeks ushered away the tepid warmth of the Glowing. Howls mixed with the currents, the multitude of raging voices sending the agents reeling in pursuit of the source. Target reticles rose and shifted to various locations, finding only the emptiness of open air.

Shadows melded and stretched with movement, rising above and around Rodriguez. A looming figure emerged from the darkness. The width of its shoulders flanked the agent on each side, its long sinewy arms hanging with blackened claws flexed and curled. Spiked antlers appeared above Rodriguez, who turned only to find their sharpness driven into her stomach.

"Patty!" Corwin screamed.

The agent cried out in pain, flailing into the air at the end of the creature's mighty horns. Cavernous holes streamed with her life fluids down the creature's antlers. Droplets of blood washed over its face, never compromising its glower of baleful pupils, shimmering with nocturnal luminescence.

"I see you..." whispers invaded the agents' thoughts, bringing a chill to their minds. *"I've always seen you."*

With trembling arms Milton lifted his machine gun. The wendigo's head lowered, and its body arched, bringing the impaled and wailing Rodriguez into view. He shifted in his steps as the creature bounded forward.

"Damn it!" John hollered. "We don't have a shot!"

"Hold fire!" Artemis ordered. "Don't hit Patty!"

"Neh, catchwa!" Pippa squealed, fleeing behind a tree with Aristotle.

Powerful currents swelled across the area. Raptor Team squinted through the numbing cold. In a silent bound, the monstrosity came upon them. Its approach ushered along the screams of its prey, until the force of her wailing rang upon their ears. Speed carried its large form as a blur amidst the darkness.

Corwin dived, rolling out of the way, his beloved's cries speeding toward him. The hulking beast's claws raked downward, ripping away at dirt and grass. Corwin rose, only to find ribbons of agony running through his back. He turned his head to see the creature upon him, its claws shredding through his armor with each swing peeling away splinters of ceramic and resin.

"Skin... meat... tender... warm... must... eat..."

"Stay low!" Artemis ordered.

Milton and the team commander unleashed a salvo, bringing incendiary rounds fizzling along the monster's backside. Salivating jaws opened with throbbing strings from its plaque covered teeth as it bellowed in defiance. The being spun to bear its quarry into their aim, circling in steps around a groaning Corwin. Shrieking winds reclaimed their vision, nipping their eyes shut with a sudden chill.

"No shot! Damn it!" Milton roared, circling. "I can't see shit!"

Patty's mouth hung agape, screaming no more. Her glazed eyes looked down to her beloved, the torn glistening meat of his back exposed with the copper reek of his blood invading her nostrils. Its claws reached, grabbing at the torn morsels to stuff into its eager maw. Rodriguez reached on her vest, her fingers unclipping the mouth of a small grenade pouch. She took the device into both hands, pulling away the pin and lowering her arms to the wendigo's head.

"Frag... out..." Rodriguez managed to gurgle the words through the blood rising from her throat.

Artemis and Milton dived to the ground.

An eruption of force spread through the area, flinging shrapnel, and expelling waves of scalding heat within the blast area. The screaming wendigo bounced across the ground, with fragments of its skull and antlers raining over the area.

Survivors rose from cover, witnessing flickers of small flames devouring the remnants of grass around a wilted circle of earth. Lithe arms and legs were strewn about the corpse of the apex wendigo. Its face was torn asunder, leaving a wilted mess save for an eye and its mouth contorted with lips twisted from the horror of its own demise. Dark crimson fluids spewed from the beast's exposed wounds, with life pouring from the fractured husk of its skull.

Blurs formulated images as Artemis staggered toward the kill zone. Her eyes fought with hard blinks knocking away the cold with the stagnant warmth returning. She gasped, stopping just before the remnants of their teammates, and dropping to her knees.

"No... I failed them... I have utterly failed everyone..."

What remained of Rodriguez's broken corpse lay next to Corwin's shredded body.

"Thank you, Patty. You were my girl, even in our darkest moment."

"You can't blame yourself." Milton placed a hand on her shoulder.

"I'm making the calls... I'm giving the orders... and everyone is dying, John... Patty was my best friend and now she's dead. This is my family and most of us are gone..."

"We're extreme climate warfare, but this is another world, Arty. These vectors are something no one in the Agency has ever faced before. They died for humanity."

Artemis' sight never left the corpses of her friends.

"Arty," Aristotle called, with Pippa trailing behind. "John is right. There's too much at stake now for you to lose your mind to lamentation. Pick yourself up, sis."

She peered over to her brother with a quick nod.

"I've been probing the mind of our guest here. Pippa has been very receptive and open during our communication. This god that is worshiped by the denizens down here, I know where he comes from. And I think I have an idea of how we can defeat such an entity, but it's going to be extremely dangerous. All we need is an opening, a chink in his armor for us to capitalize upon." Aristotle sighed.

"I don't care anymore." Artemis stood up, hands clasping tight to her rifle, while her gaze rose to the incandescent pulse of the Glowing. "We rest and bury our dead tonight. Tomorrow we slay a god."

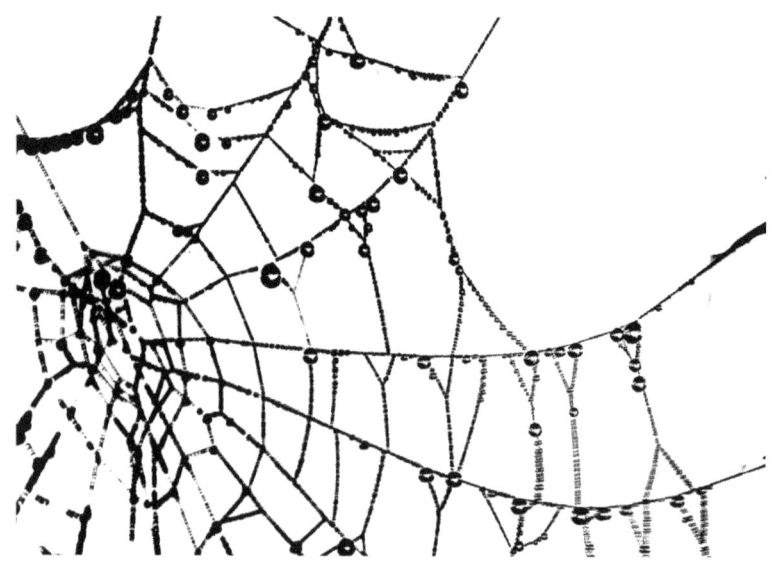

CHAPTER 20
VOICE OF THE NIGHTMARE

Tears stained the murky bags developing underneath Artemis' reddening eyes. Down her soaked cheeks they rolled, where they cascaded along her neck. Slow and solemn breaths left her nostrils. She remained statuesque in her seat at the mouth of the cave. Two mounds of dirt blared in her vision, rising from the field with an aura of orange lingering over them. When she brought her vision away from the sight, images began morphing into the mind's eye, porting her from the stagnant air and reek of the underworld.

Clear blue ocean waves undulated into the shoreline, filling Artemis' ears with the static of their tumult mixing with the cry of seagulls overhead. Sunlight radiated upon her face. A smile appeared from Patty's golden tan countenance. Her friend's long dark hair draped over thin shoulders that went into toned cinnamon arms and a rippling abdominal section revealed by the bikini top she wore. Patty swayed to the beat of the steel drums and guitar riffs surrounding them, stepping out on the sand into a hip shaking dance, much to the delight of the other tourists.

"You gotta live a little, prima!" Rodriguez proclaimed, taking a sip from the wide margarita glass overwhelming her small hands.

"I know... I just—"

"Just nothing! I brought you on vacation with me to relax. No thinking about boys, orders from ADs, missions, and especially no uglies. Come on!"

Clinking came from their table and Patty's glass as she discarded her drink and took Artemis by the hand. "Mira, girlfriend, this weekend we dance! We sleep in! We drink a lot! We eat good! For what's it all worth if we don't enjoy the world we're fighting for?"

Artemis chuckled. "That does sound like heaven. I can't argue that."

"Nope!" Patty grinned. They swayed their hips together and raised their arms to the drifting cotton white clouds above.

Always had my back, didn't you? Never gave up on me. Never let me deteriorate by my lonesome. You were one of the people who kept me in this. Kept me human and from becoming the thing I hate the most... a monster.

"And yet you still got me killed by dragging me on your vendetta, puta." Patty ceased all movement. A frown on her face was accommodated by her gaze turning to the sea.

"Wait... what... no... I didn't..."

"But you did. You call yourself my best friend? You brought me out to these fucking mountains to die for your selfishness."

"No... it's not like that..."

"You knew, but you kept us in the dark about the important details, didn't you? And now I'm six feet under, inside of hell. Not even a nice burial plot after all my service. Damn, prima... that's messed up. Even for you."

"I didn't know what it was exactly..." Artemis swallowed. She reached for Patty, but her hand was slapped away.

Artemis and Patricia stared into the ocean.

"That doesn't help us now, does it?"

"I'm sorry, Patty."

"Tell that to the man you love. He's likely going to die next, you know."

"No, I will not let that happen!"

"Like your leadership was able to save everyone else, right?"

Artemis sighed, her eyes squeezing with the pounding of sadness threatening to overflow her psyche. The team commander's lips pursed together from the stinging failure in her heart.

"Exactly," Patty said, rejecting Artemis, who turned to her.

After slow headshaking, Artemis' eyes began to pry open, daring not to look at her friend whose presence blared in the corner of her view. The green churning waters of the Caribbean Sea encompassed her vision, guided by a steadfast need to bring her mind away from the grief plaguing it.

Iridescent threads cascaded down her sight, tracing downward with a faint visible trail. Lithe legs clung to the bare skin of her chest, tapping as it crawled upward. On her mahogany bosom ran a small black spider, its bulbous rear surrounded by quick moving legs.

Artemis swatted it. Her hand passed through without incident. Up it crawled, drawing closer, its legs spreading in length, its body growing from the size of a dime to that of a toddler's hand. Long fangs extended through frontal appendages like black hooks. Droplets of venom seeped from the tips. Rows of eyes peered into hers with a determination driving it toward her face.

Others followed, streaming up Artemis' body. She continued swatting, the little creatures growing in size, passing through with the countless quick patters of their legs gripping at her skin. They went for her eyes. She wanted to close them but found no lids present. Thin, chitinous limbs covered her vision, extending from dark underbodies with red hour glasses across their stomachs. Their legs squeezed with effort, clinging to her face. Artemis swung, striking herself. Fangs aimed at her when the arachnids rose, coming down with quick and forceful bites puncturing her eyes.

"Come to me, Arty. Are you okay?" A concerned voice beckoned.

Artemis fell to the ground, rolling, clawing at the spiders. Her body convulsed, her nails shredding away at the arachnids. Legs pattered against her skin, up her back and over her shoulders. The scampering past her neck alarmed her to the assault of more. Blood and tissue gathered underneath Artemis' nails as she continued raking harder. Desperate breaths split her lips before releasing a scream, echoing around her.

"Stop it! Listen to my voice!"

Inside they crawled, wedging over her teeth, their abdomens brushing the wet innards of her cheeks. Little limbs grabbed at her tongue, pulling themselves down her gullet, leaving the forceful patterns of their movements lingering inside.

"Arty, listen to me! Damn it... forgive me."

Artemis' head turned, snapped to the side with a jarring strike. Shudders overtook her body, staring up at the vision of trembling hands covered in oozing redness. Sharp streaks of pain were left etched deep into her face. Redness washed over her blinking sight. Eyelids closed, then opened to a smiling Patty looming over her.

"Don't feel bad." Patty's voice deepened. "You worthless harlots have forever been susceptible to manipulation. Spiders, always the easiest route to terrorize you, pathetic morsels. Even with you so-called tougher types. If there is such a thing. I have yet to witness it."

Artemis scrambled backward, climbing to her feet with rapid readiness. Balled fists rose to her face as she squared with Rodriguez. Bloodstains along her fingers took her attention. Hot agony shot from the deep scrapes radiating over her face.

"You've come back to me after all these years. Oh, but your pretty face, what have you done? Such a shame. You're not going to be happy when you wake, Artemis. It wasn't my intention to cause you pain; only to show you the futility of these endeavors. That was just a spectacle you acquiesced to my delight. Free will and humanity are such double-edged swords."

"Shut up!"

"Patience is definitely not a virtue I possess, and it seems neither do you. I'll be quick with my proposal."

Spit flew from her snarling lips, blanketing over Patty's grinning countenance.

"The monkey throws a tantrum to the great chimera. Such insolence is adorable given the circumstances."

"The chimera was a female creature!"

"Be not forgetful to entertain strangers: for thereby some have entertained angels unaware."

"You're quoting the bible. But I'm no Christian."

"Not anymore. I put an end to that." Azazel snickered. "Such malleable little creatures. I honestly have no idea why she fears you. Then again, she was always a paranoid heap."

"What are you going on about?"

"Enough banter. Let's address my proposal. All of you are going to perish here. Banish the ideas of glorious martyrdom for the future of humanity. Your pride alone cannot see you through. Given the words of your own misbegotten faiths, you know that we inevitably reclaim this world—"

Artemis glowered stepping forward, her fists still up to her face in a boxer's stance.

"So, I'm offering you an opportunity to do right by the remainder of your team. The weak mortal pest that you're so enamored with—"

"His name is John!"

"—surrender yourself to me. Submit to my desires without resistance, and I will allow your precious John to leave Dudael unharmed."

"What do you mean?"

"I want a child. A mighty towering son, who will rule over the nation that I carve from my wrath. As it was in the wake of our descent, so shall it be when the judgment has expired."

"Why? What need do you have for love and family?"

"Love is such a ridiculous human concept. No, it's an extension of my will. To replace what was taken from me by our father."

Why not Persephone?

"The birthing process is rather arduous. The points of power flow strong through your family's bloodline. You're like a beacon in the ether, so easy to find."

He's reading my thoughts again. The scar along my sister's stomach? She tried, but something happened... "What about Aristotle? Can he go free as well?"

A deep cackle boomed from Rodriguez. "You obtuse

woman. You haven't the slightest clue about your dear brother, do you? So be it. Do we have an accord?"

That ritual they performed. It was the key to this madness. His presence... it feels stronger than the first time... John... I've lost so many of them already... this feels like the only way...

Rifting textures of energy pulled away from Patty. Like flakes they crumbled and shriveled, falling into the reaches of the etheric layers where they vanished. Each one revealed portions of a muscular frame, covered in coarse black fur, more akin to wires than hair. Artemis lowered her guard, stepping backward. The last visages of her friend fell away. Smoking negative energies dissipated from the fragment of Patty's face, wielding a blinking and curious eye.

Massive broad shoulders towered over Artemis, as the being stepped out. Gray membranous wings folded outward. Thick gnarled horns curved from his forehead, running up into a sharp peak. The ground clopped with his hind cloven legs drawing him near Artemis. His clawed hand extended from a thick arm, waiting to be embraced.

"This is the only way." His deep smoky voice curled the words with a sinister and eldritch ring. "Take my hand. Salvage the lives of those you care about and fulfill the destiny you have always evaded."

His enormous, calloused claw wrapped around her small hand. Artemis nodded. "Okay. Just don't hurt John. I don't want to lose anyone else. I've lost so many..."

"Indeed. You have my word. No harm will come to the one you love. I await you near the mouth of the Glowing. This is where we will consummate our bargain with the union of our wills."

"Please, wake up!"

Artemis opened her eyes to the concerned gaze of John and

Aristotle. Nothing registered save for the hot streaks of blood radiating down her face. A wet fullness had accumulated underneath her fingernails, with a throbbing sensation through her weary hands.

"She's awake!" John gave her a gentle pat. "You just started—"

"He wouldn't let me in," Aristotle exclaimed. "I'm sorry, Arty. I tried beating through the walls."

A gasp expelled from Artemis, raising her reddened fingers with tufts of skin hanging from their tips.

"—murmuring and tearing at yourself," John continued. "It was awful. I tried to wake you but..."

Artemis sat upright as they hugged. "I don't care. John, I made a deal. You're going home."

"What? You make it sound like it's—"

"Without me."

"No... no deal!"

"It's done! I can't be responsible for your death down here, too. Go home. That's an order."

Blood mixed with tears that rolled down her face, smearing when the lovers embraced. "I'll explain everything."

"You made a deal with the devil?" Aristotle sighed, looking down and shaking his head. "Arty... what have you done?"

CHAPTER 21
LUSTFUL SUBMISSION

his is it. For everything. The final effort in ending it all. I hope that fiend lives up to his end of the bargain. John, please be gone before the commencement. Leave me with that peace of mind. What happens to me after this? I am to be a slave, a tool for darkness for the hope of love.

Artemis walked alone toward the city of animal skin tents. Phantom weight lingered in her hands with the reminder of the weapon left surrendered to her comrades before traversing the reluctant walk. Glowing feral eyes appeared along the city's perimeter, as rows of beings emerged. Their outlines stood within obscurity, with hairy bodies possessing long arms and hind legs. Murmurs and growls blended when Artemis drew closer, raising her empty hands to the nods of narrowed scrutinizing eyes.

Persephone...

Standing in the middle of the road leading to the platform and the altar was Priestess Sarai. The woman's face roiled with contempt, her movements rigid from swallowing the rage growing inside. Artemis was met with a sneer, but her sister's eyes refused to connect, rolling away. She turned to escort her, burning in Artemis' peripheral with a budding glare.

"Perseph—"

"That is not my name. It hasn't been since I can remember. That heretic Pippa was sentenced to death for such insolence. Save your words. I know you're trying to appeal to my familial sense. All you survey, I rule, at his side. This kingdom, these people, this power you feel floating through the layers."

"No, this is some kind of Stockholm syndrome! Remember who you are!"

"You will be wise to understand your station. Know that there will be no pleasure derived from this. That is reserved for when I am with him. You are a brood mare, chosen purely for your genetics. There will be no regard toward you other than that, usurper."

Such steadfast jealousy. Probably rehearsing those sharp lines in her head the moment she knew the bargain was struck. She's madly in love with this fiend...

"*I'd watch my thoughts if I were you,*" Sarai snapped into her mind. "*While the High Queen has allowed you pitiful wretches to run amuck of your own world, disrespect is not tolerated in this kingdom.*"

"*Thanks for the warning.*" Artemis swallowed her inner dialogue, silencing the rampancy and focusing only upon her steps.

"*Ah, so there's some discipline and training within the muddled mess you call a psyche. Regardless, you'll be hard pressed to keep your secrets from us. No amount of half-hearted scryer training will see you through this.*"

Artemis stared ahead, ignoring the penetrating scowl she felt from the corner of her vision. They approached the large platform. With a fierce point of her finger, Sarai ushered her onward, up the steps, across the stage. Artemis glanced at the basin, to the stains of red that darkened over its stone surface. Shrill cries replayed in her mind, with the images of the wailing child, the knife and the desperate mother, Pippa, struggling in the clutches of the towering denizens.

A blanket of heat immersed them. Swathes of it poured from the backside, growing with each step that drew them closer to the inferno. Orange and yellow shone from the gaping earthen mouth below their position. Cragged teeth-like rocks extended around a descent leading into a morass of swirling energies, churning with the scorching waves of magma and the crackles of pulsing light. Artemis turned from the brightness, shaking away the ache pounding from the momentary glance.

There is something... I can feel it separate from the forces radiating within that pit.

Shifting energies appeared in senses beyond the body. The presence of life lingered in the distance, hollow in their energetic fields. The understanding they were not alone faded, only to reappear as a blaring alarm to the senses.

Beings are living within the descent to the inferno. But how?

"Didn't our darling brother teach you more than just the basics?" Sarai scoffed.

"I'm not a trained scryer."

"That gaggle of rank amateurs with no official indoctrination from heavenly entities? They are but housecats playing with yarn."

"Enough bravado, Persephone. What is this array of light?"

"What you're feeling are energies from the inner earth, limitless in its potential to create and sustain life. The residual power that flows from its center was used for locks to a prison. But I have been taught to harness it through our birthright, to use its sustenance in maintaining the spirits of those who are most precious to me."

"The children you failed in bringing to term?"

Sarai's grip on her knife tightened until trembling. Her lips pressed together and her brows arched. She stepped toward Artemis, guiding the blade's aim to the small of her back. "I want to cut out your kidneys and relish in your screams as you die slowly."

"You're a mother too, Persephone! How could you have done that to Pippa's child back there?"

"That bothered you? She shouldn't have birthed one of your ilk. Life on the surface has made all of you so weak, daughter of El. Blind to the impending war of reclamation."

"Where I come from, harming children isn't strength. It's cowardice."

Sarai leaned to the corner of Artemis' view, hissing through her teeth.

"You don't scare me, Persephone. I'm not an infant and I've faced tougher monstrosities than a lunatic cult leader like you."

"He'll forgive me if I slit your throat, cut out that annoying tongue, and feed the remainder to the ravenous ones. My beloved will be upset but he will forgive me..."

"No. I won't." Azazel's deep curling whisper washed over their ears like a breeze. "Stay your hand, Sarai. Focus upon the goals of my kingdom. Your jealousy and pride will cost us the forthcoming of my avatar."

"As you wish, my master." Retreating steps of slow reluctance withdrew Sarai's threat, until she sheathed her weapon. Hatred exuded through her narrowing eyes upon a fierce glare, burning into Artemis.

John... I hope you are long gone from here. Tears swelled over within Artemis' frown. A droplet escaped, rolling down her face where it clung to the point of her chin. She turned away from the being, hearing slow steps carrying his presence until a towering shadow loomed over her.

"You have my word, that your beloved mortal will leave the kingdom unharmed." Sulfur washed over Artemis, carried by a breath exuding a temperature rivaling the Glowing. "We are to know each other. Our union need not be arduous. Embrace me as your lover, woman. Come and I will show you pleasures beyond material comprehension."

A sigh rushed from Artemis' parting lips. Her eyes shifted under wrinkles of apprehension. She deflated the moment his palms connected with her skin, the closing of fingers along her delicate shoulders.

Artemis carried her vision to the yellow eyes peering from the darkness beyond the reach of the Glowing. Hundreds of undulating stares connected to the pair, with breaths gathering pace from anxious vigor boiling over. More unblinking denizens gathered as inhuman nocturnal pupils shimmered in the distance adding to the crowd.

No... I...

"There's always a choice," Azazel announced. "Not even I can limit your free will. Everything you have endured to this moment is what you have chosen. Your hesitation is simply a byproduct of not realizing that yet. This was always your fate, my dear. Unite our lines and ascend into legend as the mother of a demigod."

Artemis' view scoured through the distorted parodies of humanity, to the cragged earth rising and falling around them, and the pulsing light washing over her. In one of the elevated adjacent crevices, three silhouettes gathered, then lowered to a kneeling position. The center one bore a long and large instrument laid upon a shoulder.

"Okay." Artemis' nodded, another sigh fleeing her mouth in quivering apprehension. "You're right. John is safe. I need to uphold my end of the bargain. I will give you what you deserve."

When she turned, golden luminescence shone from the skin of the towering man before her. Artemis' head rose to the underside of his chiseled pecs, leading down into a tapered waist of rippling abdominal muscles. A large throbbing member erected just below her view. She peered up into his stern face. His pupilless eyes shimmered from his squared forehead with a white brilliance that resonated into her core with a vibrating aura.

Azazel's hand rose. The earth responded with a rising flat pillar of rock and soil appearing behind Artemis. Flowers sprouted from the makeshift bed, immersing it with an array of yellow and white. He lifted the woman into his arms, cradling her until she was placed upon the bed. She nodded, rising to grab at her pants.

"*Yes...*" the hissing voice of ethereal figures called from the Glowing. Traces of their images pushed from the reaches of the etheric layers, bringing shape to nothingness as they forced themselves into reality. Their voices traveled into the minds of those witnessing. Artemis paused, staring into the pit of light. "*We await our vessel...*"

The figures hovered within it, their withered and elongated appearances fading from view before another straining return. From the opened mouths of their elongated skeletal visages, hung rows of sharp teeth. Long talon like fingers rose from them, pointing at Artemis, commanding her to continue.

"I give myself to you... son of the heavens..."

Azazel stood upright, his face widening into a smile. His bulging arms rose upward in triumph over his shining glory. Artemis reached up for him as he leaned over with his mass, kissing her. His lips rubbed against hers, the sizzle of energies flowing through her body, gathering in an explosion of wanton desire between her legs. Heavy breathing racked her body. The tingle of yearning coursed through her fingers and toes, climaxing at the tips of her ears that were cuffed in the warmth of anticipation.

Eyes of brown and gold locked between them, before closing with another kiss.

CHAPTER 22
WAKING THE BEAST

Artemis' soft hands ran over Azazel's golden chest. Her fingers traced through the chiseled crevices of muscles rippling with each of his movements. His bulging biceps squeezed together from raising his hand to caress the long curls of her hair, matted from the helmet she'd worn for so long. Oaken locks unfurled with his efforts, a smirk coming to him while he stepped back to admire the effect.

"I will not endure this," Persephone grumbled, shaking her head while turning in rigid steps, quaking with growing anger.

"Ignore her," Azazel said. "This is our moment."

"Tell me, my beloved god?" Artemis queried. "When you appeared as light to my team, you seemed incorporeal. I must say that is a relief. I didn't think you were solid and was beginning to wonder how we would consummate our union."

"That was merely a projection of my will. A taste of my power and authority over the layers. There are still some rules that I must obey in the material realm or be cognizant in my efforts when defying them."

"You are incredible."

Azazel grinned, his full lips peeling away from the layered rows of sharp teeth aligning gums of marble black. The being's eyes carried to the heights of the cavern, his breaths growing heavier. Artemis rolled away, landing to the opposite side of the small plateau. Azazel peered down, brows firming, his smile evaporating into a scowl.

"Clear!" Artemis hollered. "I'm clear!"

"What are you going on about? If this is some attempt of deception, then I warn you that my patience will be expired. This will be a most painful and arduous experience for you."

"Backblast area clear!" John screamed from the hillside. "Rocket away!"

Smoke billowed in the distance, spewing from the mouth of the SMAW Serpent, as a payload sped toward Azazel. Artemis pressed her face into the dirt, rattling during the ear ringing eruption that mixed with the being's screams. Pellets of earth rained over her, the heat from the blast passing through like a scalding shower. A cough forced its way up from her heaving lungs.

Artemis rose, drawing an M1911 with an extended magazine hanging well below her tense grip. Her sights fell on Azazel, aligning with the now pointed golden head of the being. He clung to the edge of the Glowing, its lights rising around his dangling body. Crackling smoke rose from charred portions of his form, sizzling with a grimace inducing pain.

"You piece of shit!" Artemis roared. "Like I would ever give myself to unholy, inhuman filth like you. This is for my team, you bastard!"

A double tap sent two thick .45 caliber rounds snapping Azazel's head back. The being's nails scratched into the ground, sliding back until losing his grip and plummeting into the Glowing.

"Good riddance! May you rot forever in your burning prison!"

Unintelligible murmurs were exchanged among the spectators. Wide eyed dismay was traded between them with prolonged glances. Whispering conversations sparked around them.

"No!" The word hissed from those dwelling in the etheric layers above the Glowing. Their glares trembled and claws flexed with raging anticipation.

"You will never live again!" Artemis yelled. "The earth belongs to the rightful creations of God!"

"Your arrogance belies you, mortal." Their words shot back in slow and simultaneous whispers. *"The denizens from beyond will never relent. Your vigilance has its limits. Our hatred does not."*

Footsteps tapped along the ground, closing behind Artemis. She turned, seeing Persephone, long faced and wide-eyed. The priestess approached with slow steps, peering to the mouth of the Glowing, to the gouges along the edge where her subjugator left his last marks on the world. Glistening tears swelled in her eyes. A blink brought the first droplet rolling down her cheek.

"Big sis... is it over? Is... it really over?"

"Yes... it is." She lowered her weapon, looking to her younger sibling. "He held you prisoner here; violating your body, making you do those vile things, and harming others, didn't he? Fear is what kept you locked away here, from the world. But it's over. Come home with me, Persephone."

"Home..."

Tension melted away from Artemis' torso, with arms dropping to her sides, the heavy breaths of adrenaline fading. She smiled at Persephone, reaching to embrace her with a hug. They held tight to one another.

"Let's rendezvous with the rest of the team and get the hell out of this place," Artemis announced. "You can stay with me. We'll get you to the surface and back home safely, Persephone."

"My..."

"Are you okay?" Artemis leaned back, examining her sister's lowered countenance, following the path of tears culminating at the tip of her chin. "Perse?"

"My name is Sarai!"

The glint of sharp metal rose into Artemis' peripheral vision. Sarai's dagger slashed into her hip. Streaking pain coursed through the Raptor Team leader. Artemis groaned, convulsing from the wound's stinging torment. Another stroke followed, cleaving into her arm. Artemis stumbled over the earthen bed, scrambling backward despite the agony of warm blood spilling from the deep gashes.

"Go home with you? Up there? With the blind, imbecilic children of El?" Sarai screamed. "I am a goddess down here in Dudael! I am gibborim!"

Pistol sights lifted, but a quick slice of the knife brought Artemis' arm reeling out of aim. Sarai climbed over her like a spider. The hard points of her knees dropped into her sister's arms, pinning her.

"You have nothing for me. I held my tongue while you were given the greatest of honors! It was my king who offered you salvation, and how did you thank him? You stupid bitch! See how your technological weapons ultimately mean nothing?" Sarai howled at Artemis, bashing her numerous times over the face with her fists. "Your friends will die, too. Dudael will devour them; there is no escape! Now die!"

Through the redness streaming into view and the blows that shifted her vision, Artemis caught a glimpse of Sarai's dagger raising, its sharp point aiming for the heart. A weapon barrel's roar spewed buckshot, striking the raging priestess, sending her flying off Artemis and rolling to the floor.

"Good shot!" Milton said. "Not bad for your first combat operation. You learn quick."

"Iye kun nutti, Persephone!"

"Yeah! Whatever that means..."

Artemis turned, seeing her comrades arriving with John patting Pippa, wielding Patty's shotgun. Aristotle ran to their team leader, helping her shaking frame rise from the bed.

"She did a number on you, Arty!" Aristotle exclaimed. "Sorry we were out of range and didn't want to risk hitting you."

"I'll live. Fortunately, she didn't stab. It's all superficial. Painful but nothing vital was hit."

Pippa cocked the shotgun, ejecting the smoking shell, and chambering a fresh round into place. The weapon remained trained on Sarai, writhing as blood spilled from the many holes in her flesh. Through deep weaving breaths, the priestess scowled at them from the flat of her back, fingers reaffirming a grip on the knife.

"You've... won... nothing here." Sarai's gargled declaration rang with contempt. "You... will... all die... this... I promise... painful... death awaits."

Artemis looked to Pippa with a nod. The woman pulled the trigger, spewing another blast that sent fragments of the bone necklace, and chunks of meat darting over Sarai's face. The priestess' head dropped back, rolling to a shoulder. The composure of life escaped from her body.

"I'm sorry, my love." John hugged Artemis. "I know you did your damnedest to save her."

"It's over. Let's not dwell on it."

"Agreed. We patch you up and get the fuck out of here. Luckily the locals haven't swarmed us yet."

"They just watched their god and goddess taste defeat." Aristotle chuckled.

"We're bringing Pippa with us?" John asked. "There's no way that I trust her surviving down here after siding with us."

"Indeed," Artemis answered. "I'm sure the Agency can give Pippa a good life somewhere. She can have a fresh start away from this madness."

The blaring of horns throbbed into their ears, blanketing all who beheld it with a pulsing resonance. Cold apprehension ushered away the tepid environment's embrace, pumping through their muscles with a rigid negative frequency. Deep was the sound, rumbling into a growl at the end of each note, only to restart with the shrill outburst ringing with rage. The high and low frequencies pushed from the Glowing, with every rising vibration, until the area around them trembled to proclaim his arrival.

Dark wings of thick hide stretched with a massive span, flapping hard to propel a hulking mass into the air. The agents' sights wrestled through the booming tumult, bearing witness to scaled claws protruding from a lion-like body. Their weapons raised, combat sights meeting the glowing whites of a pupilless glare from a head wedged between wide pillars serving as arms. A multitude of shriveled swaying limbs dragged on the ground beneath its undercarriage. The beast coiled its body into a challenging arch.

Artemis raised her M1911's barrel, following it to the glare above the lower head. Another set of eyes stared back from a second head bearing upon them with a rumbling snarl. Flaps of skin dangled around of its face, hanging from a slow opening maw, that released the blaring frequency between flat teeth and a thick sloshing tongue. Long horns rolled back from the forehead, curling with a thickness that encompassed its crown. Her attention was snatched away by a thinner shape rising along the backside of the skewed frame. Jaws opened from its serpentine head, hissing with a fury trembling down the length of its neck, serving as the beast's tail.

"What the fuck?" Milton exclaimed.

"Icke neh obin treis!" Pippa turned and screamed to those watching in the distance. Pointing her shotgun at Persephone's corpse. "Obin treis ut chbala!"

"It's him," Artemis said.

Murmurs passed around in the darkness with the feral gazes of denizens shifting about in low and rumbling growls.

"Icke neh—"

With blinding motion Azazel went for Pippa. The large frame bounded, landing with a thudding calamity that mixed with the crunch of the hapless woman's bones.

Artemis, Milton, and Aristotle dove from the crash site. A shotgun blast fired along Azazel's underside. Pippa's grip loosened on the weapon, the integrity of her body breaking under the clamping jaws of the lower maw. Her screams raked over the area with a harsh desperation, mixing with grunts and the deep panting of shock.

No! Pippa! How do we defeat this... we can't... I can't do anything for her!

Shots from Artemis' gun punched into the membranous flesh, leaving gaping holes in the creature's skin, glistening with ooze. Her finger pumped until the weapon was spent. She pressed the release, dropping the empty magazine, slapping in another from her pocket, and continuing with rapid trigger pulls. The beast's shoulders rolled inward, bringing Pippa's body farther, her cries becoming muffled when she entered the gullet.

Persephone was right. Our firepower is doing nothing...

"Neh, coro dot!" Anger bellowed around them.

"Neh obin treis!"

A horned man sprinted from the shadows, his hind legs clapping with each desperate stride. In his hands a long knife was raised, aligning for Azazel. The point of steel went deep into the beast's hide, bringing deep bellowing roars from the lower head. A shuddering noise erupted from its caprine head, guiding the blaring roars of trumpet like sound upon the attacker.

He hurt Azazel? But how?

Ears rang with aching beats. Jolts of apprehension carried from the layers, into their bodies with a grip that slowed their movements. Artemis bared her teeth. John groaned, battling against the frigid waves of negative frequencies. He lowered the rocket launcher, taking a knee to retrieve the next warhead from the side of his pack.

Azazel spun to the knife-wielding man, poised in a crouch before leaping forward. The flapping appendages reached for him, digging into his body with the grasp of a dozen hands. Nails dug into his clothing; without effort they pierced, tearing into his skin. The beast's shoulders widened from its coiled pose, giving way to the large maw's extension. Rising streams of smoke and glamour of light rose from its innards. A river of flames sprayed from Azazel's mouth, melting the screaming man's legs into a mixture of sizzling blood and bubbling swathes of meat.

Aristotle leaned forward, his face scrunching with sheer focus. Light channeled through the etheric layers, struggling to find its momentum in the negativity that immersed it. He strained, pushing with all his effort until the ball of psychic energy illuminated within view of his mind's eye. The scryer's hands shot out, launching the projectile at Azazel. A bellow expelled from the beast, as light crashed into his rear, stretching over his back with a clamping energy.

"Scryer!" Azazel's roar spread through the layers, knocking Aristotle to his rear. *"Your wandering soul will now shatter under my wrath, and I will feast upon the morsels of light, so that those who dwell in his name will hear your lamentations!"*

"Resist! With everything you have!" Aristotle yelled. "Do not give into his will! You are stronger than him, Arty!"

"John, reload the launcher!" Artemis urged. "Hurry!"

"I'm trying... the noise... it's locking me in... place!" Images around him melded into a blur. Fatigue weighed heavy on his mind, bringing his eyelids to a slow close.

Artemis rushed over, pushing her body through the throbbing call of surrender from the other side. The bite of negativity ran deep through her limbs as a force that wanted to emerge from beyond perception. Alarm ran through her thoughts, with the knowing that should her resistance wane, it was ready to devour her whole.

I... I... can't... no... I must... for retribution's sake. Persephone was right. Aristotle is right. I haven't the training. But I must resist!

The energy's dark embrace dissipated.

Citizens of Dudael roared in defiance in a unified charge. From the craggy outskirts they poured, wielding weapons of steel and stone, clamoring with rage from generations of torment. Their numbers gathered around Azazel. The beast rose with an arched back, swiping at the first with a mighty arm, sending the man flying back into the group of his comrades. All three mouths bellowed at the crowd. They continued pressing, sending spear points forward to stab at the creature.

Long and deep hisses expelled from the thin serpentine head arched over the rest. It reeled back before launching forward. Fangs sank into the torso of another denizen, the sharp venomous tips puncturing through with ease. The man was lifted into the air, held by a clamping bite. A ferocious jerk from the beast hurtled the victim into the distance with his fading cries.

Artemis grabbed the warhead from John, whose rigid movements came to a near halt. Trembles ran through the large agent, deep breaths escaped between clamped teeth.

"Artemis... the pain..."

"Fight it, like I did, John!" She placed the rocket into the launcher. "Dig deep! I need you!"

A slow nod came from Milton. His hands moved, wading through the thickening resistance to take the launcher from his beloved. "Thank you... for never giving up on me."

Artemis kissed her love, closing her eyes to the warm caress of his mouth. She pulled away, turning to face the beast. *I confront my destiny with faith and courage. I am the daughter of the creator. This is my kingdom! Not yours!*

Arms sped from Azazel in another vicious swipe. Blood squirted from neck lacerations, ripped open with bladed claws that raked across rebel denizens. Gargled screams muffled under the choking of their seeping wounds. Azazel's second head peeled backward, its mouth splitting wide. The flat teeth lead to a pit of swirling darkness pushing forth the trumpet's deafening call to ever greater levels.

"*Insolence demands decimation!*" His eldritch voice scoured over them, like slow pouring water. "*What I once asked for, shall be taken. I shall feast on your essences, until all you know is the suffering of my devouring hunger, the wrath of my eternal hatred for creation."*

"Faith, Arty," Aristotle said. *"With me. Masculine and feminine, together, overriding the imbalance. As it was in his grand plan."*

"I understand now."

Artemis looked to Aristotle. Grim-faced nods were exchanged. Her fingers loosened their grip, allowing the pistol to slip away, where its metal frame clattered along the rocky ground. The twins' hands rose in unison.

"No!" Artemis screamed.

Inhabitants looked to see the three of them positioned against the flank of the beast. Many scrambled away, gawking at Milton. The agent stood upon the bed, aligning the SMAW, bringing the illuminating lights of the targeting system over Azazel's body. A locking square hovered over the snarling beast, blinking with a searching beep. It rang out, the reticle turning solid with a definite lock.

"Backblast area clear!" John groaned. "Rocket away!"

The blaring warhead raced forth with great velocity, leaving a trail of exhaust billowing in its wake. Thunderous flame spewed calamity in a massive explosion, buckling Azazel's side. The beast roared, its bulk dragged by force to the Glowing's edge. Azazel's back legs dangled over the light, his wings struggling against the ground for flight. With shaking limbs, John reached for the last rocket.

Light emanated from the twins, pushing against Azazel's defiant growls. Hateful glares were exchanged. The trumpet's cry resounded again from the screaming ram's head. Negative energies coursed through Artemis. Agony traveled up her spine, jerking her head backward. Her eyes reddened with the swelling of tears. Bruises rose along the surface of her skin, pounding against her with flares of anguish.

Images flashed within Artemis. Arms buckling, as the sensation of a shredding pain forced its way into her womanhood. The lashing of a tongue crawled over her back, leaving a slime trail that encrusted into white flakes. Claws reached from the darkness enveloping her vision, gripping her body with piercing nails into the most tender regions.

"Artemis!" Aristotle cried out. "Listen to my voice! Fight him! Do not give into his will!"

"Torment beyond measure awaits when you inevitably fail." Azazel's laughter wrapped around their psyche.

Hollering erupted from the denizens of the Glowing. Convulsing possessed those closest, until they fell to the ground, bouncing on the stone surface. Ribs gave with successive audible cracks. Fingers bent, shattering from vain attempts at clutching the ground for stability. Bodies arched, stomachs reaching toward the ceiling, grinding vertebrae into each other until loud pops left their broken bodies flaccid.

"I was there when your predecessors stepped into the material world. And I shall endure even after this misbegotten experiment to replace us has failed!"

"Rocket out!" John yelled.

The warhead sped to its target, crashing into the lower head. The blast carried away Azazel's grip, sending the flailing beast plummeting into the Glowing. Howling faded, as it dropped into the boiling depths of light and magma. Hissing rose from the lost souls, their skeletal countenances opening jaws of sharp teeth, flexing their long curling claws.

"Close it!" Aristotle exclaimed.

Azazel's claws scraped against the walls of the Glowing until locking in place. Reaching upward, his limbs working with rapid succession, propelling his mass. Bladed nails ripped away at stone. He climbed, his growl rising into a surging war cry. The trumpet's call resounded from the horned one, the orb of darkness pulling the remaining negative energies from Dudael, concentrating it through the beast's will.

Artemis raised her arms, stepping forward against the tumult of negative frequencies burrowing against the pit of her soul. Flakes of the light began to fade from her being, floating to the consuming darkness of Azazel's rising presence. Quivering limbs buckled, her kneecaps pressing out sideways, until pulling from her legs. Artemis wailed, as ligaments and tendons ripped away, the cap shifting within her skin to the outside of her femur. The shattered remnants of her legs drove into the ground, her knee pads absorbing the hard thump.

"I can feel your pain. I relish it. The promise of gentleness has been extinguished. I rise again, to claim what was pledged. Know that I will violate you, even in your throes of incalculable pain. It will get worse. Your beloved twin will witness from the layers. This I swear."

A golden spear tip lowered into view above the Glowing. Artemis reached upward, witnessing six streaks of light extending from the back of a being. Sweat cascaded from her weary brow into her blinking eyes, only to find nothing when her vision returned.

"Never!" Artemis bellowed, pressing her invigored will outward. Aristotle buckled gasping at fragments of his sister's soul exploding with rippling power. Light saturated them, forming a barrier over the Glowing. Large hands heaved the fallen agent from the ground. Artemis' weary eyes met with John's.

"We finish this together!"

The lovers nodded, John carrying her to the edge of the

Glowing. Azazel glared at them from beyond the translucent dome of radiance. Milton sneered, lifting his middle finger. Artemis raised her arm, closing her eyes. The temperature escalated until sweltering. The Glowing's illuminance rose. John reared his face away. Artemis stared into the brilliance, pushing until seeing the rise of magma. Azazel screamed as the rumbling energies of the earth engulfed him.

Claws held tight to the walls of the Glowing, the trembling beast cried out. Orange, yellow, and red immersed him, charring every part of his body. Black flakes crumbled away, disintegrating into smoking nothingness. Screams erupted from the roasted husk. Stones disintegrated in its frantic grip. The remnants of the beast peeled away in a decaying shower. There was only a man now peering back at them. He buckled, revealing his bare back with four deep and lengthy scars stretching along his upper side. When he rose again, a cry of desperation expelled from his quivering lips.

The Glowing snatched Azazel, the earth's agonizing embrace elevating his wails until they echoed through the vastness of Dudael. Down it pulled, sinking the being into the lowest depths. Mouthfuls of endless burning torment silenced his cries, matching the limitless misery surging through the rest of his being. Rumbles ushered from the earth, closing the pit of light, leaving only a cracked glowing scar across the ground.

Something isn't right... part of me is missing... this isn't just fatigue... I'm deteriorating...

"The nightmare is over..." John sighed with relief.

From the shadows stepped the survivors, gathering around the couple with their glowing yellow eyes. Heads bowed with lowered frames, as the denizens of the underworld knelt before the agents. John reached for his side arm, only to stop at the gentle touch of Artemis' hand.

"It's over for them, too."

Milton nodded.

"Let's go home, my love."

CHAPTER 23
A PROMISE KEPT

Tires of a large van scratched along the repaved roads of the small mountain town, coming to a halt before the small gas station. They parked at one of the brand-new pumps, the plastic nozzles shining in the afternoon sun, below the digital computer screen with the words 'Welcome to the Mountainside fueling station.'

The large cargo doors slid open, with a young woman and man hopping out of the vehicle's large body and stretching. The later raised a large black video camera to his shoulder, pressing buttons that brought the illumination of its interior monitor to life.

"We're here!" The young blonde lady smiled, fixing her black leather jacket after yawning. "This is going to be the big score. I can feel it."

"You always say that!" the man snapped, pressing his glasses to his nose. "Michelle, you know I'm deathly afraid of deer ticks and the thought of getting Lyme disease! I swear if I get bit by—"

"Oh, hush it, Stevie! Such a big stupid baby sometimes. You

call yourself a professional? Just keep that camera rolling and don't miss any good stuff." Michelle turned to her drivers. "And you two, don't forget to buy some snacks and fill it up while we interview. Now let's see..."

The station door opened with Jasper stepping out. The old man waved and smiled at the duo. Michelle smiled, urging Stevie to follow.

"Hello, sir!" she greeted him. "It's a pleasure to meet you. I'm Michelle Mitchells and this is my reluctant and disgruntled cameraman, Stevie Wilburson—"

"Not disgruntled enough," Stevie grumbled.

"I host and run one of the most popular internet shows and podcasts on the supernatural. We travel around the country interviewing folk about weird happenings, pursuing the rumors that surround them."

Jasper and the woman exchanged smiles.

"And judging by that big handsome grin, you've got something for me?"

"Not sure why you're in Jefferson, ma'am." Jasper responded and shrugged. "We're just a small peaceful town of mountain folk. Nothing exciting going on here except a little huntin' and hikin'."

"Let's just stop beating around the bush, Mr..."

"Just call me Jasper."

"Oh, that makes sense." Michelle nodded toward to the writing on the large window proclaiming, 'Jasper's Mountainside Gas and Jerky stop Est. 1800.' The outlined picture of a large fish and spear appeared below it, leaping from a lake encircled by mountains. "So, your family has been in these parts for a while?"

Jasper shook his head. "Nope. I'm the first and only from my family to live out here."

Michelle's brow rose in confusion. She and Stevie exchanged glances. Stevie shrugged.

"I watch over the place," Jasper continued.

Michelle's attention fell on two small cases in a stand behind the window. They were opened, presenting the blue ribbons culminating into golden eagles surrounding a white star.

"I know what those are! They're Presidential Medals of Freedom!" Michelle grinned, looking to Jasper, closing on the display reading the words. "Awarded to Honorary Deputies of the U.S.A. Department of Homeland Defense, Philip and Robert Clemenson for bravery and courage in the face of overwhelming odds in the defense of humanity!"

"Two very good friends of mine and a lovely couple." Jasper smiled. "President Biden was kind enough to sign off on them receiving these in a timely manner despite it being a posthumous award. I'm holding those in their honor because their families had disowned them many years ago. And despite all that, those two still came through for what was right, when they were needed the most."

"So, it did happen! Please, tell us about the U.S.A!" Michelle slapped Stevie's shoulder. "Don't miss anything!"

She cleared her throat, taking a stance next to a smiling Jasper who waved at the camera.

"Mr. Jasper—"

"Just Jasper, ma'am. I'm nothing special. Just a servant of the good lord like yourselves."

"I apologize, Jasper. Can you tell us more about this U.S.A. that is rumored to exist?"

"Well shucks, ma'am. Ain't no rumor. This here is the good ole United States of America. Land of the free, home of the brave. And it's been my place of residence for quite a while."

"Umm... I meant the Unholy Slaying Agency that was rumored to be operating in your town."

"Oh, well, can't say I know what you're talkin' about. I tend to mind my own business."

Michelle sighed. "Tightlipped like the rest of them. You're not going to be of help are you, sir? Please, the world needs to know the truth!"

"You're right. They do need to know the truth."

Michelle rubbed her hands together.

"Well... young lady. The truth is that all the hardships people endure are for the betterment of not just their lives, but the soul that travels beyond the conscious confines of this world. For better or worse, it stays with you, resonating as those compounding energies, and you grow ever stronger from it. Sometimes there're things that may seem so arduous it's insurmountable. But what I've learned in my long time here, is that human beings are amazing, capable of returning from the brink of defeat when times seem the grimmest, because after all... well, Genesis 1:27; God created mankind in his own image, in the image of God he created them; male and female he created them. And it shows in those moments when the darkness is shed. Nothing is beyond your reach when you have courage and most importantly faith. And that's why he works through you, not for you."

"Who?"

"God Almighty."

Stevie rolled his eyes. "Sir, with all due respect we're trying to research the paranormal, not listen to sermons."

"Why is everyone so tightlipped about this organization?" Michelle groaned, palming her face. "We're not getting anything here, are we, Jasper?"

"Not unless you want to."

"Damn it!" Michelle grumbled.

"Thanks for nothing, old timer." Stevie cut off the camera.

"Paranormal Undercover New-Age Klick, let's get going," Michelle snapped. "We'll find someone in this town that will talk."

"PUNKs?" Jasper grinned. "How fittin'."

"Don't call us that!" Stevie grumbled.

"It's actually kind of catchy," Michelle murmured.

"My apologies." Jasper waved as they drove off. "I think I'll close up early today and go fishing. Reminds me of the old times with my buddy Tobias."

The electronic imitation of a doorbell rang through the speakers near the suburban home's living room. Hector stood at the kitchen sink, turning off the running faucet and grabbing a paper towel to dry his hands. Flashing light from his cellphone illuminated his face while his finger skipped through the menu options, until bringing up the feed of security cameras along the door.

Waving into the lens was a smiling Carver, holding hands with a black-haired beauty who wore a leather jacket matching his own. In her grasp was a vase filled with fluffy white baby's breath and bright yellow wildflowers.

"Coming, bud." Hector spoke through the cellphone. "Just finishing up some dishes."

Sunshine and smiling faces greeted the old agent. He continued drying his hands on the red and yellow sweatpants, labeled 'Marines' down the side of his leg.

Carver reached out, clasping hands with his comrade and superior.

"Good to see you under better circumstances, sir."

"Likewise, but I wouldn't necessarily call this better." Hector's gaze remained firm, despite wandering low.

"This lovely lady is Lucy." Carver introduced his girlfriend.

The dark eyed beauty waved from behind Carver, shrinking back with a meek smile.

"She really digs me!" a grinning Carver leaned in to whisper. "She even approached me!"

"Wow, ma'am, you look like you could easily be a super model," Hector complimented before turning back to Carver. "A cutie for sure but what happened to Jessie?"

"Couldn't get over it... no matter how much I tried to help."

"That sounds all too familiar."

"Is Actual... okay?"

Hector waved them inside to follow. "No, Son. You have to see it. Nothing has been the same since that operation. Artemis has been deteriorating since she left that place. John and I take turns looking after her. AD Hughes has been here a few times to visit, too. But she's not the same person anymore. Whatever's happening it's... unpredictable and constantly changing. Artemis can go days without saying a word, then burst into screams or mad rants, making zero sense. Scryers, doctors, everyone's been here, but none have been of any help. Her eyes... it's as if she's peering into something at times, following things that aren't there." A deep sigh escaped Hector.

"I... I don't know what to say."

"It's good that you're here." Hector patted the young man. "I'm not a healthcare consultant or scryer, but I think seeing familiar faces could help. She lost something down there, after facing off against that vector. I just wish she could tell us what happened beyond John's details. So much is missing from the After-Action Debrief, the official mission report has gone inconclusive to the resolution of the vector's final status."

"You guys are military, right?" Lucy asked. "Is a vector a name for a terrorist or something?"

"Yeah." Carver nodded. "Umm... it's a more humanizing way of labeling them, you know instead of the old derogatory names."

"That makes sense."

After they finished traversing the staircase and hallway, Hector stopped at the door, placing his hand on the knob. "Brace yourself. She's not exactly how you remember."

"Okay..."

The door opened to a large room. A king-sized bed sprawled out to its center from the back wall, surrounded by nightstands covered in half empty water bottles. Hunched over, in an olive USMC sweatshirt, seated in a wheelchair was Artemis. Gray streaks wove from her forehead, into the once luxurious shining hair that had looked akin to rich chocolate. Her sunken face carried years beyond the truth of her age, bearing heavy wrinkles and large drooping bags below her intense unblinking eyes.

John rose from the corner of the bed next to Artemis, turning with a weak smile and a handshake to greet Carver.

"Good to see you, big guy."

"Likewise," John said.

Carver stared at Artemis, following her dilated gaze to the frilled patterns running along the closed white curtains. "Hey, Actual!"

The unblinking stare continued.

"Can she hear us?" Carver asked.

"I don't know." John sighed. "I don't know anything

anymore. I wish I could understand what happened but it's a spiritual thing. The scryers... when they came to visit, they stated numerous times how they wish Artemis had trained with them, to prepare her mind and spirit for that moment. But she was too devoted to us. Now I wish she hadn't been..."

"I'm going to try." Carver took the vase from Lucy, walking over to Artemis and placing the flowers on the nearby nightstand. "Hey, Actual. We've missed you a lot. Glad to see you're alive and kicking after that hop. I want you to know that what you said before that mission lit a fire in my ass. It got my mind right for all we endured out there. I wouldn't have survived without it. Thank you for that. You're a great leader, Actual." Carver leaned in with a smile, to nothing. He lowered his head before patting her shoulder.

"Aristotle..." Artemis called out. "Is that you? We did it... we got justice for our family... no one has to ever face... what we did... lose what we did... thank you... for being there with me..."

Carver walked back to join the others. "Who's Aristotle?"

"Her twin brother," Hector answered. "He perished with the rest of her family on that night. Torn apart by vectors. Artemis told me that he held them off so she could escape."

"She mentioned something in passing a while ago," John added. "Never spoke much save his last words on that night was a promise to catch up and be with her."

"Aristotle..." Artemis murmured then smiled. "We did it..."

THE HUNT CONTINUES:

CASES OF COMATOSE CHILDREN APPEARING AROUND THE NATION

Stay tuned for the next installment of the UNHOLY SLAYING AGENCY series, DOOR TO DARKNESS.

Some nightmares bring more than just chills and shakes. When several children are found comatose after casual slumber, the agency sends former Filipino ranger Gabriel Agapito and Team Butcher to hunt down a dream-walking shaman they believe responsible for the nocturnal terrors. But Team Diver intercepts their sorcerer hunting brethren, brewing hostility between all the agents involved. Little do they know something awaits both sides of this cold civil war. In a nightmarish realm from beyond, the souls of those who dare to sleep are tucked away for dwellers to feast upon.

Sign up for my newsletter to be notified when new books are released.

guyquintero.com/recruitment

ABOUT THE AUTHOR

Guy Quintero is a former reconnaissance soldier with three deployments under his belt. Quintero combines his military background and a life-long fascination with the occult, bringing a mix of bone-chilling horror and heart-pumping action. His inspirations are Stephen King and Tom Clancy. He hopes to follow in their footsteps someday.

GuyQuintero.com

instagram.com/guyquintero
facebook.com/guyquinteroauthor

CPSIA information can be obtained
at www.ICGtesting.com
Printed in the USA
BVHW020420230123
656730BV00048B/79/J